★ ★ ★ ★ ★ ★ ★

PRIME
CANDIDATE

ALSO BY GORDON COTLER

★ ★ ★ ★ ★ ★ ★

PRIME
CANDIDATE

GORDON COTLER

St. Martin's Press

New York

❧

Design by Pei Koay

Library of Congress Cataloging-in-Publication

Cotler, Gordon.
    Prime candidate / Gordon Cotler.
        p.   cm.
    "A Thomas Dunne book."
    ISBN 0-312-14028-2
    I. Title.
    PS3553.07643P75   1996
    813' .54—dc20   95-40612
                                       CIP

First Edition: February 1996

10 9 8 7 6 5 4 3 2 1

FOR MARTA

Patriotism is the last refuge of the scoundrel.
　　　　　　　　　　　—Samuel Johnson (1709–84)
　　　　　　　　　　　Lexicographer

Dr. Johnson was evidently unfamiliar with 'My opponent cheats on his wife.'
　　　　　　　　　　　—Paula "Poppy" Hancock (1963–)
　　　　　　　　　　　Election Campaign Manager

MONDAY

1 I was no more than ten minutes late, but I leaned on the accelerator all the way up the Henry Hudson Parkway and I managed to pass everything headed north but a low-flying private plane out of Teterboro. That contest was still in doubt when I pulled off the parkway at Kappock Street. I hadn't drawn a police car. It was the last good thing to happen that day.

Mort Beaufoy had set our meeting for one o'clock at his apartment in Riverdale, the clean-shaven enclave that hates to admit it's part of the five-o'clock-shadow Bronx. Late was not the message I wanted to give in the early stages of a relationship with a new employer—an employer, at long last, I could respect—and my weary Honda may have depressed real estate values among these solid prewar homes and sleek high-rises as I propelled it through the mellow, sun-dappled streets.

By the time I reached the entrance to the basement garage of Beaufoy's boutique apartment house, I was almost back on schedule, but I probably didn't ease off the gas pedal as much as I should have, and the Honda plunged recklessly down the ramp.

I didn't expect anyone to be hanging out in an apartment-house garage in the middle of the day. I had to brake hard to avoid running into two people standing in mostly empty space.

They seemed to be locked in an embrace—a big black man in overalls and a skinny white woman in a dress, both about forty. At first I thought I had interrupted a furtive sexual liaison, a snatched moment of happiness meant to be hidden from a disapproving world. An instant later I realized this was something else entirely. The woman was distraught and clinging to the man not in passion but for support and comfort.

He didn't seem to know what to do. He rested one arm lightly on her shoulder and patted the other shoulder occasionally, as though he was testing a hot iron.

I climbed out of my car and walked toward them. "You people need help?" Now that I was on time I could spare a minute out of simple courtesy.

"I don't think so, thank you. I already called nine-one-one," the man said.

"What's the problem?"

"It's Miss Kleiman here. The police will handle the matter. They should be here any minute."

He was reluctant to go into it with me, since he would have to explain it to the police anyway, but I had asked and I was clearly expecting more. He said, "She became upset, don't you see, when she saw this dead lady." He had not so much an island accent as a lilt. Haitian.

I looked around the garage, a concrete block enclosure nearly devoid of cars. "Down here?"

"In a car. The black one. As I said, the police are coming."

My blood froze. There were four cars in the garage—mine, a minivan, a lipstick-red sports car, and the lumpy black Buick that belonged to my employer, Morton Ezra Beaufoy, the senior senator from New York, chairman of the Senate Foreign Relations Committee. I stared at it.

"In that car?" I asked stupidly, hoping there had been a miscommunication.

★ 4 ★

The man nodded. "It belongs to a tenant."

"You're sure she's dead?"

"Oh, yes. I made sure I didn't touch anything, just her wrist. The rear window is open. I reached in and felt for her pulse. Nothing."

By now I had forgotten about time; late had lost its importance. I walked around the little two-seater to the Buick. Miss Kleiman, if that was her name, had stopped trembling and was mopping her eyes.

The man said, "I wouldn't go touching, sir. The police are on their way." He was really laying in that point.

"That's okay, I know what not to do." I had been around more than my share of corpses.

I peered in the rear side window, open. A woman lay sprawled across the backseat. Her shoes were on the floor of the car, as though she had kicked them off to take a nap, but she wasn't sleeping; it doesn't take special training to tell the difference between sleeping and dead, even when, as here, there was no blood, no sign of foul play.

She was probably in her early to mid-thirties, nice looking so far as I could see through the honey hair draped across her carefully lipsticked and eye-shadowed face. She was wearing a bright green dress that was hiked far enough up one thigh to reveal the clasp of a garter she had fastened this morning with a quick, practiced move; someone at the morgue would unfasten it this afternoon with slow, clumsy fingers.

A pinwheel was doing lazy turns in my stomach. "Does this woman live here?" I asked.

"She does not," the man replied. "I have never seen her before."

I had put in four years on the police beat before I got boosted to City Hall by the sleazy tabloid where I labored for a tortured decade, and my nerve endings were honed to a fine sensitivity to scandal. I didn't need it here. I didn't even need the garters, which I think of, especially for day wear, as special event equipment—possibly a delight to her man, but a pain in the ass to the woman in harness.

Even without supporting evidence, a good-looking woman dead in a place where she doesn't belong may call for an explanation from some nearby man, and this honey-haired woman was dead in Senator Morton Beaufoy's car eight days before the primary. There would be no problem for Beaufoy if she had come into the garage feeling ill, had stumbled by chance into the backseat of his car to gather her strength, and had died quite suddenly of a massive heart attack. Yeah.

My nerve endings were tingling. The tab reporter was rising in me like the ears of a firehouse dog at the sound of the bells. I had to remind myself, before I went hunting for a phone to call the paper, that I was no longer with the paper, that I was on the other side of this possibly brewing scandal, the "cool it" side.

As though it had been triggered by my hunger for a phone, I heard something like a ringing somewhere. "Are you the super?" I asked the man. "Is there a phone in here?"

"Yes. I mean yes, I'm the super. No sir, there is no phone in the garage, just the building intercom," he said. "That makes a buzz. I don't know where that sound is coming from. Maybe we should wait until . . ."

I had already left to follow the sound, not that easy in the empty, echo-y space. I found its source on the other side of the Buick and bent to it. A cellular phone lay under the curve of the rear wheel. I fished out a Kleenex and picked up the phone by its edges and flipped it open.

"Sir, do you think it's wise to be doing that?" the super called. "The police will—"

I said, "The police will want to know who called this phone." I punched the On button but didn't speak.

A rich baritone voice came through the phone. "Hello . . . ?" And when I didn't answer, "Hello, Sheri . . . ?"

I said, "Who is this?" For an instant I thought the voice

was the senator's, because that's where my head was.

"Who are *you?*" the baritone demanded. It wasn't Beaufoy; not remotely. "Will you please put Sheri on?"

The best I could manage was, "I'm sorry, she can't come to the phone right now."

"What do you mean? Where is she? You've got her phone. And I repeat, who the hell are you?"

"I'm afraid there's been an accident." I was beginning to feel my way. "Would you please identify yourself?"

"Oh, my God. What happened? I'm her boss. Clifton Oliver. Oliver Realty. Is she all right?"

"The police will be in touch, Mr. Oliver." I hung up and started to bend to put the phone back down where I found it. It rang again and, conscious of a disapproving look and a clucking sound from the super, I pushed the On button again.

This time there was a long stretch of dead air. I waited it out, and eventually a male voice—undistinguished, not the baritone, definitely not the senator—came on.

It said, "Hello . . . ?" And after a moment, "Hey, Honeybuns, where are you?"

I waited, expecting more. When there was none I said, "Are you looking for Sheri?"

The line went dead. I held the phone for a minute, hoping for a callback, but none came. I put it back pretty much where I found it, under the rear wheel.

When I straightened up, a police car was coming down the ramp. I said a silent prayer of thanks that Mort Beaufoy was anchored in Apartment 5A waiting for me to show.

The cop car pulled up next to mine. Two uniformed officers climbed out, adjusting their uniforms, moving slowly but purposefully. They were young and they were green: one-celled creatures in the law-enforcement food chain. A Times Square display sign could have been hung over them, with rippling lights in an arrow flowing to the single flashing word, ROOKIES.

Two rookies in one car. Why not? An older partner of one may have called in sick; no big deal. This was the crime-free part of the Bronx, where a major police action would be writing a summons to the Good Humor man for littering. Up here the illegal object bulging in a school kid's jacket was likely to be an overdue library book.

Cop One, the short, button-nosed one, pulled out his notebook. He said, "Okay, folks, we understand somebody's deceased in here. Where at?"

The super pointed to the Buick and Cop One went to it, peered in, and opened the door with his bare hand. He would never make it past the probationary period. The super looked pained.

Too late, the cop realized his boner. He had the good grace to say, "Uh-oh," but the damage was done. He reached in, intently scrutinized the face he saw, and felt for a pulse. "She's dead, all right," he called to Cop Two.

Cop Two had exercised his right to express his individuality, by wearing his hair so that it streamed from under his cap like an overflowing tub. He was talking into his hand mike. In twenty seconds he would have a computer feedback of the Buick's registration. Twenty minutes later it would be all over New York that there was a dead woman with honey hair in the backseat of Senator Morton Ezra Beaufoy's Buick.

But it turned out that a license plate check wasn't what Cop Two was up to. He called to his partner, "Yo, Ed, I'm getting EMS dispatched."

Emergency Medical? Was he hoping for a resurrection? I decided it was to my side's advantage to move things along, find out if there was any real damage to be controlled here. Maybe I had too much tabloid suspicion in my makeup; it was still likely there was a simple, guilt-free explanation for this death. As gently as I could I said, "Don't you want to report this to your supervisor at the precinct?"

Cop Two's response was, "Who are you?"

"My name's Jock Caprisi."

Cop Two's eyes widened. "The columnist, right? From . . . uh, the *News?*"

"The *Ledger,*" said Cop One.

"Right," I said. Not anymore, but damned if I was going to tell them who I worked for at present; not until I had to. I shifted their attention to the now reasonably well-composed Miss Kleiman. "That's the woman who discovered the body."

"I called nine-one-one," the super volunteered.

Cop One nodded his appreciation of both pieces of information, and while Cop Two called the precinct he approached Miss Kleiman, notebook poised. He said, "Miss, why don't you tell me when it was you came in here and exactly what you saw? In your own words." He may have been afraid she would use my words; I was the columnist.

Miss Kleiman's voice was quavery and it lacked density; it matched her fragile body. "I live in the building. I came down for my car. The minivan. Ten minutes ago? About, I guess. Out of the corner of my eye"—she was beginning to break down again—"I happened to notice . . . It caught my eye . . . The dress. That green dress . . ."

She was sobbing, and the words wouldn't come. This painfully thin woman was stretched; pluck any string and it would break. The corpse was hardly gruesome, but I supposed in Miss Kleiman's world people died in hospital beds, between clean sheets.

Cop One was wriggling uncomfortably. They hadn't briefed him at the academy on tears control. "So you noticed the dress," he said at last, trying to be helpful, "and then the woman."

"Yes, the green dress . . ."

"How long ago was this? At what time? Approximately is all right." Apparently he had missed that part of her story.

"I don't know." She turned to the super. "How long ago, Mr. LaPierre?"

"Yes, ten minutes. Not much more."

I had to get out of there. I didn't want to witness this lumbering interrogation, and I certainly didn't want to answer any questions myself. I was possibly unduly concerned, but if I did have to do some shoring up, I had better get upstairs first and huddle with Beaufoy.

"I guess you won't be needing me," I said to the cops. "I didn't drive into the garage until after the super here made the nine-one-one call. I don't see how I can help."

Cop Two said, "You don't live in the building?"

"No, I'm just visiting."

The cops exchanged a glance, each checking to see if the other could come up with a reason to hold me. I could think of several, but they couldn't, and Cop Two said, "No reason for you to stay, Mr. Caprisi."

Cop One said, "We can always reach you at the *Ledger*."

"They'll know how to find me."

I didn't tell them about the calls to the cellular phone. I wanted to get out of there before they thought to ask me who I was visiting.

2 I was in Mort Beaufoy's employ because of a blip in his career that came along at about the time there was a turning point in mine.

The *New York Ledger,* where I put in nine years and seven and a fraction months, was founded in 1837—"by Washington Irving," the masthead proclaims, conforming to a policy at the paper of misstating, enhancing, or simply sidestepping the truth at every opportunity. The *Ledger* was actually founded by a distant cousin of Irving; Irving's contribution was a few humorous sketches in the early years. He received a pittance for them, and that's the tradition the *Ledger* has made every effort to honor writers with down to the present day.

The "Washington Irving" masthead is meant to counter a competing tabloid, the *New York Post,* which trumpets Alexander Hamilton as its founder. Hamilton, after all, was a foreigner, a banker, a lawyer, and an elitist, not the best image for a workingman's paper; Irving was a true son of New York and an earthy celebrator, in his writings, of the city.

None of the above is relevant, except to indicate that I loathe the *Ledger*—for its sleaze, its Neanderthal editorial policy, and its slaveowner attitude toward the hired help. But I had gone to work for the rag when I was twenty-four, when it was the only paper in New York that made an offer.

I came to the *Ledger*'s attention through an overheated account under my byline in the small south Jersey daily where I was working at the time. It was a hostage-standoff story that involved a Dominican mother and her two small boys, a thug with a nine-millimeter pistol, and the college-bound black teenager who made the fries at the burger joint that was the scene of the drama. The standoff ended when the teenager scalded the thug with fry oil. No one else was hurt, and once I fired up my computer the story practically wrote itself.

At the time, I was sixteen months out of the Columbia School of Journalism. I had gone to classes by day and proofread copy at *The New York Times* at night. I was naive enough to think that working in the *Times* building gave me a shot at a reporter's job there. No such luck, so I had gone to the New Jersey paper. The *Ledger* was my New York chance. I dug my toe in the sand while I agonized over the offer. The *Ledger*? After a day I took it.

I went to the tab with my fingers crossed and my own editorial policy—to tell the truth the best I knew how, because the truth shall make you free. I confidently expected my attitude to light up some of the dark corners at the paper.

That didn't happen, but I did have a big-city newspaper job. If I hung in I would get a better one. And I held fast to my editorial policy. On a storm-lashed coast I was a forty-watt beacon of integrity.

For whatever reason, I caught the attention of the *Ledger*'s readers. Back then the rag cost them a hard-earned thirty cents a day. I was competing with a Snickers bar, and I was determined to provide some nourishment and an absolute minimum of hot air. And because the readers' daily struggle with the city caused them pain enough, I tried wherever possible to lace my daily take on it with the saving grace of humor and a touch of compassion. Most of that was cut by the copy desk, until I built

★ 12 ★

enough clout to make them edit me with a lighter hand.

I was rewarded for my popularity, not my attitude, with a promotion from crime to politics. I faced up to wearing a shirt and tie and struck back at the discomfort by occasionally puncturing a public windbag. And then, about two years ago, age thirty-two, I was given a column of my own, "City Beat," five days a week. Now I got to pick my stories and to write them as I pleased. I chose not to affect the high-school dropout/ex–copy boy style that works for some columnists. I couldn't; I had been to college and graduate school. My concerns were the concerns of the average Joe, but I wasn't going to patronize him by writing down.

Five columns a week were too many, but the paper's corporate owners were shrewd; they knew how to get value for their dollar. In my case they had pushed the right buttons. The job became everything to me: work, hobby, home. The column was a jealous lover and it consumed me. Every time, for instance, that I tried to cheat it with a flesh-and-blood relationship, the woman would give up on me sooner or later—here comes my tab sensibility—defeated by that painted slut, the *Ledger*. Deep down I wanted a wife and kids (I am that rare American who actually comes from a functional family), but the whore's allure was too strong.

And then, a few weeks ago, my integrity got tested one time too many. The *Ledger*'s corporate owners dumped the paper to concentrate on their profitable television stations. The buyer was a slumlord from Baltimore who had as much interest in journalism as he did in urban architecture. He dealt with the paper's employees the way he dealt with his low-rent tenants—anyone he couldn't make money off, he found a way to force out. He used every dirty, humiliating device that might work, up to, but not quite including, unleashing a pack of weimaraners to snap at their asses.

The rag went from dreadful to worse. When the two people I respected most on the editorial side picked up their severance checks, to be replaced by the star reporter for a super-market weekly that specialized in weird births (DOCTORS AMAZED), I knew it was time to go. It took a month to work up the courage. Three days after I quit, Mort Beaufoy made his offer.

We had crossed paths often enough in press conferences and an occasional one-on-one interview. Beaufoy had served three terms in the Senate and was as much a New York staple as gridlock or the annual twin budget crunches in Albany and City Hall. But he was far from your boilerplate politician. A distinguished professor of medieval history at Columbia when he was first elected, he had written several books on Charle-magne and the Holy Roman Empire that were standard works in the field.

Beaufoy had come on the political scene during one of those periods when a wave of disgust at professional politicians seizes the electorate and they will elevate to high office almost anyone who doesn't smell of the clubhouse. That usually means a wanna-be with family money to spend on Academy Award–quality TV advertising. Beaufoy didn't have a dime. But he had made some insightful, deeply felt observations on foreign policy during a television debate and that started the ball rolling. He was invited here and there, and his thoughtful views, expressed without cant, could rarely be reduced to sound bites.

That refreshing fact did the trick almost by itself. The clincher might have been his sturdy, no-nonsense wife. Clara Beaufoy was handsome without having to work at it—a scrubbed-clean New Englander, who had the additional virtue of being smart. Free standing, she was worth a hundred thou-sand votes.

When the elderly Brooklyn pol who was the incumbent an-nounced his retirement from the Senate, the party nominated Mort Beaufoy almost by acclamation, despite his protests that his teaching schedule for the following year was already printed in the university catalog. He was forced to take a leave of absence.

That first time he ran he barely squeaked through. But then, unaccountably, he was reelected twice by margins so wide there really was no contest. Unaccountably, because Beaufoy didn't work at holding on to his constituents. He voted well enough for New York's interests and he pulled a few morsels out of the pork barrel for the cities, but his main focus was on international affairs; in eighteen years what he did mostly was ride herd on the State Department and help cool some hot spots in sub-Saharan Africa, Central America, and Southeast Asia, none of which were causing sleepless nights to the residents of Utica, Poughkeepsie, or Genesee County. All I could figure was that New Yorkers were proud to be represented in Washington by a man whose gaze was fixed well above the level of petty politics—a statesman, a fitting spokesman for a great state.

Every six years poor Beaufoy had to submit to an election campaign. He would make a pro forma swing across the state, giving beautifully composed academic speeches that sailed over the heads of many voters but made them feel they would be ungrateful wretches if they failed to pull the lever for Morton Ezra Beaufoy.

This year had shaped up differently. For many reasons, some economic, some prompted by another "turn the rascals out" phase in the political cycle, the voters were unhappy. Sensing their mood, Congressman Herbert Turnbull had slid out from under his rock to challenge Beaufoy for the party designation in the primary. In record time he gathered twice the number of petition signatures he needed to get on the ballot.

Herb Turnbull was prime slime. From a base in the Hudson Valley where he began his political career as head of a neighborhood improvement association, his titles—and, not incidentally, his income—had grown ever more impressive. As a local office holder he had sold building permits, zoning variances, and county construction contracts. He had never met a bribe or a kickback he didn't like, but he had never lost an election—town leader, town councilman, town supervisor, congressman. He was now completing his third loudmouth term in Congress and the polls gave him a fighting chance for the senatorial nomination.

Turnbull's appeal was that although he was on the take, he also delivered. Even with his finger in every pie, there seemed to be pie enough for all. A la mode. In three congressional terms, he had not only retained every air and military base in his county but he had actually established a new one, the funds for which were provided by cuts in the Federal Aid to Education program.

His most recent triumph was a new IRS service center for his congressional district; it provided hundreds of permanent jobs to his constituents and gave a shot in the arm to the local economy. The coup prompted several grateful contractors who had already fattened his personal pocketbook to load his campaign war chest to the brim.

Turnbull campaigned for the Senate nomination by promising to be a "full service" senator—"full service," as in wiping your windshield and checking the air in your tires. No problem of a constituent was too small for Herb. He avoided only the big problems. The only legislation he introduced was relief bills for voters who had relatives with immigration problems. His political philosophy he kept under wraps; he had none, except that he was for sale or rent to any special interest that needed him.

Since Turnbull had no record to stand on, his main campaign strategy was to zero in on his opponent's vulnerabilities. He sounded the alarm on Beaufoy's health and age—Mort was sixty-eight—and derided him on what others thought of as his strengths. I saw in this last tactic the hand of his new, cutthroat campaign manager, Poppy Hancock, a hired gun who had never lost a campaign. Poppy Hancock, a dragon lady if ever there was one.

★ 16 ★

With Hancock supervising Turnbull's scripts, Beaufoy became "the senator from Afghanistan," "the people's choice in Mali," and "the caring representative of anybody whose basic diet is snails." Turnbull advised the citizens of Buffalo and Yonkers that if they wanted the attention of their senior senator, they would be well advised to secede from the union.

This tactic, of course, was totally unfair. Beaufoy's focus on foreign affairs had helped avoid several brushfire wars and helped extinguish a couple of others. He knew when to threaten and when to placate. He had rescued the United States from some hopeless entanglements, and he had probably saved the lives of American soldiers and protected the pocketbooks of American taxpayers.

Given the most favorable circumstances, these intangible pluses would have been difficult to explain in the heat of an election campaign. But Mort Beaufoy hadn't even been able to address them in his usually never-fail professorial manner. During the previous few weeks he had been completely out of action, sidelined by a freak injury. While carrying a bicycle across the street for a grandchild, he had severely dislocated his back. He had spent the next nearly three weeks in the hospital. Now he had been out a few days but his doctor was still strictly limiting his mobility. Some campaign. That's where I came into the picture.

Beaufoy took an interest in me, not necessarily favorable, the first time we met, at a press briefing. I thought he was misreading the cause of an unresolved border crisis between India and Pakistan. This was way out of my field, but after an hour in the library and twenty minutes with the waiter in the tandoori restaurant where I sometimes roughed out my stories over a bowl of lentils, I put together a couple of questions that stung the senator to rise above routine answers.

After that, when we crossed paths he would attempt to draw a drop or two of blood. "You still with the daily that has Washington Irving spinning like a dreidel?" he would say. Or

"Isn't it time for a career move up from the *Ledger*? You could try for towel boy in a parlor house."

I never sensed any real malice in these barbs and I never took offense. Eventually Beaufoy changed his tune. "Have you considered abandoning all hope and coming to work for me?" he said one evening at a fund-raising dinner I was covering. I summoned a noncommital smile and we moved on to a topic of the day.

Beaufoy had been in the hospital about ten days when I told my slumlord publisher what he could do with his rag and the presses that printed it, and walked out. It was just about when Turnbull's campaign was heating up. Poppy Hancock's dirty-tricks department was seeding the state with new rumors that would be in full flower by primary day: Beaufoy's medical problem was not orthopedic but mental, possibly the onset of senile dementia; or Beaufoy was concealing a cancer that would kill him by Thanksgiving. Stuff like that. The senator decided he needed additional staff help. He phoned from his hospital bed and said, "Dear boy, can we talk?"

After all those years working in a place I couldn't respect and hating myself for it, I jumped at this chance. Turnbull was less than pond scum. Beaufoy was the closest thing we had in Washington to a dedicated and honorable legislator; maybe I could do him and the state a service—and at the same time be able to look myself in the eye again when I shaved.

I took a position with the campaign committee. "Media consultant," they called it, a P.R. job, but what the hell, in a good cause. It would give me some breathing space while I decided what to do with my life.

I rang the bell of Apartment 5A and waited a good bit for the occupant to shuffle to the door and unlock it. Mort's few remaining tufts of gray-white hair were in disarray, and for a man with a back problem he was carrying at least ten pounds too many around his belt line. Otherwise he looked okay, pale, except for a spot of pink high on each cheek, but pale was his natural state and he had been indoors for weeks. He was wearing the trousers of a gray business suit, and a white shirt open at the neck; his idea, I supposed, of an at-home outfit. Add a necktie and jacket and he could have conducted a Committee meeting.

"Sorry to keep you waiting, John"—he couldn't bear to call me Jock—"but I'm alone here. Clara's gone back to Silver Spring to tuck a few twigs in the nest. I am bereft." Clara had been Mrs. Beaufoy for more than forty years. Silver Spring was the site of the Beaufoys' Washington home.

He led me slowly back into the living room/study. This modest apartment was a pied-à-terre; his main residence was the Maryland house. He waved me to a chair while he cautiously eased himself back down to a nearly horizontal position on the couch.

The couch looked like it was his principal abode these days. A coffee table beside it was piled high with work-related papers, his Rolodex, a juice glass, several coffee cups, and what must once have been a linen napkin, although it contained so many folds and crumples as to suggest major abuse.

When he had made himself more or less comfortable he said, "I don't have to remind you, John, that punctuality is the politeness of kings." His tone was more playful than accusatory; if he was in pain he was hiding it well. "I assume you have an unassailable excuse for being twenty minutes late."

"I do," I said. "It's complicated. Okay if I save it?"

He didn't seem the least worried, and if Mort wasn't worried, there was no reason for me to worry. I had doubtless blown the situation in the garage out of proportion. I breathed easier, sank back in my chair, and opened the floor to a review of the campaign schedule. Based on long dealings with the police, I figured I had a good twenty minutes before a pair of detectives came knocking at the door with routine questions that would nonetheless upset Mort. I wanted to get as much of our substantive work as I could out of the way before I had to prepare him for their arrival.

Paul McClintoch, who headed Mort's reelection committee, had worked out a rough estimate of what we might accomplish in the week ahead with Mort's still limited strength and mobility. Our plan of attack comprised a clutch of twenty-, thirty-, and sixty-second spots to be shot here in the apartment for paid airings on television and radio stations across the state; a few selected interviews with local TV news anchors—in the apartment, if we could coax the anchors here; downtown, if we had to go downtown—and a single giant rally in Rochester or Syracuse two nights before the primary, to show that our man was far from disabled, that he could travel anywhere in the state to make his case. Even if this last effort put him out of action for another month, it would no longer matter; winning the primary was tantamount to winning the election.

Mort had wanted McClintoch to come up to Riverdale with me, but Paul was locked into the more important task of overseeing his boiler room fund-raisers. How intensely we would be able to blanket the airwaves in the final week of the campaign depended in part on how much last-minute money this telephone brigade could shake out of Beaufoy supporters.

Mort listened closely as I outlined the proposed schedule. He agreed that his part in it was about as much as he could manage. Then he quickly read the spots I had written with staff input, and penciled in a few quick fixes.

He was a damn good editor. He took out two glancing references to his opponent; he was taking the high road, addressing himself solely to the issues. Elsewhere he cut a nearly useless adjective and rewrote a sentence that had the smell of a campaign promise.

"To paraphrase the immortal Samuel Goldwyn," he said, fixing me with a stern look over the rim of his reading glasses, "oral promises aren't worth the paper they're written on."

After he set the spots aside, he peered around the room and decided that both the spots and the interviews should be filmed against the bookcases that lined one wall. "Books are non-threatening," he said. "Either people read and are reassured that the candidate also reads, or they don't read but are comforted to learn that they are represented by a man who does. Anyway, I hate displaying this tacky furniture. It was never meant to be seen, and it will turn off ninety percent of the women."

He was right on all points; who said he didn't know anything about practical politics?

And he was fast. We finished our business in not much over fifteen minutes. Mort had still given no hint that he had anything on his mind but the campaign, so I felt comfortable sliding into topic A. I said, "You asked why I showed up late."

"So you've finally dreamed up an excuse. Remember, I was a college professor. I've heard them all."

"Maybe not this one." I made my voice deliberately grave; I wanted him at least partially prepared for what was coming. "There's something of a problem here in your building."

He caught my tone. "Yes . . . ?"

"While I was in the garage a police car showed up. There's a dead woman down there."

"In the garage? John, my God, how awful. What happened?"

"I don't know. I left to come up here just as they were starting to look into it. The thing is"—my voice sounded strange to my ears—"the body is in the backseat of your car."

"My car? The Buick?" Again he said, "My God, how awful." His usually unlined face was knotted in distress. He propped himself up on an elbow. "How did she get there? Who is this woman?"

"I don't know. A youngish woman in a green dress. Would you have any idea who she might be?"

He shook his head and sank back down. "Not the slightest. This apartment is simply a place I lay my head when I'm in town overnight. I'm barely acquainted with the people who live here." He seemed both puzzled and concerned. "A hell of a sad place to be dead—the backseat of a Buick sedan in a basement garage. It lacks resonance."

He shook his head again. "Is this city beyond saving? I certainly hope not. This is truly appalling. I do feel for that poor woman."

"Mort, let her relatives mourn for her. My concern is for you. However the woman got in your car, there's going to be political fallout."

"No, no," he protested. "It will be quickly understood that this has nothing to do with me."

"Will it?" I did a fast revision on my estimate of his political acumen. "Let me put it this way," I said. "If Herbert Turnbull and Poppy Hancock had spotted this woman dead on the next street, they would have dragged her happily into your garage and tossed her into the back of your car. Because no matter what else, she means at least a hundred thousand votes for him."

He disagreed vehemently. "John, you wasted entirely too much of your youth on that tabloid rag. It has colored your outlook. This tragic death may generate a moment or two of incipient scandal, but it was Justice Stone, I believe, who said, 'Never underestimate the sober second thoughts of the American people.' "

"If those second thoughts take eight days to mature, we're into primary day."

"O ye of little faith," he said. But somberly.

And then he dispatched me to find out what was going on down there in the garage.

When the elevator door opened at the garage level I paused to take in the action. I didn't much like what I saw. The cast of police characters had expanded greatly, and the newcomers were clearly professional. A Crime Scene unit was at work here.

I preferred the Laurel and Hardy atmosphere of my earlier visit, but now the two rookie cops had been sent to the top of the ramp to hold back a knot of the curious. Down here, a pair of attendants were easing a body bag into a morgue van while a bearded man in wire-rimmed glasses stood by, stripping rubber gloves off his hands.

The area around the Buick had been taped off. A couple of uniformed specialists under the direction of a man in a dark suit, obviously a detective, were dusting the car and searching the area for trace evidence. A photographer was packing up his gear. The garage was getting the full forensics treatment.

Far from this action, a second detective in a Hawaiian shirt and an open windbreaker was questioning the super and the jittery Miss Kleiman. He took notes, and his pen flew. No heart-attack victim gets this kind of attention; something ugly had happened to the woman in Mort Beaufoy's Buick.

As I approached the scene the first detective turned and walked toward me. I recognized him at once—Sergeant Al Nordstrom, known on the job as "Hap," short for "Happy," because of the perpetual look of a youthful undertaker, if there are any such, on his long-jawed Nordic face. This was a break, and I might need one.

I had made Hap Nordstrom the hero in a high-profile murder case I covered in midtown Manhattan shortly after I got the column—a body-in-the-wall story, one of the best. The

★ 23 ★

wall this time was in the rectory of a Catholic church. A textbook tabloid story with rich Gothic overtones. Hap had looked exactly right peering lugubriously into the hole he had helped chop in that wall, and the *Ledger* bled the picture across five columns on pages two and three. Hap's jaw made it onto two of those columns.

Detective First Class Nordstrom had the killer in custody less than seventy-two hours after that picture ran. He was not a priest, everyone was relieved to learn, but some of the details were unfit for a family newspaper. Whoever said the *Ledger* was a family newspaper? It printed them all.

Hap had been given a merit promotion shortly thereafter, and he invited me to his wedding. "We want children right away," he whispered to me at the reception, half in the bag and struggling for breath after stumbling through some kind of energetic Swedish clog dance. Then he confided that between his odd work hours and the bride's—she was a special-duty nurse—the likelihood of their getting together when she was ovulating were about the same as for an eclipse of the moon.

It was an intimacy that cemented our bond, and every time we ran into each other the new sergeant reminded me he owed me one for his promotion. I hadn't seen him in six months. He was a smart cop, a consummate professional. What was he doing in the Bronx?

When our eyes met he said, "Jesus, Caprisi, how'd you get up here so fast?"

I told him to relax, hadn't he heard I was off the paper? I couldn't leave it at that; I had to admit I was here visiting my new boss. His expression changed. The police had done their homework; he understood who in this building my boss had to be.

The other detective called over, "Hap, I'm finished with these two. Okay if this lady goes to work?"

Hap nodded, and the weepy witness breathed, "Thank you" and made a beeline for the minivan. Hap drew me back toward a wall.

"You're working for the senator?"

"Yes, and you don't have to break it gently. I know the dead woman was in his car. I saw the body when I drove in." Better if we both laid our cards on the table, but I couldn't get out the word "murdered." "What did she die of?"

"Technically we won't know until they open her up. Approximately? A sharp impact injury to the gut."

I felt my heart pumping. "A knife wound?" Of the various foul play options, I liked that one best; it suggested a random killing by a street crazy. But it didn't make sense. I found myself saying, "Hap, I took a good look at the woman. There was no tear in her clothing, no blood. I didn't see where a knife could have penetrated that dress."

"The way she was lying, all you saw of the dress was the front of it."

"You telling me she was stabbed in the back?"

"No, I was checking to see if you moved the body." I remembered now; he could be sly. "She was stabbed frontally," he said. "But you're right, not through the dress."

"You mean her attacker lifted her dress above her waist before he plunged the knife in?"

He responded to the note of wonder in my voice. "I didn't say that," he said. "I'm not going to speculate on how the deed was done. All I'm telling you is what I know to be fact. The knife went through the flesh but not through the dress. I'll give you two more questions, Jock." He called to the forensics people, "How much longer, you guys?"

One of them called, "Maybe half an hour."

A succession of grating sounds set my teeth on edge. Miss Kleiman's minivan was lurching up the ramp. First her tires squealed and then her bumper scraped a side wall. When it was quiet again I said, "What about blood?" The more facts I had, the more I would know how to answer questions, if it had to come to that.

"She's been dead two or three hours. There was dried blood on her midriff."

My hopes rose. "It didn't soak through the dress. Doesn't that mean she wasn't wearing it when she was stabbed?" Even more than a random crazy, a rapist loose somewhere in the neighborhood would quickly shift interest in the crime away from Beaufoy.

"That's a reasonable assumption. But no more than an assumption."

"Was she raped?"

"There's no visible evidence of a struggle—no scratches, bruises, torn underclothes. No garment removed but her shoes. Was there forced vaginal penetration? Was she sodomized? How long can she have lived after she was stabbed? Do I have to tell you that many questions will have to wait till they get her up on the table? But Jock, have you ever heard of a rapist-killer who puts his victim's clothes back on?"

"Who knows what goes on in the heads of these street loonies?" I offered gamely.

He must have taken pity on my situation because he volunteered something he didn't have to. "There's blood on the floor a few yards back from the car."

That sounded like something else that could work in my favor. I said, "So that's where she was killed—back there deep in the garage. And then the killer—okay, maybe a mugger, not a rapist—looked for a place to dump the body and he stuffed her in the nearest car."

"Your boss's car." He looked more than ever the sympathetic undertaker. "Look, Jock, I said I wasn't going to speculate, but I'll stick my neck out. I don't believe this was a mugging. By the way, I assume you know we're off the record."

"I told you, I'm no longer with the paper. There's no record to be on."

"Good. Because I'd like to chase down a few leads before the media grabs this and an army of reporters starts rolling over us. A U.S. senator. Jesus."

"A senator's *car*, Hap. That's all it is. And a mugging in a garage. Probably the twentieth this year."

"I told you, it wasn't a mugging. We've got the woman's handbag. It's intact—credit cards, cash, keys."

"Then something scared him off. What you've got here is one more case of random urban violence. And they hauled you all the way up from midtown Manhattan for this?"

"I'm not in Manhattan anymore. I've been working in the Bronx for three months." At my raised eyebrows he added, "I stepped on the wrong toe and got reassigned. That's all I'm going to say."

Poor Hap. Too honest, probably, to lay off somebody with connections; his reward was an hour-and-a-half trip every day from Staten Island. Solving another high-profile crime could be his ticket back to an easy commute. I didn't want to think about that.

He said, "It's time I checked in with the senator." Reassuringly, "For the record."

"I'll take you up."

He looked at me. He was about to say, Don't bother, I can find it. We locked eyes; I wasn't going to give on this. When he did speak he said, reasonably, "Sure, why not."

He shouted to his partner that he'd be upstairs for a few minutes, and I led him to the elevator. The super hurried after us, reaching for his keys. "I'll have to unlock that for you."

Hap said, "The elevator door is locked?" He turned to me. "How did you get upstairs?"

"The senator buzzed me in."

The super said, "I explained the system to the other detective. He is your partner?"

"You can tell me," Hap said.

"Yes, sir. Tenants bring the elevator to the garage level with a key. Visitors, if they enter this way instead of above, through the lobby, call up on this intercom and their people upstairs buzz to release the elevator door lock."

"Why not make them use the lobby?"

"They can, if they want to walk around the corner. Same thing there, except the intercom is on the front door."

"There's no doorman? No elevator man?"

"Sir, they would be a waste. Our tenants are business and professional people, out all day. The apartments are small—studios and one-bedrooms—so there are no children. Almost everyone who comes here arrives by car and uses this entrance. We have never had a problem."

"Uh-huh," was Hap's response.

The super caught his meaning. "Not inside the building itself. Our tenants are very well satisfied. They feel safe. Or we would not have people like Senator Beaufoy living here."

3 Hap and I waited even longer at Apartment 5A than I had earlier for Beaufoy to make his way to the door. Was he fading as the day wore on, or—the thought sneaked into my head—was he making sure the police understood just how limited his mobility was? Either way, he did eventually end the suspense and let us in.

While I introduced Sergeant Nordstrom, "an old friend and a first-rate detective," Mort led us at a snail's pace to the living room, all the while playing the warm, if pontifical, host. Hap responded just as warmly; he said he was pleased to meet the senator, and he volunteered that he had voted for him twice.

"Only twice?" Mort twinkled. He had interrupted the long trek to the couch to ask the question.

"I'm sorry, Senator. I was a month under age the first time you ran."

Mort pursed his lips. Professor time. "Ours is supposed to be the advanced civilization," he said, "but you probably know, Sergeant, there are social entities on this planet where boys as young as twelve are admitted to tribal councils as soon as they have gone through the puberty rites."

"I guess I'd like that," Hap said. "If the puberty rites didn't make me barf."

Good for Hap. Mort had the good sense to throw back his head and guffaw his appreciation. Then he finished the journey to the couch and gradually found a way to make himself comfortable.

His demeanor now indicated that the social part of the visit was over. He said, "John has filled me in some on the tragedy downstairs. I'm anxious, of course, to help in any way I can. But I must warn you, I'm seldom here for more than a day or two, and I've never known much of what goes on in this building. Even less these days. I was in the hospital for three weeks until last Thursday and since then I've only been out of the apartment once."

"When would that have been, Senator?" Hap was opening his notebook; the social part of the visit was over for him too.

"Last evening. My wife was here playing mother hen until yesterday afternoon. She did stock the kitchen before she went back to our home near Washington, but once she was gone the walls began to close in. Long confinement to that hospital bed has made me a touch claustrophobic."

"I can understand that. Where did you go?"

"I managed to hobble—not without cost—to the little Italian restaurant a block north of here. At the time it seemed more like a mile. I managed to choke down some salty pasta, shook a few hands, and came home. Not worth the detour, as Michelin might put it."

Hap was writing. "The restaurant. That's the Piazza Roma?"

"I believe that's its name. Tell me, are you making a call on everyone in the building?" The question seemed to come less from personal concern than from a mild curiosity about police procedure.

Hap said, "I'm afraid we'll have to do that. The super tells me you're the only one in at the moment. Senator, do you know a woman named Sheri Bannerman?"

Mort seemed to rise half an inch above the couch. His relaxed air had vanished. "My God, is that the woman who died?"

"According to her wallet and car registration."

"Yes. Yes, I know her." He shot me a look of surprise and pain while he fought to control a trembling lip. "This is terrible. A terrible tragedy." He was twisting the already mangled linen napkin between his hands, as though to wring it out. "She was here this morning."

"At what time?"

"Our appointment was for ten. She was prompt. She stayed for perhaps half an hour. Not much more. My God, she seemed such a vital young woman, totally alive." He looked the way I suddenly felt. He breathed, "How did she die?"

"Sir, this will go faster if I ask the questions. It's okay with you, is it, if I ask a few?"

I cut in. "Mort, you don't have to sit still for any of this, if you don't want to." The ground seemed to be dropping out from under me.

He said, "No, no, by all means, Sergeant, ask away. My God."

"Okay. To answer your question first, she was murdered. Apparently stabbed with a knife."

"God." Mort had turned chalky white. "God, how dreadful."

I said, "Mort, are you all right?"

"Yes, yes. I'm just . . . How tragic." He was drawing deep breaths. "How terribly sad."

Hap gave him a moment to steady down. Then, "I agree, sir. We're living in ugly times. Can you tell me how you happen to be acquainted with this woman?"

Mort took a final deep breath. He seemed in control now. "She's—was—my real estate agent."

"You're looking to buy, what, a house?"

"A small apartment. But bigger than this one." Some of the color, such as it was, had returned to his cheeks. "I'm afraid I can't afford a second house." He was talking now to calm himself. "I'm one of your rare Senate birds who lives basically on salary." His voice was steady, but he was gripping the edge of the coffee table, grinding the crumpled napkin into it.

"So this Sheri Bannerman was taking you around, showing you apartments?" It was a sly question.

"Not in my condition, no. We did it all here. Ms. Bannerman came in with a few preselected floor plans, some pictures, and so on." He slowly shook his head. "Not three hours ago she was sitting about where you are now. My God."

He was still badly shaken, but I was beginning to feel more secure. The situation was taking a more reasonable shape.

Hap kept writing, his long, sad face pressed against his necktie; he was for all the world the funeral director taking burial instructions for the recently departed. He said, "The visit this morning. Was it your first meeting with Ms. Bannerman?"

"No. I saw her on one previous occasion when I was up from Washington. Some time before I went into the hospital. To give her some idea of the sort of place I was looking for."

Hap said, "Excuse me for asking, but if I don't, someone else will. Picking an apartment—isn't that usually something husbands and wives do together? Mrs. Beaufoy was here with you until yesterday. I would guess she was available to look at floor plans too. But the Bannerman woman didn't come to see you until today. How come?"

Mort put the napkin down. "A very good question, Sergeant. I'm glad to see that John's calling you a first-rate detective was substantive rather than hype. Fact is, my wife knows nothing about Ms. Bannerman."

Jesus Christ. While my stomach dropped into my shoes Hap said, "Excuse me?"

"You see, the new apartment was going to be a surprise for her. Still will be, I hope."

Hap was searching for a delicate way to phrase his next question, and I couldn't think of anything to say that wouldn't lead to more trouble, so I kept my lip buttoned. After a beat or two Mort picked up the slack himself.

"Clara and I have a wedding anniversary on the horizon. Believe me, after you've celebrated a few dozen of those you run out of gift ideas. This is a rather clever one, don't you think?"

Hap found his voice. "Very." Now he was beginning to look like young Abe Lincoln in the grip of one of his black moods. "And you say you've been planning this surprise—a new apartment—for some time?"

"Before I went into the hospital it was no more than a vague notion, more in the realm of speculation."

Beaufoy began speaking more softly now, almost to himself. "But during the weeks I was a prisoner in that hospital bed— a prisoner, as well, of pain—my imagination began to make up for the failings of my body. I couldn't do, so I let my dreams take wing. During the day I concocted wishful solutions to the problems in my professional sphere, those of nation against nation and sect against sect.

"At night I scaled down my dreams to help me sleep. What I found most relaxing was arranging and rearranging the rooms in a perfect apartment—as perfect as my resources will allow. Thus inspired, I summoned Ms. Bannerman to actualize my dreams. Subject in the end, of course, to my wife's veto."

Hap allowed a respectful moment to go by. He scribbled in his notebook and then said, straight-faced, "Thank you for sharing that, sir. I promise to try not to spoil the surprise for your wife.

"A final question or two. When the Bannerman woman was here this morning, did there seem to be anything bothering her? Did she seem at all nervous or fearful?"

"You mean, as if someone might be threatening her? Not

that I could tell. As I said, she was vibrant and cheerful, seemingly untroubled."

"Do you remember how she was dressed?"

"I'm sorry, no. I'm a total failure in that department. I never seem to notice. Sometimes not even what I'm wearing myself. I am the despair of my wife."

"It's the same with my wife. Senator, Ms. Bannerman had to have been killed within minutes of leaving this apartment. With that in mind, looking back on your meeting can you think of anything else that might help me? Any sort of lead, no matter how slight? Someone she might have mentioned, someplace she was going or had just been, something she was thinking about, wondering about?"

"I'm sorry, we stuck pretty much to the matter at hand. I had calls to make and to receive in connection with my campaign, and with Senate Committee business. She sensed that my time was limited, and she took up no more of it than was necessary. I respected that."

Hap closed his notebook with a mournful sigh and got to his feet. "Sir, I do appreciate your help. If I can think of some further way you might help, I suppose I can find you either here or in your Washington office?"

"I'll be in New York at least through primary day. I'm sorry I couldn't be more useful. I wish you every success in finding the killer of this young woman. I cannot tell you how deeply I feel this tragedy. What a waste. What a terrible waste."

I walked Hap to the elevator. When we were in the corridor he turned to me. "Would you do something for me, Jock? You can do it without ruffling feathers. Get me the name of the senator's doctor. The one who put him in the hospital."

"The orthopedist? Sure." I should have let it go at that but I had to say it. "You want to know if that old man is strong enough to carry a dead weight across the garage and heave it into his car—a dead weight of what, a hundred and twenty pounds?"

"Beaufoy may know Bannerman's weight better than either of us."

"That was uncalled for."

"Sorry. Look, whatever I think, I'd be nailed as incompetent if I didn't follow every street to its dead end. Don't take any of this personally."

I didn't reply to that. I was mad. But I had nothing to gain by making Hap an adversary. When the elevator arrived, I held the door open while I described in detail the two calls I'd picked up on Bannerman's cellular phone and hadn't reported to the rookie cops. He nodded, stepped into the elevator, and said I'd done the right thing to answer the phone. We parted on good terms. As the door closed he had pulled out his notebook and was scribbling an entry.

Back in the apartment, Beaufoy was lying on the couch, talking with his Washington office. The call turned out to be a long one, and I took the opportunity to snoop. I ran my eye over the books, mostly on European history, glanced at the homey family photos, and took a closer look at the furniture Mort was eager to exclude from his TV spots. He may have been wrong about the furniture. The pieces were undistinguished Grand Rapids modern, decades old, and worn. They spoke of a man who hadn't been bought.

One of the things I had always admired about Mort Beaufoy was his refusal to profit financially from his position of power in the Senate. He had never, for instance, accepted a fee for speeches. "I lectured sixty times a year at Columbia on a professor's salary," he once told me. "I'm not going to accept twenty grand from some global corporation for a forty-minute talk that would put me in their pocket forever." His only out-side income came from the scholarly books he turned out every four to six years.

I stole an occasional hard look at him on the phone. His cheeks were back to their original pink and white. His face was unlined, almost childlike. I didn't for a minute entertain the idea that he was capable of murder, but there was no way I could swallow whole the loopy story he had told Hap.

How much of it was true? I hated the *Ledger* because it shrank from the truth the way a cat does from a hot stove; had I bound myself to another employer for whom truth was a sometime thing? God, I hoped not; I wanted to believe in Mort Beaufoy.

After he had hung up he said, "You look troubled, John. Did your policeman friend rattle you? He came on somewhat heavy, but he was only doing his job. I'm glad I cleared the air. The thrust of this story will be moving elsewhere."

"Not just yet," I said. I couldn't keep the edge out of my voice. Was he that obtuse? "I guarantee that at least one tabloid tomorrow morning will run side-by-side photos on its front page of you and the deceased. Bad enough you're at least twice the woman's age; her picture will show her at eighteen, because some enterprising reporter will have lifted it from her high-school yearbook. That will make you look nearly four times her age."

"I can live with that. Thank God, John, everybody doesn't have your tabloid mentality. Come to think of it, a whiff of scandal might do me good. Turnbull's people paint me with one foot in the grave, dribbling a trail of milk and crackers. So how come I still seem to be kicking up my heels with some young chick?" He bit out the last word as though he had never uttered it before, and maybe he hadn't.

He was really ticking me off. "Mort, if you want the spot-light off you, would you please give serious thought to keep-ing your story straight?"

"Where have I failed to do that?"

I had been carrying a heavy burden, and I dropped it without ceremony. "I described the dead woman to you not half an hour ago. Didn't you tell me you had no idea who I was talking about?"

"You described her? I don't remember a description."

"I said a young woman in a green dress. Did that misrepresent her?"

"I do remember your saying that. In all honesty, it did nothing for me. As I said, I rarely notice how people dress. If I shut my eyes now, I couldn't tell you what you are wearing."

"Mort, a bright green dress."

"It didn't register. I don't know why. . . ." He lit up. "Wait a minute, I have a notion. At my request Ms. Bannerman made me a cup of instant coffee. When she carried it from the kitchen some of it spilled, I believe, on whatever she was wearing. Was it green? I think possibly not. Probably not. She had other clients to see today. Could she have kept an emergency change of wardrobe in her trunk and slipped it on in her car? Because I'm certain now. I never saw a green dress."

He was in dead earnest. He seemed to believe he had just put forth a viable theory. He was impossible. He would have to be saved from himself.

4 Even a no-holds-barred pair like Herbert Turnbull and Poppy Hancock were not likely to persuade New York's voters that Morton Beaufoy, the professorial chairman of the Senate Foreign Relations Committee, had stuck a knife in a honey-blonde. I devoutly hoped not. But they would readily believe—it wouldn't take much to convince them—that Beaufoy and the blonde were involved in a relationship.

"Relationship" was too classy a word, considering the age difference. Sugar daddy said it better—grateful older man showers gifts on compliant younger woman. That threat had hung over me from my first glimpse of the Bannerman woman's garter. Although the term was rarely used anymore, sugar daddies were still staples in the diet of the tab press and tabloid television. As cooked by Poppy Hancock, this savory dish would be devoured by the media, hot, cold, and as leftovers, every day until the primary. The voters would have more than enough time to reevaluate their previously squeaky clean senior senator. Unless the smear could be stopped before it started.

I was already at work on a theory to do just that when I drove out of Mort's garage. Hap Nordstrom and his people were still there, combing the scene. If Hap was right and the blonde wasn't killed in a random street crime, the perpetrator had to be someone who knew her schedule this morning or whom she had asked to meet her in the garage. Nailing that person would effectively squash the sugar daddy scenario. Rule One for furtive liaisons: don't invite friends, relatives, or business acquaintances to your married lover's garage.

If a killer known to Sheri Bannerman could be identified before the media got wind of the crime and whipped innuendo into firestorm, Mort Beaufoy would be spared political incineration. For Mort, every hour counted. For the police, hours meant nothing. Knowing Hap Nordstrom, I figured it would be an hour or two before he started following leads. By then I hoped to be able to point him toward a solution.

That was not as brashly ambitious a goal as it sounds. Contrary to crime fiction, most real murders are five-finger exercises in cause and effect; to anyone who takes the trouble to look, the perpetrator usually stands out in Day-Glo colors. The police solve most homicides in three or four days of routine investigation. And that includes assembling evidence that has to stand up in court.

In three or four days Mort Beaufoy could be in too deep a hole to be hauled out by primary day. But I didn't have the problem of satisfying a grand jury. All I needed was a viable suspect, one who fit my hopeful take on the crime.

I learned early on covering homicides that if you can knock out robbery and rape as the motive, you can bet dollars to dimes a married woman's killer is going to be her husband. Never underestimate the power of domestic friction. I had noted the gold wedding band on the dead woman's hand. A husband was out there somewhere. And a husband was the perfect murderer for my scenario. If Sheri Bannerman told hers where she was going to be this morning, it was likely with a clear conscience regarding her dealings with Mort Beaufoy. And if the husband then came to Mort's garage and murdered her, he must have been motivated by something entirely unrelated to Mort Beaufoy. That was my scenario—I suppose because it was the one I needed. I didn't want to consider any other.

But of course I had to. How could I ignore the possibility that the husband had trailed his wife to Mort's place and killed her precisely *because* the two were having an affair? If that was the case, I had better learn the truth before anyone else, so I could try to put a favorable spin on it. Good luck.

I hadn't a clue where the Bannermans lived, but it was likely to be near where Sheri sold real estate. The Bronx phone book in Mort's neighborhood Italian restaurant listed two Bannermans in the Riverdale area. The first one I called gave me liftoff.

A female voice on the answering machine at the home of one Bryce Bannerman was warm and throaty: "Oh, dear, Sheri and Bryce are at work again, those drudges. He can be reached at Bannerman and Bailes in Manhattan, and she's at Oliver Realty in Yonkers. Or leave a message, please do, you lovely whoever."

I didn't leave a message, but I felt a twinge of compassion as I hung up; Sheri sounded, as Mort suggested, very much alive.

I figured Bannerman and Bailes for a law firm. The Manhattan book gave an address in the far East Fifties. I didn't call. I could be there in under half an hour—with luck, a shade before Hap Nordstrom. It wouldn't be the first time I'd beaten the police to the next of kin.

It turned out to be a storefront in the heart of the home-furnishings district. From the street it looked like the shop of a London bespoke tailor, but the burnished gold lettering across the top read "Bannerman & Bailes, Antiques." The single display window was empty except for an amphora circled by placid wrestlers, and an inlaid harpsichord draped with what looked like a sari. For the window of an antiques shop, very understated.

The interior was just the opposite. Shelves to the high ceilings along two dimly lit corridors barely contained the pileup of objets d'art. They were of many periods and appeared to be of varying quality. Vases, lamps, bowls, figurines, ornamental trays, and so on, seemed poised to cascade onto my head. The floor was so crowded with antique furniture and statuary that I had to move crab fashion to advance through it. This was what I imagined William Randolph Hearst's warehouse of San Simeon rejects must look like.

The atmosphere in the airless, dust-laden half-light was oppressive. There were no other customers, and although a bell had dinged when I opened the front door, no one came to help me. At the back of the shop a crack of light spilled from under what was probably an office door. It was my fond wish that Bryce Bannerman was back there working up the courage to confess his mad act. I would even settle for his being back there polishing his alibi.

Directly in my path as I pushed rearward was an umbrella stand painstakingly fashioned into the head of a trumpeting elephant. I stopped to stare. Unbelievable. At that moment I sensed, rather than heard, someone at my back.

I turned to face a man in a double-breasted blazer. He had a lethal jaw, a healthy tan, and a head of streaky blond hair that was combed straight back. He looked under forty. If I had to guess an occupation, I would have ventured hired captain of a racing yacht.

He turned out to be an antiques dealer with a trace of prep school in his voice. He murmured, "You happen to be looking at one of my favorite pieces in the entire collection."

I said, "That a fact? I really hate it a lot." Confrontation might be the quickest route to confession.

Hammer Jaw didn't miss a beat. "I know what you mean," he said smoothly. "It's not to everyone's taste."

"What do I know?" I said. "I've never really understood African art."

"Me neither. Actually, this is nineteenth-century Tamil. South India."

"Indian even less." Enough foreplay. "I'm looking for Bryce Bannerman."

"Bryce is out. I'm his partner, Hilton Bailes. Perhaps I can help you."

"You probably can. You can tell me where to find him."

"May I ask who's inquiring?"

"My name's Jock Caprisi."

His eyes widened, then narrowed. He was comparing me to the picture that used to run beside my byline. "Yes, of course, the columnist. I don't often see the *Ledger* but I occasionally pick one up in a taxi."

"Same here."

He took a second or two, then said, more prep school than ever, "Would you care to step back to the office?"

That sounded promising. I said I only had a minute or two, and we went single file back to the room the light was spilling from. En route he called to a thin young man I now saw high on a ladder, dusting, "Eric, will you please take the conn?" Yacht captain could be right on the money.

Believe it or not, the office was crammed with more antiques—in case, I supposed, there was a run on the merchandise in the shop. A space had been carved out for a kidney-shaped desk that was piled high with paperwork but was probably also for sale, and a couple of very tired French Empire chairs, likewise.

Bailes motioned me to one of the chairs. I was afraid if I broke it I'd bought it, so I remained standing. Anyway, I didn't want to look as if I had time to settle in for a chat. Hap Nordstrom was probably no more than a beat to my rear.

Bailes perched on a corner of the desk and said, "Okay,

what's he done?" He made sure there would be no misunderstanding. "Bryce."

Cagily I said, "What makes you think he's done something? And I'm not sure I know what you mean by 'done.' " We seemed to be edging in the right direction.

I noticed now that Bailes held his head tilted awkwardly high, whether out of pride or to maintain the clean line of that formidable jaw I couldn't tell. He said, "Mr. Caprisi, I've seen the stuff you write. Your column. Strong New York stories. You're not here because Bryce saved a cat up in a tree."

I said, "It could be because he saved a child from a burning building. But you expected to hear he was in trouble."

"Damn right." His mouth was grimly set.

"Because . . . ?"

"Only if you tell me why you want him."

"Okay. You first."

He sighed wearily. "This is all off the record," he said. "What do they call it—'deep background'?"

"I'll agree to that. None of what you say is for publication." It was as easy a promise as I'd ever made. Apparently Bailes hadn't been in a taxi lately.

He hesitated only a moment. "I've been thinking of putting a private investigator on Bryce."

My pulse quickened. "What do you think he's up to?"

"That's it, I don't know. Until now I thought he's been cooking our books. But that wouldn't interest Jock Caprisi. It must be something big—smuggling drugs in our imports, running guns. Maybe laundering mob money. You tell me."

"What roused your suspicions? Does Bannerman have income he can't account for?" I didn't know where we were going but I liked the idea of money poisoning the well.

Bailes picked up a heavy silver letter opener that was holding down a pile of invoices. "He sure as hell does. Business is rotten. In the long run antiques go up in value. Always. But not in the current economic climate. Collectors won't take the necessary short-term risks. We're heavy on inventory, light on cash."

He ruffled the papers with the letter opener. "Overdue bills. You know the joke. *We* can't sell antiques, but the man who sells us antiques—brother, can *he* sell antiques. This business is dead in the water. Becalmed. We've waited two years to raise a breeze." Bailes worked his nautical metaphors like a bilge pump.

He was becoming more agitated as he spoke, and he began using the letter opener—it looked like a Florentine dagger— to drive home his points. "Bryce and I have been drawing damn little from the business. I've cut my living expenses to the bone. Christ, I've even taken a leave from my club. But the Bannermans? They've redone their living room and now they're putting in, for God's sake, a swimming pool."

I said, "And you think the money for all that came out of the shop?"

"They sure as hell didn't win the lottery. I know, it's a standard business complaint: 'My partner is fucking me over.' But it's easy to do here. Is Bryce selling pieces on the sly? We have very loose inventory control. We built this business on a basis of mutual trust. We saw eye to eye, aesthetically as well as on running the business. But these days . . ." He trailed off disconsolately.

"Yes . . . ?" I encouraged.

His upraised chin had dropped a few degrees, the jawline softened a bit. "I don't know exactly. He's remote, withdrawn, absent from the shop sometimes without a good reason. And then there's this free-spending mode. . . ."

"Couldn't the cash flow be from Mrs. Bannerman's real estate deals?"

"Exactly what Bryce says. Please, it hurts when I laugh. Real estate has been flat for years. People don't have the guts to buy a house. Sheri is dealing mostly in condos and co-ops, apartments for sale or rent. She may have some action, but it's small potatoes."

I said, "Still, potatoes. And you have no matching source of outside income?"

"You mean, am I married, with its offsetting pros and cons for the emotions and the pocketbook?"

"Okay, are you?"

"Not unless you count my recent separation from a temperamental sloop. But none of this affects the price of beans in Bulgaria." He said abruptly, "Your turn. What do you want Bryce for?"

We were running long. Stepping up the pace, I said, "I came to let him know his wife is dead."

Bailes dropped the letter opener, and it landed heavily on the floor. For a moment he said nothing while his face wrestled with shock, pain . . . and something else. Secret pleasure? But when he spoke it was in a hushed voice that had lost its sour edge.

"No. How? What happened?"

"She was murdered in an apartment-house garage not far from where they live."

"Holy Mother." Shaken, he slid off the table and bent to pick up the letter opener. He needed the moment. When he stood up he was more composed. "A mugging?"

"It's too early to say." I was watching him for clues. Clues to what? This wasn't the same as working the scene for an eight-hundred-word character sketch for the column; I was still learning to play detective.

Bailes was fumbling with the letter opener and for something to say. Finally he said, "Awful news. Awful. Bryce and I go back a long way. I feel terrible for him. . . ."

Did I detect a slight emphasis on "him"? There was more he wanted to get off his chest. "And still . . . ?" I prompted.

He spoke slowly now, measuring his words. "Of course it's

Bryce who concerns me. I must sound cold-blooded, but for Bryce, in the long run, when the shock wears off, frankly, this may be for the best."

"Tell me."

"Not if it's going to get back to him."

"It won't. Or anywhere else. I agreed, we're off the record."

He put down the letter opener to give what he had to say his full attention. "Sheri was bad news for Bryce from day one. The woman tried and failed to make it as an actress and she had an attitude. You know the type—flashy, out front, always 'on,' overcompensating. She made up for failure by conspicuous consumption. In the end she had pretty nearly consumed Bryce. If he *is* cheating me, it was to feed Sheri's compulsion to spend. No, he is well out of it."

If, as I hoped, Bannerman had chosen to help get himself "well out of it" by way of a knife thrust to Sheri's gut, I might be able to wrap up this business and hand the package to Hap Nordstrom this afternoon.

"Do you have any idea where he is now?" I asked.

"He's at home."

"I phoned and got a machine."

"Did you leave a message?" I shook my head, and he said, "Bryce listens but doesn't pick up. We have persistent creditors. He should be there. He had a good excuse today. He was expecting his swimming pool contractor." His head was elevated now. "It's going to be a hell of a lot of pool for one person."

5 Driving hell-bent back to Riverdale, I weighed the value of Hilton Bailes's assessment of the Bannermans' relationship. I tried not to credit it too highly. Bailes had made a case for an abrupt termination of their marriage vows, but was it clear-eyed, or the view of a possibly woman-hating homosexual?

I stopped right there. What made me assume Bailes was gay? Because he was over thirty-five, unmarried, and worked in the interior decorating district? I was not that much *under* thirty-five, unmarried, and I occasionally watched Joan Crawford movies on cable TV. Snap judgments can be dangerous. And of course I wanted Bailes to have gotten it right. I *needed* Bailes to have gotten it right.

Nearly an hour and a half had gone by since I left Beaufoy, and I was becoming increasingly edgy about the likelihood that the story would break. Or had the floodgates already opened? The senator had my cellular-phone number but I knew he would be too proud to holler for help—and probably too P.R. naive to know when he needed help. I tried calling him three or four times during the drive. His line was continually busy. Was that a sign of trouble or was he on campaign business?

Meanwhile I kept my radio tuned to the all-news station. After monitoring an entire eighteen-minute cycle without hearing a reference to a female body in a garage, I breathed easier. Hap Nordstrom was possibly managing to keep a temporary lid on this thing for reasons of his own, or as a small favor to me. Or should I just be thankful that news flowed glacially from the far north corner of the Bronx where this drama was unfolding?

There was punishment in keeping the news station on for the full twenty-five-minute drive: I had to endure not once but twice Congressman Herbert Turnbull mealymouthing his way through an answer to a reporter's question: No, it was not for him to declare whether his opponent was medically fit to serve another six years in the senate. But to quiet voter concerns, wouldn't it make sense for the senator to submit to an examination by an impartial panel of doctors?

The bastard. If there were voter concerns about the senator's health, they had been planted by Turnbull's dirty-tricks department, and that bunch could be guaranteed to produce a quack who would cast doubt on an examination of Beaufoy by a panel of Nobel laureate doctors. My response to Turnbull's challenge would have had Beaufoy agree to a physical exam if Turnbull submitted to a *moral* exam by a panel of judges, philosophers, and clergymen charged with determining if he was ethically fit to serve. There was no point in making the suggestion. Mort would never go for it.

When I gave up on reaching Mort I spent three of the remaining six minutes of the drive on a call to the Reelect Senator Beaufoy campaign headquarters in Manhattan. That phone was answered after twelve or fifteen rings by a harried volunteer. I gave my name and asked for Paul McClintoch, and the volunteer bellowed, "Paul! Paul McClintoch! Pick up, please." State of the art.

Paul came on at once with a mild, "Where are you, Jock?

I've been trying to reach you for at least an hour. What's going on up there?"

Mild didn't mean McClintoch wasn't concerned; mild was his way, even in crisis. I said, "It'll go faster if you tell me first how much you know."

"Mort called me half an hour ago on fund-raising business, at the end of which he mentioned that a woman he knew slightly had been found dead in his basement—"

"In his *car*, Paul," I exploded. "In the back seat of his Buick. Stabbed to death."

"Jesus," he breathed. He took a moment to let this sink in. "The only reason he mentioned her was to ask me to send flowers to the funeral, 'With deepest sympathy, Morton Beaufoy.' What do I do?"

"You'll have to do it. The whole story will come out soon enough. Mort may have been the last person to see the woman before she was killed—"

"I see."

"—and if he doesn't send flowers he's going to look like a cold fish."

"How, um, bad is this?"

"Not as bad as it looks, but until the killer is found it's going to look terrible. So, the sooner the better. Paul, is anyone else on this line?"

"No, we don't do that here."

"Okay. Just between us, is Mort a chaser?"

"Jock, are you telling me this is an attractive woman?"

"With honey hair. Is he?"

"Absolutely not. Uh-uh. Not as far as I know. I've never seen anything, or heard anything. Not remotely. And I've been with him twelve years."

"That's good. Don't get your hopes up, but I think I have a shot at shortstopping this thing before it gets started."

"Do it. Before Poppy Hancock gets tired of snapping at our

ass and moves up to the jugular. I don't have to tell you, Jock, nobody does it better."

I knew, and I tried to push the knowledge aside. "A last hopeful thought," I said. "Pray that when the voters hear about the body in their senator's Buick they focus on the ancient Buick and not the body. It could become a populist icon, like Harry Truman's frame house in Independence or the hole in Adlai Stevenson's shoe. It speaks of a politician neither on the make or on the take."

"I'll take what comfort I can from that," McClintoch said, and hung up.

I turned off the radio. McClintoch had put Poppy Hancock into my head. I had taken pains to avoid thinking about Hancock in connection with this mess, because if it wasn't cleared up in a hurry she would be all over us. I didn't look forward to that. She was a ball breaker so artful that her opponents sometimes didn't know their balls were broken till they tried to use them.

Poppy Hancock was possibly a year or two younger than me but she had been in politics ever since her graduation from the University of Michigan. Correction, she had always been in politics: grammar school politics, neighborhood politics, gofering at her local political club in Flint from the time she was fourteen. She had counted cadence at marches, carried signs at demonstrations, and trampled on them at counter-demonstrations. She was, in short, a force to be reckoned with wherever three or more people gathered to press a point.

She was the complete political animal. "Who isn't?" she once told an interviewer. "Everything we do has a political side. We persuade, we deal, we leverage, we compromise, we maneuver, we overcome. In life, in love, in the laundromat."

In the past several years she had built a reputation guiding underdogs in the Midwest and Northeast to election victory—

two mayors, a congressman, and a governor. This present campaign was a career marker. A Herbert Turnbull win for the Senate nomination in New York against the well-entrenched Mort Beaufoy would make Hancock a major player on the national political scene.

The television cameras ate her up. She had thick dark hair cut short and bouncy, a curvy figure just this side of zaftig, the innocent face of a sixteen-year-old cheerleader, and a strong, clear voice that cut like a chainsaw through the background noise in arenas and airports. Her looks and her vivid, in-your-face use of language combined to make her the queen of the sound bite. "Our opponent is not on the take," she declared under the turning blades of a helicopter during one hairy race. "He is a public-spirited recycler of Pepsi cans, whose vacation palace and Olympic pool were built one refund nickel at a time."

One of Hancock's campaign signatures was the untraceable leaflet or letter to the voters, circulated too late to be answered, that made some outrageous charge against the opposition. After the election she would deny any connection to this scurrilous document and speculate that it was a dirty trick of the other side, designed to make her man look less than honorable.

I first met Poppy Hancock two years earlier, just before I was given the column but not long after people started mentioning her name. I had called for an interview. Not for the *Ledger*, which couldn't have cared less; I knew I could sell a piece to *The New Republic*. She was passing through town and she said she'd give me an hour.

We met in the bar of her hotel. She showed up exactly on time, dressed in tailored pants and a silk blouse and looking even better than on the tube. Her clear blue eyes gave off glints of violet. She had a glow. Her hello was crisp and businesslike but by no means cold. Her handshake was firm. I bought the drinks. She ordered a Virgin Mary.

I don't know how or why, but she already knew I was from

South Jersey, that my father was a jazz musician, and that I had financed my way through the University of Pennsylvania working construction before I went to the J School. While we waited for the drinks she bombarded me with sharp questions about Italian-American politics in South Philadelphia. She knew at least as much on that subject as I did.

It was my interview, and when the drinks came I opened my notebook. Before I could ask the first question she had engaged me in another bout of verbal arm-wrestling. It was not the first time a subject had tried to take control of the interview, but I found myself unaccountably on the defensive. I had to explain that although my dad was away a lot the family ties were strong, the home anchor was sunk deep, my mother was a saint, none of my siblings to this day lives more than a ten-minute stroll from the family home, blah, blah, blah. What was she up to? Before she submitted to the interview she had to show me that the decision to do so was entirely hers.

The next forty minutes of Q and A went smoothly enough. She would rattle the ice in her hoked-up tomato juice while she framed a reply, and she annoyed me by stealing too many glances at her watch, but she fielded my political questions crisply. She had served her professional apprenticeship on the staff of a highly regarded Michigan congressman, now retired. She wouldn't say where her own political heart lay these days. She admitted to being a technician; she wanted to work for pols she found exciting—doers of various political persuasions, "the ones who hack away the underbrush instead of getting caught in it." I got a few good quotes (I was the interviewer she gave the "In life, in love, in the laundromat" line to).

Then we got around to the obligatory, sometimes tricky, personal stuff. I said I knew that her real first name was Paula; wasn't "Poppy," a childhood appellation, a little cutesy for the hardball league she was now playing in? Not, she came back sweetly, if you fix in your mind the powerful drugs derived from the flower of that name, drugs that had shaken our world

★ 52 ★

and turned it upside down; and wasn't "Jock" needlessly macho, and the *Ledger* a puerile outlet for a grown man who ought to know better? Or was my writing suitable only for people who couldn't absorb anything more complex than carbohydrates? The serpent's tongue had flicked out.

Despite the putdown, or maybe because of it, I felt a surge of sexual feeling for her. This woman was a major turn-on. I didn't even offer in my defense that the "Jock" had been pinned on me in college when I failed to make, in succession, the baseball, track, and swimming teams.

I took a moment to regroup. I asked a couple of harmless questions while her violet-flecked eyes darted twice more to her watch. I thought I had my lust well under control when I remarked that her public image was of a workaholic; did she have much time for a private life?

She said, "Is this for the piece or for your little black book?"

"For the piece, of course. I don't have to tell you, readers want to know that stuff."

"Do you ask men in politics who it is they're dating? Bachelor governors, divorced senators?"

"I'm more curious about who the *married* ones are dating. But I can't ask them, so I limit myself to anyone in politics who's unattached and might have some appeal to the opposite sex. Isn't sexual energy a clue to political energy? Look at Clinton, Johnson, Kennedy. Any Kennedy."

She leaned forward to reply, thought better of it, and instead picked up her glass and rattled it a last time. She said, "Jock, I'd love to sit here and cut up libidos with you, but if I don't get upstairs and pack, I'm going to miss my plane. Nice meeting you."

I wanted to offer her another drink, a real one this time. I wanted to offer her my body. But with a tight smile and a curt nod, she had left for the elevators. She made as satisfying a picture going as she had coming.

When the interview was published the next month, I got a

penciled note from her from somewhere in the Midwest: "Thanks, I've seen worse." It was signed "Paula." Nice touch. We met again about a year later, this time in Washington. I was covering New York's mayor on one of his periodic pilgrimages with a paper cup to beg for federal funds. After a long day of meetings and an endless dinner with a group of wine lobbyists, where the samples flowed freely, I got back to my hotel after midnight, ready to sack out. I noticed on the lobby events-board that there was a political function in the ballroom. I felt obliged to at least poke my nose in the door and see if anyone present was worth buttonholing briefly.

There was a speaker on the dais. I didn't even notice who, because I had already seen Poppy Hancock, far across the room but weaving her way toward the door. She was wearing a long-sleeved sheath with a neckline that plunged discreetly but allowed for extrapolation. She looked unsteady on her feet.

When she got closer I could see that her face was chalky. She was bent on getting the hell out of there, and not until she was at the door did she notice me. When she did she said without hesitation, even though she looked near death and we had met only that once, thirteen months ago, "Hello, Jock."

I have always marveled at how people in politics keep a thousand names and faces in their heads and never make a mistake. I said, "Hello, Poppy," held the door for her, and followed her as she wobbled into the lobby. "Can I get you something?"

"A breath of air."

I took her arm, firm under the sleeve, and guided her through the long lobby and out the front door into the cool night air. She stood on the sidewalk and took half a dozen deep breaths before she spoke.

"I got boxed into drinking. Dumb, dumb, dumb. I almost never drink. I hate to drink. Of all the wastes of time, drinking is the most pointless." The color was coming back into her face. She was all right, but still a little buzzy from the alcohol.

She became aware now of my hand on her arm. "I'm okay," she said. "Thanks. I'm going up to bed."

Regretfully, I removed my hand. I said, "So am I."

We went back into the hotel and got in an elevator together. She smelled wonderful; if that was perfume it was well formulated. Essence of desirable woman. She pushed a floor button and turned to me.

I said, "That's my floor too." It was.

All she said was, "Uh-huh."

Neither by word or body language had there been an invitation from her to anything approaching intimacy, but I felt an electricity in the air. Or wished it there. Maybe my antenna had been oversensitized by the free-flowing product of the California Viniculture Guild.

We rose in painful silence. If only to break it, I said, "That was a hell of a job you did on the DelMano campaign. You deserved every bit of the credit you got."

"Not really," she said. "The other guy was a zombie. Campaign of the Living Dead. And he made a fatal mistake on his income tax."

"It was a very small mistake."

She snapped, "Not when I got finished with it." That serpent's tongue again.

The elevator stopped and I followed her out. We got to her door first. She had already taken her key from her tiny evening bag, and she opened the door a crack and turned to me, hovering behind her about three inches.

She said, her speech still slightly slurred, "It's after midnight, I'm a little drunk, I think you're a little drunk, and here we are at my hotel room door and I've opened it." What was this? I went lightheaded with anticipation.

She said, "It's a configuration that sometimes causes near strangers to fall into bed together. I'm sure you know it won't happen to us, in spite of my political energy that you believe is tied to sexual energy. I consider mindless sex, next to drinking, just about the greatest misuse of time there is—a bare half-cut above stock car racing."

I came down gently from my high. "I can assure you," I said gamely, "nothing like that even remotely entered my mind."

"It didn't?" she said, and seemed surprised. "Okay, then, no harm done. Thanks again for your gallantry, and good night."

She tilted her face up and touched her lips to mine. Sweet. Suddenly she thrust her tongue deep into my mouth. It had a life of its own, very animated. I felt a surge of excitement, and I reached for her. But she stepped back, slipped inside the door, and closed it, leaving me looking dewy-eyed at the brass room number. Her voice floated through the door, laughing. "Sleep tight."

I didn't.

Reasonably early the next morning I phoned to invite her to breakfast. She had already checked out.

I hadn't seen her since.

The Bannerman house was set well back from the curb on a generous plot with landscaping that had been given a good sixty or seventy years to mature. The house itself, like all the others on the block, was a solid-looking Tudor; on this street you would think there had been no advances in architecture since the seventeenth century. The single anachronism was on the Bannerman property: a mud-caked pickup truck blocked the mouth of the long driveway. I parked in the street.

Walking toward the house, I read the door of the truck: "Pools by Puller," and an address and phone number. And then I saw under some trees toward the back of the property a few sacks of concrete, a wheelbarrow, and some other equipment. The new pool was behind the house.

Except for the construction material the grounds were impeccably maintained: hedges newly trimmed, grass lush and weed free, bushes flowering profusely, old trees freshly pruned.

The house too was in mint condition. The roof looked new. I could see where Hilton Bailes, if he was really struggling to make ends meet—having ditched both his club and his beloved sloop—might get his back up when he came to visit his partner.

I was still a dozen or more yards from the front door when it opened and a massive, heavyset man in work clothes filled the opening and stepped out. Another, slim and somewhat shorter, stood just inside the door; they were apparently saying goodbye. The shorter man—I took him to be Bannerman—spotted me and looked . . . what, nervous?

I hoped, but I couldn't let hope lead me by the nose. It was also possible he was merely surprised to see an uninvited stranger coming to his front door; it was not that kind of neighborhood.

He shook the big man's hand and said what sounded like, "Thanks, Mac. Tomorrow, then?"

One thing was clear: the police hadn't been here yet to break the bad news. I suppose Hap hadn't seen the need to make that his first priority. With the murder still under wraps, no one else would drop the bombshell on the unsuspecting widower.

The big man came down the driveway and threw me a frank stare. His slicked-down hair had an oily sheen. He wore an open work shirt and jeans with a heavy silver buckle. His neck was exactly as big around as his formidable brow—head and neck made a single unit, like a fireplug. His shoes were a knockoff of those favored by Frankenstein's monster. This hunk wasn't selling encyclopedias; he must be the pool contractor.

After he passed, something made me glance back over my shoulder. He was reaching for the door of the pickup but looking back at me, still curious.

I said, "My car blocking you?"

He continued staring, finally grunted what I took to be a

negative, and climbed in his cab, slammed the door, and quickly backed out of the driveway.

I turned back to the other man. He was leaning against the doorjamb with an inquiring look as I climbed the front steps. He was probably in his late thirties, dark, fine boned, with large, liquid eyes that were also dark. His receding hairline suggested he would be bald in three years, but on him it worked. He had on cords and a pullover knit shirt, and an ancient pair of sneakers. "Meek" is a word I don't use much, but this guy appeared meek. And untroubled. I wouldn't have taken him for a man who had killed his wife this morning. This wasn't looking good for my team.

When I got to the top of the steps I said, "Mr. Bannerman?"

I was hoping for something like "No, I'm watching the house; he hasn't been here all day; I don't know where he is." What I got was a cautious, "Yes, please?"

I searched his face for a clue that he was putting up a front. I saw none. Then again, he'd had five hours to compose himself.

Now what? There was nothing for it but to plunge right in. I told him my name and said, "I'm afraid I have some very bad news." His balding head flushed pink. I added, "Okay if I come in?"

He was turning ghastly looking. "What do you mean, bad news? What is it?" His mild voice became tight with fear. "Please, tell it to me here."

There was no way to ease into this. I said, "Your wife was on her way to her car in a garage this morning when someone attacked her with a knife."

"Please . . . My God, no . . ." His eyes were pleading for some word from me that she wasn't seriously hurt. He could probably read that I had nothing good to offer.

I said, "I'm sorry. I'm afraid she didn't make it."

He was searching my face, unable to absorb the truth. He said, "She's . . . ? Please, she's not . . . ?"

"I'm terribly sorry."

He uttered one more "Please" before his knees buckled and he leaned against the doorjamb in a kind of half faint, his face dead white and his eyes rolling back. I caught him by the waist and got his head down until I saw some color returning to it. My heart sank—partly in sympathy for his apparent grief, and mostly because this poor bastard was turning out to be a big disappointment. He was almost certainly not his wife's murderer. Among other clues, there were too many "pleases."

There went my theory, admittedly shaky and prayerful, that was going to separate Mort Beaufoy from this mess. I eased the desolate widower into the house.

6 A few minutes later he was slumped on the leather couch
in his living room, sunk in despair. He dutifully sipped
the cognac I had poured for him from the bar section of
a wall unit, and he apologized with endless "pleases," almost
like a mantra, for being so much trouble—practically for being
alive.

While he collected himself I glanced around the room. For
an antiques dealer with a Tudor house, he had decorated this
room defiantly modern and spare, with plenty of chrome,
leather, and glass. Or maybe this was Sheri's taste. Whichever,
it worked. The few antique accents stood out dramatically in
this setting, better than they would have in a period room.

During ten years on the *Ledger* I had seen the relatives of
crime victims react to the bad news along a wide range of emotions, from nearly catatonic to rug-chewing hysteria. There
was no predicting. After Bannerman's dramatic collapse it
took him only a few minutes to steady down. When he had
choked back half the brandy, he asked in a voice that wrenched
my gut where they had taken Sheri and could he "please" go
to her.

I said by now she'd be at the morgue and that the police

would be taking him there soon enough to identify the body. I didn't claim to be the police myself but he must have assumed I was. It didn't occur to him to ask me to identify myself and I saw no reason to volunteer. As I've said, this wasn't the first time I had beaten the police to the victim's family with the bad news. Whoever first observed, "He travels fastest who travels alone," wasn't just whistling "Dixie."

I sat next to Bannerman on the couch and when he finally finished the brandy I asked if there was anyone I could telephone for him—family, say. He turned his liquid eyes on me and said his family was in Minneapolis and Sheri's was in Pasadena and what was the use? He would wait with both those calls until he had seen the body and knew more about what had happened; there was no point in hurrying bad news.

I said, "How about your partner? Would you like me to call Hilton Bailes down at your shop?"

He didn't seem surprised that I knew he had a shop and a partner. He considered my offer and quickly dismissed it. "Thank you. Thank you, no. There would be very little comfort in that. Hilly Bailes was never a big fan of Baby's."

"Baby?"

"Sheri. My pet name for her. Baby."

"Right." This didn't seem the time to ask who it was that called her Honeybuns. Anyway, he would likely be the last to know, poor bastard.

The brandy loosened his tongue. He set the empty glass down and began a grab bag inventory of his wife's virtues—how infectious her laugh was, how she adored children, how seductively she danced, how thoughtful she was on birthdays and anniversaries, what a gift she would have been to the theater (and now the world would never know). Please.

Talk was his way of convincing himself the ugly deed had really happened. I find it sad that at times like this, no matter how deeply felt the sentiment, it comes out sounding recycled.

He wound up with, "She was so damn *up* when she left this

morning, so full of expectation for the day. She looked especially pretty."

"She had a big day planned?"

"She always looked good," he protested. "But yes. She was full of hope, full of confidence. You have to have confidence to sell. It makes all the difference." He looked at me as though it was important to make me understand that. "Sheri was good, the best in her shop." And then, without missing a beat, "Did she die quickly? Please, was she in pain?"

I didn't have the least idea about either, but I said, "I don't think there was pain." It was the least I could do. "I believe she died quickly."

"Good. That's good. You know, we were best friends. That's the part of marriage people overlook. Don't they? You can't be married as Baby and I were for eight years without children unless you're best friends. Are you married? Do you have children?"

"I'm afraid no, on both counts." The personal question had taken me by surprise. A sense of emptiness, of loss, touched me for an instant and that surprised me too.

He was saying, "Have they caught him? Please, the mugger—whoever it was who killed her?"

"They don't know for sure it was a mugging. They don't know what it was. Did she have any"—"enemies" seemed too harsh a word at the moment—"well, people who may have wanted to harm her? Anybody?"

"Baby? No, impossible. Everybody loved Baby. Please, please. At Clifton Oliver—where she worked—I never saw jealousy. Even though she did so much better than the others. Everybody loved Sheri. She had a knack, a way of getting around people. The theater groups she worked with? Never that big—off-off-off-Broadway, I suppose you'd call them. They never gave her a real chance, never recognized her talent. But that didn't keep them from loving Sheri. Please, everybody did."

"Except, as you say, Hilton Bailes."

He waved an arm. "Hilly is Hilly," he said dismissively. "Hilly has his own problems."

The doorbell rang. "I'm not expecting anyone," Bannerman said. "Please, would you send whoever it is away?" He had appointed me his protector.

En route to the entrance hall I looked out the living room window. I had expected this: Hap Nordstrom was standing back from the front door lamping the house, his partner in the Hawaiian shirt beside him.

I turned to Bannerman. "It's the detective in charge of the investigation. Sergeant Nordstrom. You'll have to talk to him."

"Of course. Please."

I went through the entrance hall and opened the front door. Hap didn't seem surprised. He said, "That's your heap out front, huh? What are you doing? You think you're still with the paper? I have every expectation of wrapping this thing up in a couple or three days. Why don't you go stuff envelopes for your senator? Doesn't he need you?"

"Yes. At the moment, right here." I didn't add that three days might not be good enough for my senator. I couldn't afford to insult Hap: I didn't know when I might be needing him.

All four of us were soon settled in the living room: Bannerman, Nordstrom, Nordstrom's partner, the sporty Detective Otero, and me. On the way through the entrance hall I had asked Hap if the story had broken.

He said, "I'm still managing to hold off. I estimate you've got another hour or two of free play."

At the living room door he stopped me and lowered his voice. "Did you break it to him gently?" His face was at maximum mourning. On Hap, that was formidable.

"The man's wife was stabbed to death," I whispered. "How

do you break it gently? I broke it." Nordstrom had a heart of drawn butter.

Even after Hap let Bannerman know I wasn't a cop but merely "a concerned citizen," Bryce asked me, please, if it wasn't too much trouble, could I stay? In his grief I had become family. Hap shrugged his acquiescence; he knew when not to rock the boat. And he made sure to spend a minute on condolences before he eased into asking questions.

His first was, "Mr. Bannerman, do you remember how your wife looked this morning?"

"Of course. I told Mr. Caprisi, she looked beautiful. As always."

"I meant, do you remember what she was wearing?"

"Her green shantung dress, ivory pumps"—his voice broke and he took a moment to steady himself—"a matching leather bag, and I think a double strand of fake pearls."

"That's very good. You're sure she was wearing a green dress?"

"That shantung was a favorite of mine."

"I'm sorry. Shantung is . . . ?"

"A kind of silk in a rough weave."

"Thank you." Hap was writing in his notebook. "And you saw her leave the house in it and drive off?"

"Yes. Exactly." He was so eager to help that it hurt.

Hap was laying on this green dress thing with a trowel but I didn't blame him; like me, he was hard put to find a reason the dress had come through the crime undamaged.

"So your wife did leave home before you?" he persisted, and when Bannerman nodded patiently, Hap said, "That was your usual routine?"

"Please, no. I usually leave first, because I have to take the bus down into Manhattan."

"What made today different?" The questions were pointed, but Hap's manner was nonthreatening; he could have been asking for driving directions to Yonkers.

★ 64 ★

"I didn't go downtown today. I was expecting the pool contractor. Mac Puller."

"I saw him, Hap," I cut in. "He was leaving when I arrived."

Hap turned to Bannerman. "Your contractor was here all day?"

Bannerman said, "He showed up late and we had a lot to go over. The bulk of the work is done. We're down to the finishing details. That's where all the options are. I had decisions to make." There was a catch in his voice again. "Please. Sheri and I wanted that pool to be perfect."

"Then you didn't leave the house at all."

"That's right."

"Did you try to consult with your wife by phone about any of the choices you had to make?"

"No. We had agreed generally on what we wanted. And there was no point in calling her at the office. She said she was going to be out all day showing properties."

Hap nodded. "But she still could have been reached. I'm sure you know she had a cellular phone."

As benign as Hap's manner was when he asked his questions, I could see that Bannerman, despite his grief, was beginning to sense that the questions themselves may have had a purpose not entirely benign. He said in a flat, firm voice, "Sheri asked me to stop calling her on the cellular phone."

"Why was that?"

"I was always getting her with a client and breaking in on a sales pitch. Okay?"

Hap knew he had pressed too hard. He said, "I can see where that might have bothered her. These Dick Tracy phones don't give you a minute's peace."

Having made nice, he shifted gears. "Mr. Bannerman, we have a small problem maybe you can help us with. The client your wife was visiting just before her tragedy says she showed him floor plans of apartments she thought he might be interested in. Do you know how she would have carried those?

We've examined her car but we haven't found any floor plans or anything that might have held them."

Nordstrom, you son of a bitch, I thought, I can't believe this. You're checking on Mort Beaufoy's account of Sheri's visit; you've actually put him down as a suspect.

Bannerman said, "You didn't find her dispatch case?"

"She carried a dispatch case?" Hap asked.

"Yes. A black, hard-sided leather case, a good-sized one. She had it with her when she left this morning."

"You didn't mention that."

"Please, you asked me what she was wearing." Bannerman's mild voice had taken on an adversarial tinge. "Would you call a dispatch case wearing apparel?"

"You're right. I stand corrected."

That seemed to satisfy Bannerman. "It's made of English leather. Beautifully crafted. I bought it for an anniversary. Our sixth. Sheri loved that case." He had softened again, and if someone didn't stop him he was going to backslide into a few more mournful reminiscences.

"It will turn up sooner or later," Hap said comfortingly. "When it does, we'll get it back to you."

Bannerman attempted a smile of gratitude. "Please."

Hap quickly asked, "Do you happen to know which of her clients your wife was meeting today? In general, what her plans were for the day?"

The faint smile faded. "No, why would I? We kept out of each other's day-to-day business affairs." He glanced my way, as though to recommend the practice to me should I ever marry.

Hap said, "Is there anybody who would have known her schedule?"

"I doubt it. The office, possibly. That's Clifton Oliver Realty. In Yonkers."

Hap had run out of questions. He closed his notebook and thanked Bannerman for his help "at this difficult time." Then he proposed that he and Detective Otero run him down to the morgue to identify the body.

Bannerman turned pale again. "Yes, of course. Thank you." He looked at me pleadingly. "Mr. Caprisi, could I impose on you to come along? Please?"

Hap said, "I'm afraid there's a rule against that." He had just made it up.

I said, "I'm sorry, Bryce. I couldn't do it anyway. I have to be someplace."

Yonkers was over the city line, out of Hap Nordstrom's jurisdiction. He would have to do some kind of administrative song and dance before he could go up there. I didn't have a jurisdiction. I might still squeeze in one more inquiry before this scandal broke through the ozone layer and caused severe burns.

7 My chief regret about the virtual outlawing of public smoking in New York is that you rarely run across discarded matchbooks anymore. During my *Ledger* years, matchbook covers twice led me to clear beats on stories. I could have found Oliver Realty in the phone book, but out of nostalgia for my tabloid past I took it from a matchbook I lifted off Bannerman's bar. I read the ad in the car: "Clifton Oliver Realty—the complete real estate service since 1971," followed by the address in Yonkers. It would take maybe fifteen minutes to get there, about the length of a cycle on my all-news station.

Having busted out on Sheri's husband I was back again to the other probable explanation for her death: her killer was a mugger forced to flee the garage before he could grab her purse. This thug was desperate enough to be working in daylight, so he was most likely a junkie and would make a mistake that would flush him out. Soon, I prayed.

He was beyond my power to pursue, but I could meanwhile look into the one other possibility that readily presented itself—a long shot that came out of theory number one. If Sheri was killed by someone she knew *other* than her husband, someone who knew where she had appointments this morning, that person could be someone she worked with. A knife is an intimate weapon, an instrument of passion. The weapon of an office love affair gone sour? Of a co-worker she cheated out of commissions? Or of her boss, Clifton Oliver, for whatever reason, who then called her cellular phone when she was dead, to cover his tracks? I was reaching; the Oliver office was a long shot. But it was the best use I could make of the rest of this lousy afternoon.

The item I had an ear cocked for came on the all-news station less than two minutes into the drive. The senator's name was never mentioned—thanks again, I suppose, to Hap Nordstrom—but the story still led the local crime stories. No surprise there. A middle-class white woman found stabbed to death in an upscale apartment house—even the garage of one—takes precedence over all other violence in a city that always has a wide selection to choose from.

All that mattered for the moment was the absence from the story of the senior senator from New York. The young woman's name was being withheld "pending notification of next of kin." There were no suspects in the crime, no leads, no motive; the police investigation was just getting under way. The newsman moved on to a drive-by shooting in Queens that had put a seven-year-old and her grandmother in the hospital.

I turned off the radio and tried calling Beaufoy. Sometime in the next hour—if not, God forbid, already—some hustling reporter was going to put the body in the garage together with the address and make a scattershot call to Senator Morton Ezra Beaufoy to get his reaction to a murder on his very doorstep. I had to stop him from taking that call.

Miraculously, I got through on the second try.

"Mort? It's Jock Caprisi."

"John, I'm glad you called."

My nerve endings came alive. "Yes . . . ?"

"I was afraid I wouldn't find you. Paul McClintoch has

arranged for the film crew to come up tomorrow morning to make the television spots. I want to make sure you'll be here."

That was it? "Of course I'll be there." I could feel muscles untense. "Listen, have you had any calls from reporters? I mean in the last half hour or so."

"No. Why? Should I?" This man was from a planet in a distant galaxy.

"You will. They'll be wanting to know about Sheri Bannerman."

"That poor woman. I can't get her death out of my mind. Of course I'll want to say something to the press about that brutal, tragic crime."

"No. Mort, I don't want you to take the calls. No calls from reporters. Don't answer your phone."

"Dear boy, I have to answer my phone. I have pressing Committee business in Washington—foreign affairs don't stop for local elections—and there are fund-raising matters here in the state that only I can attend to. I cannot simply not pick up the phone."

"Yes, you can. You have a—"

"I can handle the reporters," he cut in. "I've handled you in the past. I'll tell them the approximate truth: that I don't know a damn thing."

"No, that's the worst. It will start them speculating, and they'll end up spinning nightmare scenarios. If it's at all possible, I'd like to keep the media at arm's length until you're well out of this mess. Until the killer is caught and there's no longer anything for them to wonder about."

"And when is that likely to be?"

"The police are on top of it," I half lied. "I'll let you know. Meanwhile, you have an answering machine. Monitor your calls. If it's someone you don't recognize, don't pick up."

"A damned nuisance. But all right, if only to please you." There was a moment of dead air and then he said, "John, that young woman. I haven't been able to get her out of my head.

Are the police really making progress? Are there clues? Maybe they found something in her car that will help them?" For the first time he sounded anxious. Good; reality was impinging on his improbable world.

"They found nothing in her car," I said. Because he had been so exasperating earlier, I added pointedly, "Not even the floor plans you say she showed you."

"I see. All right, goodbye then." Now he sounded a million miles away. Maybe there was a transmission problem, maybe his head was in a committee room in the Capitol.

As soon as I punched off, the phone rang. Paul McClintoch. Behind him there was a hum of keyed-up voices. I said I had heard from the senator and of course I'd be at the taping in the morning.

He said, "Fine. That's not why I'm calling."

"Don't tell me you've already had a call from some reporter about the dead woman."

"God, no. I pray for never," he said mildly. "I've been thinking about what you asked me before."

I didn't like his tone. "When?"

"You know, about the man we were discussing. Hopkins." There was no Hopkins, but McClintoch was overly hyped on secrecy. "Whether he was a chaser."

I had another sinking feeling. "Don't say it. You've taken a new reading on that. What did you do, ask around?"

"I'm not that dense. But something did occur to me. Maybe it's nothing. I never would have thought of it if you hadn't broached the subject."

"Paul, what?"

"There was a woman who used to be the New York office manager—coordinator, she was called. Krista Grolik."

My blood was chilling. "I've met her. She was there for years, wasn't she?"

"She left two years ago to have a baby."

"You're not going to tell me—"

"No, no, nothing like that. My God. She has a husband, an engineer. Anyway, Krista and I go back a few years. Her last night on the job I took her out for a drink. She ended up having two, or she probably wouldn't have told me what she told me. She's a team player. A very solid woman."

My nails were digging into the steering wheel. "Paul, tell me what she said."

"No. It was strange. There's no way I can begin to convey it. I'm not going to play middleman on this, certainly not over an open line. If there's some reason you have to pursue it—and I can't see why you should—you'll have to get it directly from Krista's mouth."

"Paul—"

"Uh-uh. They're in the Manhattan book. Harry Grolik. Look, they're yelling for me here." Before I could press further he had hung up.

I was not going to pursue it. I didn't want to bait another hook. I already had as many lines in the water as I could safely watch.

Almost in Yonkers now, I went back to the all-news station. I supposed there wasn't much happening today; I came in on a long-winded live interview with Representative Herbert Turnbull at the Syracuse airport, in front of what the announcer described as an enthusiastic gathering of well-wishers. I had to hand it to the Turbull campaign for their advance work.

"Mr. Beaufoy," Turnbull was saying, "hollers that the State Department's stand on Dalmatian independence is a hundred and eighty degrees wrong and a hundred and eighty percent dangerous. So why doesn't he roll on down to Washington and conduct some hearings? I doubt his committee cares whether he chairs from a chair with wheels or one with legs. But I will tell you this—more and more his *campaign* looks like it has no legs." That got more applause and laughter than it deserved.

The son of a bitch. I had never heard Mort utter a word about Dalmatians. Turnbull had set up a straw man. Nor had Mort ever used a wheelchair. As for the campaign-with-no-legs crack, it was too clever for Turnbull. I suspected the fine hand of—

But I stopped speculating to catch his windup. "By the way, my friends, I personally don't care a rat's overbite, nor does any other New Yorker I know, about Dalmatia. Damnation is what bothers us. Mort Beaufoy's dithering is pushing us taxpayers right into the fiery pit."

Close behind him there was a burst of forced laughter, and I was sure I recognized the bell-like voice of Poppy Hancock. No surprise there, only confirmation.

I turned the damn thing off.

I suppose real estate brokers get those terrific houses they use as offices on the same principal that gives theater people the choice seats to hit shows: you've got to be in the business. Clifton Oliver Realty occupied a small but perfectly preserved gem of a Victorian house on a street where all the other buildings were postwar cinder block and aluminum siding. If you took away the discreet sign in front of the lilac bush on Oliver's postage stamp front lawn, you would never guess a commercial enterprise lay behind the gingerbread front porch, the cupola, the quaintly broken rooflines, and the gables.

It was a little after five o'clock, later than I had hoped, when I stepped onto the porch and went in the front door. Two smallish front rooms had been made into one largish one, and six or seven desks were tucked this way and that in the space. The workday seemed to be ending, at least here in the office. Lively cross-talk of no particular consequence filled the room while the staff straightened desks, gathered up the things they were taking with them, and, in the case of a couple of the women, freshened makeup.

I felt that jolt of energy that hits offices around quitting time, although I gathered that at least a couple of these people weren't quitting but were on their way to meet clients. If any of the five of them had heard of the death of their co-worker they were hiding it well.

For about thirty seconds nobody paid any attention to me, so I was able to give them a quick once over: four women and a man, a standard real estate office mix. Two of the women were middle aged and cozy looking—nicely dressed but non-threatening. They were probably good at bonding with the wives of house-hunting couples while the husbands went exploring for termite damage; they could talk about the school system or show how easy it would be to turn a walk-in closet into a guest bathroom.

The other two women were younger, more with-it in their dress, not bad looking, possibly cutting-edge aggressive. One had spectacular red hair. Too bad she had fussed with it; that had been bad judgment. The other wore a leather miniskirt and heels high enough to cause her pain if she was obliged to climb to attics that could be finished for practically nothing. I suspected these two were most effective at selling properties to newly transferred executives who had left the wives and kids in Topeka while they scouted the territory.

The lone man was mid-forties, fit looking, still probably more than a match for his teenage son at one-on-one basketball. His rapidly retreating hairline failed to detract from a look of virility; just the opposite. And to show that he had as much hair as the next man, although not necessarily in the same place, his ran down his back for half a dozen inches in a pony-tail. The guy looked as if he could talk mortgages and taxes. You would listen when he sat down with pencil and paper to see "how we can make this work for you."

That was the lot. At first glance I wouldn't have tagged anyone in the room a killer. When one of them did finally take notice of me it was the redhead. She had an easy smile and good teeth. She said, "I'm sorry, can I be of help . . . ?" She hoped not; she was anxious to get out of there.

"That's all right," I said, and walked past her to the ponytailed man. I would have to declare some purpose. "I'm looking for Clifton Oliver . . . ?"

"Sure, if you'd wait just a moment," he said. I had assumed he was Oliver, but this wasn't the baritone voice I had heard on the cellular phone. He glanced through the mostly closed door to a room behind this one and turned back to me. "He's on a call, but I think he's winding it up. Why don't you take a seat?"

He pulled out his swivel chair for me—his desk was nearest the back office—and I thanked him and went to it while he called through the doorway, "Someone to see you, Cliff."

When he turned back to me I said, "Ms. Bannerman's not in today?"

He said, "Are you a client of Sheri's?"

"Not really." I sat down. "We've run across each other."

"I haven't seen her today. But I've been in and out. Probably she has too."

"Mostly I know her husband. Bryce. They make a hell of a couple." A crapshoot, but it beat sitting and swiveling.

Or maybe not. All I got from Ponytail was a curious stare.

He opened his desk drawer and took out a pamphlet. "Some light reading you might find interesting while you wait," he said, and dropped it in my lap. "Sorry to leave you like this. 'Night."

He headed for the front door. The others were drifting out, calling some version of " 'Bye now," or "Have a good one" to each other. I would have liked to bar the door and grill them separately on Sheri's work habits, on their whereabouts this morning, on a dozen related matters. But there was nothing I could do but grin stupidly and watch them go.

The redhead was the last. She said, "If Cliff keeps you waiting, you just holler," and flashed the good teeth once more. "Good night." I was alone.

What Ponytail had given me was a brochure: "Prime Properties in Southern Westchester," with his name stamped across the bottom, JARED PHILLIPS. I put it back on his desk—bare except for a photo of, yes, his healthy teenage son. Everything here—everybody here—was about what I should have expected. More and more I had the feeling I had been spinning my wheels all afternoon, propelled more by hope than practical good sense.

I looked around the room. There were two regional maps on the walls, otherwise nothing. My glance settled on the adjoining desk—Sheri's: I found myself looking into the eyes of a smiling Bryce Bannerman, years younger. In this silver-framed photo he was wearing a blue blazer with brass buttons and he was holding a martini glass. He had a regulation hairline and he looked as if he never said "please" to anyone.

Sheri's desk was close enough to Jared Phillips's so the two could have played footsie, if they so chose, right beneath Bryce's oblivious smile. I noticed now that there was no photo of Mrs. Phillips next to that of the Phillips boy.

Alone, I was ready to go fishing in Sheri's desk drawers. For what, I hadn't a clue, but I was desperate enough to fantasize a death threat on letterhead paper, I didn't care whose.

Before I snooped I would have to make sure Oliver was otherwise engaged. Through his mostly closed door I had been hearing an occasional grunt into the phone, as though he was disagreeing with whoever was on the other end of the line and doing most of the talking. I stood up and edged my ear close to the narrow opening in his door.

The rich baritone I remembered from Sheri's phone came through reasonably well. At first it murmured mostly "no"s and "no way"s, but he finally got his chance. "Dilys, we don't have to do that," he exploded. "In no way is that necessary. Have you any idea what that would come to per head? Without the extras? Have you any idea . . . ? Dil . . . Dil . . ." Dilys had taken over again.

This could be more rewarding than Sheri's desk drawers, and I hung in. Next time Oliver managed to speak he said, "Can't this wait till I get home . . . ? Yes, I am. It's my turn to stay till seven o'clock, but I am leaving the office in three minutes. . . . Right . . . Right . . . Dil, I said right." He hung up with a groan that spoke volumes.

I gave him a moment before I stuck my head in the door. "Mr. Oliver, do you have a minute?"

His face was already pinched with tension when he turned to me with a "What now?" look. He said, "Are they all gone out there? Yes, of course." He got wearily to his feet and roused himself to affability. "Come in, my friend. What can I do for you?"

This was it; if I didn't come up with something now I would have to let nature—meaning the police and the media and time—take its course. My string had run out.

I am never completely at ease with a man who spends as long grooming his mustache as the next man does his poodle. Clifton Oliver sported a luxuriant steel gray guardsman's brush. It was impeccably maintained.

Behind it was a muscular man in his mid-fifties with thick, pepper-and-salt hair and a rambling nose that demanded attention. He was wearing the trousers and vest, but not the jacket, of a suit of good British tweed, no doubt custom made. Under the vest was a snug white shirt with French cuffs held by gold links almost massive enough to join a pair of I beams. His necktie called for almost as much respect as his nose. Except for his tense and haggard look he was a fine figure of a man; I would have been embarrassed to ask him to show me properties at under a million dollars.

The walls were crusted with civic awards, industry commendations, and other souvenirs of his years in real estate. But the main attraction, directly behind Oliver, was a slick oil painting of a chestnut horse. In the saddle was a young woman with shiny hair and crisp riding gear—the daughter, captured forever during her most precious year, probably sixteen. She had daddy's nose.

Oliver, no surprise, was not a reader of the *Ledger*. I introduced myself as a reporter for the paper and the man who had given him the news, over Sheri Bannerman's cellular phone, that she had met with "an accident." The reason for his strained look became quickly apparent; he told me he had kept this information to himself all afternoon, reluctant to share it with his staff until he knew more of what had happened. He had been waiting anxiously, hoping the news would not be too bad. He looked at me expectantly.

I gave it to him unadorned: "I'm sorry to have to be the one to tell you. You'll probably get the official word from the New York City police. Mrs. Bannerman was found stabbed to death this afternoon in the basement garage of an apartment house in Riverdale."

Oliver absorbed this almost as if it was what he had expected. He said nothing while he rubbed each of his cuff links with the middle finger of the opposite hand. Then he checked the trim of his mustache and blinked rapidly. Finally he said, "We're living in an ugly world, Mr. Caprisi. I don't have to tell you. A bitch of a world."

"Yes, it is." I would let him take the lead.

"I saw Sheri for a few minutes just this morning. She came in early, carrying a couple of low-fat muffins. Insisted on pressing one on me, knowing I am in a continual war with my cholesterol. That was the essential Sheri. Never forgot a birthday, knew every special event in everybody's life."

"She wasn't troubled about anything?" I was playing a reporter now. I could ask questions again.

"She was in high spirits when she left the office. This is very hard for me to accept."

"I can understand that."

"Very hard. And yet . . ."

"Yes . . . ?" I leaned forward in encouragement.

"I'll tell you something you may want to share with your readers. If you care to hear it."

"Please."

"I've always been prepared for something like this."

"Have you? Why is that?"

"May I call you Jock?" I nodded. "My people are almost all women, Jock; married women at that. Why? Women are the nesters, and nests are what we are in the business of selling. And in today's real estate market, who but a woman with a gainfully employed husband would be foolish enough to work on straight commission, no salary or draw?"

"I would guess very few," I said dutifully.

Unchallenged, he continued with quiet emphasis. "The women who do this work put themselves at risk every working day of their lives."

"In what way?"

"Much of their time is spent in the field. They are showing properties to clients, many of them men. They are sometimes alone with these men in empty houses in secluded areas—men whose only bona fide is their claim to be looking for a residence, but whose agenda may be sexual assault. The only wonder is that something like this hasn't happened before."

He observed me sad-eyed over the formidable nose while I absorbed this. It was just what I needed not to hear. The headline lit up in my skull: SLAIN WOMAN'S BOSS SUSPECTS CLIENT. And the devastating subhead, "Senator Beaufoy Was Last to Confer with Blonde."

The phone rang and I waited for Oliver to pick up. He

★ 79 ★

didn't; he was watching me. Eventually the answering machine light blinked on.

I said, "If you want to take that . . ."

"Not at this hour. I'll leave it to the machine. I've decided my workday is over."

So, I decided, was the period of contemplation he had imposed on me. I said, "You think Mrs. Bannerman's attacker was a client?" My job was to get him off *my* client. "That's a possibility, I suppose. One of many."

"What else, Jock? Are you suggesting some sort of enemy? Dear, generous, openhearted Sheri. I can't imagine her with an enemy in the world."

"Did you know her entire world?"

"I'm not able to say that. . . . Still, I can't believe . . ." The mustache was twitching. "Could she have been a mugging victim? Robbed and then murdered?"

"It's too early to say."

"God, I hope so. I hope there was no . . . no sexual assault. Listen to me—praying my friend was merely murdered. Some world." The mustache twitched violently and subsided. "You must cover a great many crime stories. What do you think?"

"I think we'll both have to wait for the autopsy report. But I'd guess the police will want a list of her clients. I suppose there must be dozens."

"She may have had that information with her. Clients are a salesperson's most valuable asset."

"Mrs. Bannerman was good at her work?"

"Sheri was a self-starter, a true dynamo. Yes, she was good, damn it to hell. Despite that business these last years has been so lousy."

"You wouldn't know that from the work done recently on the Bannerman house. And now they've put in a pool."

He didn't miss a beat. "That was a sound move. A pool will add double its cost to the value of a property like theirs. And of course Sheri's husband would be footing that bill out of his antiques business. You've seen Bryce, have you?"

"To break the news. He took it hard. Apparently it was a good marriage." I pushed a little. "At least he thought so. How did it look from this end?"

"I make a point of keeping out of the personal lives of my salespeople. Sheri claimed he was wonderful. So what? By training, Sheri was an actress; she'd have convinced me Benedict Arnold was wonderful. We have another gal here who says she's crazy in love with her husband. I know she has someone on the side. I know, but I don't want to know. About any of them. It's better that way."

He was getting to his feet. "I could sit here and talk Sheri all day. Duty calls. Multiple duties." He was sloughing me off and that was making him even more expansive. Anyway, he wanted me to know. "One, we're making wedding plans, believe it or not, for my princess. That's Kelly up there behind me, sitting Balthazar."

Before he went on he gave me a moment to admire the portrait and to offer my sincere best wishes for Kelly's future. "And two, if I don't get home to dress for a function at the club, her ladyship will nail my hide to the wall."

I didn't have to ask—I didn't really care—but he took the trouble to spell it out anyway. "My wife. I'll walk out with you."

He led the way. I expected him to slip on the jacket of that magnificent tweed suit, but I saw now that there was no jacket in here, no place even to hang one. He passed through the doorway to the larger front office and paused at Sheri's desk.

"A damn shame." He ran his fingers across the gun-metal surface and tapped it lightly in a sort of farewell.

A thought popped into my head. "Sheri's husband says she left home this morning with a briefcase."

He snapped out of his reverential mode. "A black dispatch case. Her traveling office. That's where she's likely to have kept notes on clients."

"The police didn't find it in her car. Could she have left it here in the office?"

"I don't know. As I said, she did come in first thing this morning. Do we look? Or do we leave it to the police?"

"Why don't we look?"

Oliver didn't need urging. Maybe he had an agenda of his own: Why let that list of hot prospects slip into limbo? He pulled out the two drawers in Sheri's desk big enough to hold a dispatch case. Nothing. I checked under and around the desk with the same result.

Oliver was now opening a couple of drawers in the adjoining desk, Jared Phillips's. He caught my look of surprise and mumbled, "You never know. Real estate can be a dog-eat-dog business."

We both surveyed the room, and when nothing presented itself, that pretty much ended the search. Oliver opened the front door and held it for me. We walked out onto the porch and I waited while he went through a locking-up routine. This would be it.

I hated coming up empty, and I made my first stab at something resembling an interrogation. "I met your people. Nice group. Mrs. Bannerman got along well enough with all of them? No big problems?"

Oliver lifted the mighty nose from its contemplation of his keys and stared at me. He knew what I was getting at and he chose to look offended. "I said it was a dog-eat-dog business. Not a murderous one."

I let it go at that. We wished each other a pleasant evening and I watched him walk toward a black Cadillac at the curb. A last thought occurred to me and I called to him.

He turned and I said, "That call you made to Sheri's cellular phone? The one I picked up? What was that about?"

It was none of my business, even as a reporter, and we both knew it. He scratched the nose and pretended to think for a moment. "Damned if I remember. Some client thing, I suppose.

Her death put it clean out of my head. Why?"

I shrugged. The best I could manage was, "It's something the police may want to know."

He nodded, got in the Cadillac, and drove off. He was still not wearing the suit jacket. Maybe he didn't want to crush it under his seat belt.

I climbed in my Honda and turned on the motor. Pulling away from the curb, I caught a car in my rearview mirror I thought I recognized. I drove slowly and kept watching. It stopped in front of Clifton Oliver Realty and Hap Nordstrom appeared, trailed by his partner, Detective Otero. Five minutes over the city line, these New York cops could only be making a courtesy call. Like me.

I had been half a step ahead of Nordstrom all afternoon. It didn't matter anymore, I had taken my shots. Wrapping up this mess was not going to be the one-two-three business I had half expected. We were going into a new phase. There was no longer any way I could keep the spotlight from being turned on Mort Beaufoy. The best I could hope for was to soften that light with an amber gel.

I headed for the parkway to the city.

8 I kept the radio tuned to the news during the drive south toward home. The story still hadn't broken when the parkway rolled me into Manhattan, but a thin fissure opened just before I passed under the George Washington Bridge. I usually get a tiny kick of pleasure when I come around the bend below the toll station and the bridge comes into view, soaring to make that improbable leap across the Hudson. This time the good feeling was effectively squashed by the news from the radio.

An update on the murdered woman in the Riverdale garage now included the address where the body was found. No mention of Senator Morton Beaufoy's Buick—due, I was sure, to still another "Thank you for past favors" from Hap Nordstrom. But could another hour go by before some reporter got curious enough to ask the right questions? This town had too many newspapers and television stations, too many investigative journalists raking the same muck.

I weighed my options. Should I go home and catch the six o'clock local TV news? Or should I head for Reelect Senator Beaufoy headquarters and seek comfort in numbers?

"Home," as I called it for want of a better word, was a two-room "suite," as management called it, in a respectable if depressing residential hotel in the convenient West Fifties. Think of a building that reminds you of the galoshes your grandfather wore for thirty years.

The Stanley's clientele was a mixed bag, but mostly geriatrics too stubborn to leave Manhattan for a sensible Florida condo. There were several retired songwriters living off ASCAP royalties from hits that dated back to World War Two and earlier; this bunch got out of their yellowing bathrobes only to dress for an occasional tribute dinner at the Waldorf. There were a fair number of widows and slightly younger surviving mistresses of Broadway hustlers. The latter carried yappy dogs when they ventured out on thin ankles and perilous heels, dressed as though another Mr. Right might present himself at any moment. There were a few pasty-faced, doughy-around-the-middle, unhealthy-looking men, occupations unknown, who never made eye contact in the elevator and gave the impression they had been brought as infants in swaddling clothes directly from the hospital to this hotel, or another like it, and had spent their entire lives here or in similar hotels without ever exchanging a word with a living soul.

The Stanley wasn't cheap, and I couldn't afford it until I got the column. I moved there, I think, as part of my ongoing war with myself over being the only one of my siblings who wasn't married and shouldering the responsibilities of a family. The Stanley was a judgment, a self-punishment. I had consigned myself to a kind of limbo.

The Stanley had advantages: a location in the very aorta of the city; the fully equipped pullman kitchen and the complete, if well worn, furnishings that saved me the chore of shopping for same; and regular maid service. I could make myself a pot of coffee in the morning and toast a bagel, and the maid would come in and rinse the plastic dishes and change the linens. Could a wife be expected to do as much?

While I was on the *Ledger* I banged out the column on a

word processor set up on a card table in the suite's "drawing room." I almost never went to the decrepit *Ledger* building down on Hudson Street that may already have been an eyesore in Washington Irving's day. My umbilical cord to the paper was a modem; I never saw hard copy until the paper came out, if then. If my deadline pressed and I was nailed to the computer, a member of the hotel staff would fetch me a nearly warm meal from one of the greasy ethnic restaurants and coffee shops nearby. What wife could be asked to do that?

Plenty of them, my mother believed, beginning with a lot of work improving the decor. On the one occasion she visited the suite on a trip to New York with my older sister, a pediatrician, she shuddered as she took a quick look around, and said, "I'd rather be in my coffin."

My father also dropped by once when he was doing a New York gig. His observation was, "For Chrissakes, get yourself a life." As if I needed further confirmation of the charm of my digs, women I knew who were offered a return visit to the Stanley and were still willing to see me usually said, "Why don't you come over to my place?"

Sometimes when I entered the suite, decorated as it was in shades of mud, I had a flash glimpse of a future that sent a chill through me: the aged reporter, now as overstuffed as his furniture and blending with its color scheme, wearily pounds out his copy with a vodka bottle and a damp container of moo goo gai pan at his side, no longer even aware that a world beyond these walls might offer something better.

So, no surprise, I was tilting against going home to the Stanley just yet. Added to the obvious reason was my expectation of the bad news sure to come off the TV at six o'clock; I preferred not to face that alone in my brown-and-gray bedroom. Better to check in with Paul McClintoch at campaign headquarters and surround myself with sympathizers.

I called Reelect Senator Beaufoy as I came off the West Side Highway. Whoever picked up said McClintoch couldn't come to the phone right now. I got off and took a stab at connecting with the senator; by now he might have an update on the situation. He picked up on the second ring and said, "Yes?"

"Mort, you promised you weren't going to answer your phone."

"Is that you, John? Too late. I forgot and answered it a few minutes ago."

I waited.

"It was a woman—a reporter, I assumed, pushy, very sure of herself. Wanted to know my reaction to the violent murder in my building of a young woman. I knew by then I had made a mistake. But at that point, dear boy, what could I do? I said that of course I was shocked, dismayed, disheartened, and who was this calling? She gave a name and asked if I was acquainted with the victim."

"And what did you say?" My fingers were digging into the phone.

"I told her she would have to excuse me, since I was on a Washington call. I got off."

"Okay." Not great, not even good, but not a total disaster. "What paper was this woman from?"

"She didn't give a paper. Just her name. Paula something. A strong, clear voice, but the last name was hard to catch."

Now my lips were stiffening. "Hancock? Was it Paula Hancock?"

"No, I would remember Hancock, because, as you must know, that's the last name of Turnbull's campaign manager. Poppy Hancock."

Thanks, Mort. "Right. So what was it?"

"There's no way I can tell you, because there was a moment of interference on the line. Why? What's the difference?"

"None, come to think of it." Why upset him more than nec-

essary? "Mort, once again, please don't answer your phone."
I got off as quickly as I could.

I was sure it was her. Had to be. The bitch.

Beaufoy campaign headquarters was in a temporary lash-up in
a recently failed supermarket on York Avenue where I had
covered a bungled robbery attempt a few years before. One
dead, two wounded. The scene now looked no less chaotic. The
one television set was in Paul McClintoch's rat's nest of an office, safe from the urgent hum of the fund-raising crew working the phones, and the chatter of volunteers assembling
last-minute mailings. I arrived in time to catch the tail end of
the Channel Four news. One staffer or another had more or less
monitored the local news since five o'clock, but nothing had
come out I hadn't already heard on the radio, and the show
ended without any late-breaking bulletins. I had expected that;
it was too soon for Hancock to have worked her magic.

She worked it sooner than I expected. The network news
shows came on at six-thirty; by six-forty ABC had inserted a
brief, breaking story—brief because they didn't yet have much.
The video portion was mostly file footage of Mort in happier
times. McClintoch's secretary made an audio dub:

"New York Senator Morton Beaufoy is up for election to
his fourth term this year, and for the first time has a viable rival
in the primary in the person of Congressman Herbert Turnbull, who won a place on the ballot by petition. Turnbull is a
strong vote-getter. Now Beaufoy's problems may be com-
pounding. Early this afternoon a woman was found stabbed
to death in the garage of a building where Beaufoy maintains
a New York apartment and is currently in residence. There is
some reason to believe the dead woman may have been known
to the senator. At the very least, you can expect questions to
be raised by the Turnbull camp."

The shoe had dropped.

*   *   *

The first call came less than five minutes later. It was from Jerry Scovil, the *Ledger* reporter who had been hired off the supermarket weekly. McClintoch and I had already roughed out, if not quite a defense, at least a holding action.

Paul was the right man in the right place. An instantly likeable butterball in his forties, he was well served in crises, thank God, by his bovine placidity. It fit in nicely with Beaufoy's low-key style. I supposed that was why they had been together so many years. I had banged out a statement, and Paul read it to Scovil as if he was improvising:

"The senator spoke with me earlier today about this. He authorized me to say that he feels personally moved by the tragedy, since it happened so close to home and since he had actually met the victim briefly on a business matter. He has conferred with the detectives on the case in the hope of offering some help in its solution. They asked him to say no more at this time so as not to give inadvertent aid to the perpetrator."

This statement was not going to seriously discourage the wolves—Scovil snarled at it—but maybe we had thrown enough meat off the sled to slow the pursuit. I read it to Beaufoy over the phone. (He waited to pick up, praise God, until he heard my voice on the answering machine.) He approved, asking only that I change "moved" to "deeply moved." Done.

In the next twenty minutes Paul had to read the statement to half a dozen reporters who phoned. He did it with increasing assurance. Eventually the phone stopped ringing, and we figured that would be it for the day; the media people most likely to take this thing by the throat had all checked in. There wasn't much more we could do tonight, nor could the reporters. Paul was itching to get back to his other duties.

Before he left me for the chaos out front he remembered something that had, understandably, gone clean out of his head. We were alone and he closed his door. "Remember my telling you about Krista Grolik, the woman who used to manage the New York district office? How she shared with me something awkward that happened between her and the senator?"

"Something of a sexual nature, yes."

"Well . . ." He hesitated, then went on. "I felt it only fair to tell her I had spoken to you about that, so I called her. She wants to talk to you."

"What's the point, Paul? Nothing she can tell me will do our side any good."

"She was upset. She wants to set the record straight. She's a longtime friend and I owe her that much. Jock, give her a few minutes."

I wasn't going to do it if it was going to be a big deal, but the address Paul gave me was not that far north, off Second Avenue. I figured what the hell, and made the call. Krista Grolik picked up.

She sounded pleasant, if strained, and said she remembered me well, that we had run across each other a few times. I asked if she'd like to meet me in the neighborhood for a cup of coffee or a drink, but she said, No, her husband was at a meeting that was running late and she was baby-sitting; would it be too much trouble for me to drop around to her place at about eight-thirty, after she put her child to sleep? I said sure, fine.

It really wasn't that fine. I would have to kill an hour until eight-thirty, and then probably another twenty minutes being polite to Mrs. Grolik at a time when I should be giving heavy thought to how we were going to counter the massive onslaught tomorrow from the media and the Turnbull-Hancock team.

I found a low-end Italian restaurant on First Avenue that

wasn't crowded, and sat with a half carafe of the house red and a bowl of pasta my mother would rather have been in her coffin than eat, and tried to figure out where the dam was likely to spring leaks and how many fingers I would need to plug it.

I made a mental list of the evidence that would go into building the Love Nest charge against Mort: it wasn't good that Sheri Bannerman had been attractive and well groomed and a honey-blonde; that she and Mort met in his apartment when his wife was out of town and unaware of the meeting, or even that her husband was looking for a new apartment; that he had denied remembering Sheri was wearing a bright green dress; that he claimed to be absorbed in apartment hunting at a time when all of his limited energy should have gone into the primary campaign; that Sheri was supposed to have shown him floor plans, but no floor plans ever turned up; that her shoeless body was found in his car; and that she was wearing—why did this still bother me?—garters.

The garters were the easiest to dispose of. The police wouldn't let out that tidbit to the media; it could be used as a check against the validity of a confession from the kind of nut who surfaces in high-profile murder cases. The green dress, come to think of it, was just as easy. Nobody was present but Mort and me when he denied that he knew the woman was wearing a green dress; it would remain our little secret. As for Sheri being a dish, and smartly turned out, so were a high percentage of real estate saleswomen. Should Mort have demanded that he be served by a crone?

Moving right along, this was as good a time as any for the senator to begin a search for a new apartment. Trapped at home for a few days by his bad back, and monitoring the campaign and tending to Senate business by phone, he could look at plans between calls, then wait till after the campaign to drive around and eyeball the likeliest possibilities.

Mort's dream of keeping the apartment hunt a secret from his wife would have to be abandoned, but absolutely. Mrs.

Beaufoy, the rock-solid Clara, would have to be brought up from Washington and briefed to declare she knew all along that Mort was going to surprise her with a new apartment; his attempt to keep it a surprise had been a pathetic failure.

The other negatives I didn't yet have answers for: the absence of apartment floor plans from Sheri's effects, the presence of her body and her shoes in Mort's Buick. But murder cases didn't always tie up into perfect packages. There was bound to be some fallout. And, with luck, more answers would turn up along the way and some questions might never be asked. As the drama played out, we would have to do some improvising. I was feeling somewhat reassured as I paid the check.

By now Beaufoy's Washington office would be shut down for the night and his line might be free, so before heading for the Groliks' I called to brief him on the game plan. I got through on the first try. Mort was sticking to the phone-answering drill; he again waited for me to identify myself before he picked up and said, "Yes, dear boy, what's up?"

I laid it out straight. We were going to have to shore up our defenses against the inevitable questions from the media about Sheri Bannerman, and in that connection we would need Mrs. Beaufoy to come up from Washington.

"Clara? What on earth for?"

"I'll explain when I see you. I suggest you have her take the first plane she can get on tomorrow."

"John, this is ridiculous. She only went home yesterday. She has a million housekeeping chores she's had to put off, and I can't ask her to simply turn around—"

"I'm sorry. You'll have to do it."

"You'll have to tell me why."

"Because you made me your media consultant, and I'm going to try like hell to earn my entire miserable fee in the next day or two. But only if you do what I say."

Instead of arguing further he fell silent for a moment, and

then reminded me of our taping session the next morning. And after another pregnant silence he changed the subject again and reluctantly admitted that his machine had picked up a few messages from reporters with awkward questions.

I said, "How many?"

He read me the list. They were the same reporters who had called McClintoch at campaign headquarters. Plus, "And the last was that Paula something."

"You still didn't catch her last name?"

"She didn't leave it. Her salutation was, 'Hi, it's Paula again.' "

The bitch.

The Groliks lived in a faceless new high-rise with an impressive bank of elevators in the cool marble lobby. They were needed. On the Groliks' floor, the apartments along the endless narrow hallway ran up to "Q."

I remembered Krista as soon as she opened her door and flashed a quick, nervous smile. Her clear blue eyes were set in a chiseled, handsome face with high cheekbones and a wide forehead. Having a small child at her age—she had to be over forty—had worn her down some but added character to her face, if that was possible. Probably in haste, she had brushed her hair and put on a fresh shirt, but the scent of clean baby still clung to her. She used to look crisply businesslike; now she was a slightly frazzled homebody.

"I just got the baby down," she greeted me, almost triumphantly. Like many businesswomen in support positions, she was brighter than her job at the Beaufoy office required. That was true too of her present responsibility, but I could tell there would be no complaints about the drudgery of motherhood. She reveled in it.

We were old acquaintances and it didn't take more than five minutes before I felt we were old friends. We fell into concerned conversation about the Beaufoy campaign and how uncertainly it was going. By unspoken agreement we soon gravitated to the canary-yellow kitchen and sat at the formica kitchen table. Over coffee, already made, we dredged up what few reminiscences we had in common. That didn't take long, and I waited for Krista to move on to the substance of the meeting.

"Those few times you visited our district office?" she said when the shoptalk was running down. "When you left there'd always be a buzz of speculation among the women."

"About what?"

"Your availability. You were single, not at all bad looking—scruffy, but a bit leaner than now . . ."

I said, "Don't feel compelled to be totally honest."

". . . and of course, you were a glamorous, bylined investigative newspaper reporter. Even though . . ."

She had trailed off, and I finished her thought. "Even though not really for a newspaper. I was on the *Ledger*."

"Anyway, did anybody catch you? Or vice versa? Are you married?"

"You mean, have I put on these few pounds out of sheer domestic contentment? No, they come from the love of a good doughnut. Krista, you're the one I would have hit on, but I knew you were married." It was an opening. "Speaking of which . . ."

I let it hang, and she picked up. "Yes, that's what I wanted to speak to you about—Senator Beaufoy's supposed pass at me. When Paul McClintoch reminded me of what I told him a couple of years ago, I was terribly upset. I wanted to set the record absolutely straight. Because I should never have . . . *He* should never have . . ."

"The story stops with me. Paul knows that. He probably told you I'm on the reelection team."

"Yes. That's good. I'm even managing to put in a few hours a week myself. Morton Beaufoy is the dearest—"

She stopped and laughed. " 'Dearest.' I picked that up from him. 'Dear' is his favorite word. He's the kind of old-fashioned gent who's gone out of fashion. Along with the word 'gent.' The senator is especially gallant around women."

"But that incident," I prompted gently, "whatever it was you told Paul . . ."

"It was . . . well . . . strange, is the way I'd describe it." Her hands were wrapped tightly around her coffee cup; she had been bracing herself to talk about this.

"It must have been four or five years ago. The senator's car—the same Buick he has now, and would you believe, it was far from new even then?—anyway, it was in the shop. I was accompanying him on a fence-mending drive through Westchester and we'd just dropped the County Executive in White Plains on our way back to New York.

"We were in a limo I'd rented complete with driver. I'd forgotten the senator hates limos. When he was young, he's said many times, limos were for funerals. He doesn't much like police motorcycle escorts either. He once told me there was never a police escort that didn't make enemies on the road for whoever was being escorted. The senator is a refreshing mix of the naive and the shrewd, don't you agree?"

She didn't wait for an answer. "Anyway, we were on the Hutchinson River Parkway and a thunderstorm came up you wouldn't believe. Water by the bucket. This great clunk of a limo started lurching and gasping and finally limped to the shoulder and died. The driver looked under the hood but I could tell he didn't know any more about cars than to turn on the motor. He stuck his head in our door and said he would have to walk back to the gas station we'd passed, and he disappeared into the rain.

"I estimated we had a good thirty- to forty-minute wait for help. The rain was pelting the roof, and the windows were fogged up. It was too dark in the car to do any paperwork. We leaned back into the leather to wait. Bored. I suppose that's what triggered it."

"So he did make a sort of pass."

"*No*. Get that out of your head. There was no pass. I've had passes made in work situations and I know how to turn them aside without inflicting wounds. This was something else entirely, and it didn't even occur to me to try to stop it."

"Krista . . ." I was getting impatient.

"Right." She got the message. "It had been a long day. After a few minutes of sitting there without much to say, listening to the rain, we were both heavy-lidded, drowsy. And then out of nowhere—out of boredom, I suppose—the senator began this sort of dreamy soliloquy. I won't try to reproduce it. I wouldn't know how. He was just amusing us, making the time go by, having fun. Out of the wet and the isolation, I suppose, he spun up this image of us as survivors of a passenger ship that had sunk, adrift on a life raft in a turbulent sea."

She paused and looked at me for a reaction. I studiously sipped my coffee.

"That didn't take much imagination, considering our situation," she continued, "but he got caught up in the image and he began to build on it. We were not only adrift, we were on short rations. He inventoried the supplies—things like Spam and salt-water taffy and Oreo cookies and what he called Monster cheese. He had fun with the supplies." This was going very slowly.

"He said we tried to divide the little we had fairly but we didn't really trust each other. No way. We couldn't either of us close our eyes for fear the other would steal. By the ninth or tenth day we were half crazy from the tropical sun that came after the rain, and from lack of food and sleep. The salt spray had dried our skin and cracked our lips. I have to tell you, the senator certainly made the time go by."

She looked at me again, as if she expected me to interrupt. I had no intention of doing so, and she picked up her narrative. "He was really into it now—sharks snapping at the raft, giant waves rolling over us, that sort of thing. Not until our fourteenth day did he allow us to spot a distant island through the shimmering heat. And then we were inside a coral lagoon and sprawled on a white sand beach.

"At that point he said something like, 'Oh, I forgot to tell you who we are. Let's see now . . .' And with barely a moment's hesitation he spun out identities for us. Would you believe I was the ship's hairdresser, who had gone to sea to forget an ugly divorce from an abusive husband? I was off men, all men. I wanted nothing to do with them. After my working hours I would prop myself in my bunk with my charcoals and sketch pad and draw the passengers from memory. Devastating caricatures. I was really an artist, you see, and naturally very good.

"The senator made himself the chief engineer, a reclusive widower who preferred the company of his engines and his volumes of Proust to the silly socializing of the other officers in the passenger lounge. His collection of pipes had gone down with the ship.

"And now we two misanthropists were thrown together. The senator was really having fun with this. Maybe, come to think of it, because bringing natural enemies together is what he does best on the Foreign Relations Committee. The hairdresser and the engineer were going to have to make the best of a bad situation." She paused. "I must have seen something like this in a movie."

"Movies."

" 'Miss Krista' was how the engineer referred to the hairdresser, always in the third person. 'Would Miss Krista gather wood for a fire, please?' Pure camp. The details were perfect— the trees and plants and how the ocean breezes played among them, and the tropical smells and the birdsongs, and the sounds of the lapping waters inside the lagoon. He made me almost half believe, he almost seemed to half believe himself."

I said, "Remember, he's a writer." But not a writer of paperback romances. He was steeped in Charlemagne and *The Song of Roland*—epic battle stuff. I supposed this was his way of coming down from the heights.

Krista had moved on, caught up in her own narration. "The engineer, of course, was terribly clever. Under his guidance we built a shelter of palm fronds and bamboo. Our quarters shared a roof, but we carefully separated his half from mine with a wall of woven leaves and grasses. New clothing we were forced to improvise out of available material—skimpy coverings that would have been frowned on in civilization but were, the senator assured me, appropriate to our situation. The engineer fished in the lagoon and the hairdresser cooked. We ate our meals together, but that was our only social contact—if you can call it that, because we rarely spoke more than was necessary.

"And then one day when I was busy with household chores a cry of anguish rose from the lagoon. I raced toward it in time to see the engineer stagger onto the beach, blood gushing from his thigh."

"Don't tell me. He'd been bitten by a shark."

"Actually, as I remember, a barracuda. Yes, it was tongue-in-cheek, the senator's way, as I said, of making the time pass in that fogged-in limo. And now, with a trail of the engineer's blood on the coral sand, followed by his days of fever and slow return to sanity while the ugly wound closed—well, it was becoming pretty intense. It was oddball, yes. Definitely off the wall, and I was totally swept up in it.

"And then came the night the engineer woke me by shouting my name across the divider. I thought he needed help with the dressing on his wound, but no, the shout had been a warning. There was an eerie stillness in the air, an absence of all sound. And suddenly the typhoon struck. It tore off our roof before I managed to reach the engineer, and then it ripped our divider wall from its mooring and sent it flying. We clung to each other and managed to crawl and claw our way to the shelter of a giant palm. I know I'm telling this in too much detail, but that's the only way I can convey . . ."

She trailed off for a moment before she picked up the thread of the story. "With the frond sash that held my garment, I managed to tie the still weakened engineer to the trunk of the palm. We hung on to each other for dear life.

"The morning sun found us exhausted but alive. Our shelter was destroyed, our food supply scattered, our bodies, still glistening wet from the storm, nearly naked. But we were safe. And together—get this—we realized that a bond existed between us now that was stronger than a shipwreck, stronger than a typhoon, stronger even than the psychic forces that had laid out our separate paths in life."

"Oh, boy." I sensed what was coming and I didn't like it.

"At that moment in the limo, those were my very words to myself. I had been going along with the fantasy, in total admiration of the way the senator was spinning it. And only at that point did I realize that in the next minute or two the chairman of the Senate Foreign Relations Committee and I were going to be locked in each other's sunburned arms under those rustling palms, rolling nakedly toward the lapping waters of the lagoon, making wild and passionate love."

I was finding this glimpse of a hitherto unrevealed side of Mort Beaufoy increasingly disturbing. I felt unanchored, free floating, an astronaut uncoupled from the mother ship. The best I could manage was, "Yes, it must have been awkward."

"Awkward? I had become hideously embarrassed. I would have stopped the senator if I knew how to do it without becoming even more so. But you know what? At exactly that moment he himself must have realized he had painted us into a corner. He stopped almost in mid-sentence. I sneaked a glance and read his embarrassment.

"And a moment later he had smoothly shifted gears. The white smokestack of a passing ship broke the plane of the horizon and the engineer ordered the hairdresser to light the signal fire. I did so, and the damp kindling sent up billows of smoke. The ship turned our way.

"And that was about as far as the story went, because a tow truck was pulling up in front of the limo, and our driver was waving at us and grinning reassurance through the steamed-up windows."

After that neither of us spoke. Krista was giving me time to absorb what she had told me, and I was thinking about a Mort Beaufoy I didn't know as well as I had thought.

Finally Krista said, "So you see, there was no pass. Not then, not ever. Nor was there ever another fantasy story from the senator. Mountains out of molehills, the whole thing. Don't you agree?"

I wasn't sure; something of a sexual nature had transpired. A less generous woman might have called it harassment. Maybe incipient psychic rape. I hadn't had time to sort it out. I half wished I hadn't heard it.

But I didn't have to agree or disagree. Krista's husband had come in and was standing in the kitchen doorway, a nice-looking guy, possibly younger than she. He was sizing me up while he said, "Hi, hon."

She kissed him and made the introductions. "Harry, say hello to Jock Caprisi."

"Oh, sure, right." He had recognized the name. But he turned back to Krista; he had something he was dying to share. "So have you heard about your ex-boss?"

"The body in his garage," she said. "I tried to call you about that hours ago."

He said, "Old news, hon. The radio has the latest. The body wasn't in his garage. It was in old Mort's *car* in his garage. And the dead woman had been with him in his apartment this morning. How about that?"

The information juggernaut was continuing to roll.

9 It was close to ten when I arrived back at the Stanley. East, west, they say, home's best. Yeah.

Octavio, the peppy community-college student who manned the desk at night, came out from behind a chemistry text to hand me a couple of phone messages. The first was from Jerry Scovil at the *Ledger*. That surprised me; I had barely exchanged grunts with the shifty bastard those few days when we were both at the paper.

The message read, "He can be reached at The Ledger until midnight." Good for Scovil, nose to the grindstone. If he expected special favors from an old *Ledger* colleague he was smoking the wrong pipe.

The other message was from "Sergeant Al Nordstrom. Please call," followed by a Bronx phone number. At the least Hap owed me an apology. He should have been able to keep the scandal buttoned down until morning. Now it would be all over the eleven o'clock news, plus the early editions of the papers. Voters would lie awake tonight, stewing over what the hell their senior senator was up to. This voter among them.

I would have to leave for the taping session at Mort's not long after the crack of dawn, and no more surprises were likely tonight, so I thought I would hit my less than Posturepedic mattress right after the news. Tomorrow looked to be a busy day, and Krista Grolik's account of Mort Beaufoy's desert island fantasy had drained my batteries. I went up to my suite, tried not to look at it when I turned the light on, and took a beer from the fridge.

The first message I could dispose of fast. I called Scovil at the *Ledger*. He attempted the old-boy approach. He appealed to "alumni loyalty," something that would allow the *Ledger* to "stick it to the competition." Uninvited, the pitch was repulsive, and I was barely civil. Scovil got the point and went into his fallback position, a quid pro quo. If I could give him something sizzling the rest of the media didn't have, surprise, he was ready to give me a little something in return.

"Like what?"

"Jock, you're looking to point this story away from old Mort Beaufoy, right? I can steer you to a guaranteed quality distraction."

I had to find out if we were in the same time-zone. "Do I understand you right? You'll put me on to an angle that takes the heat off Beaufoy? But I've got to give you something raunchy enough to keep it on?"

He backed off. "I'm not asking you to nail your man. But you've had all day on this. I don't know, maybe you've got an angle on the woman—could be something that *helps* your man. Hell, I don't care if she's an ex-nun. So long as we can tag the story 'A *Ledger* Exclusive.' "

I thought for a moment. What did I know that was harmless? I rummaged through my grab bag.

"Okay. You heard it here first. Sheri Bannerman was a part-time actress, member of an off-off-Broadway company called the Hudson Players. You'll find them downtown somewhere, probably in Tribeca."

"So?" He was not impressed.

"They'll have *pictures*. I don't have to tell you, of all people, Jerry"—I had never called him Jerry—"there are no better shots of the deceased for a tab than the glossies taken by a theatrical photographer. Sheri Bannerman was perky, fresh, with legs up to her armpits. She would be alive in the *Ledger*, while she's stone dead in the competition. Doesn't that separate your front page from the others?"

Scovil weighed this. "And that's the best you can do?"

"Jerry, it's an exclusive. And it's all I have. I may know less about this murder than you do. Because my man had nothing to do with it. He barely knew the woman."

"Yeah, well, okay," he said grudgingly. "I may be able to do something with that."

I waited while he balanced those possibly leggy glossies against what he had to give me. Finally: "Here's what I've got. The drug retailing franchise in the neighborhood where the blonde's body was found is held by a Panamanian named Felix Pacheco. Pacheco has a lock on maybe eight or ten choice blocks. Three weeks ago he was nailed for possession and he was held on Rikers. He made bail last night."

"I don't see a connection. What am I supposed to do with that?"

"You're a flack, remember? Be creative. Whip something up."

I hadn't any idea what, but I said, "Where do I find this Pacheco?"

"Search me. Thank God you were once a crackerjack investigative reporter, right, Jocko? Before you sold out to the forces of moral integrity."

He was gleeful when he signed off, but I didn't linger on that; my mind was on overdrive. Maybe Scovil had given me more than he thought. An idea was forming that began with something like this: If Sheri Bannerman was making more money than a depressed real estate market warranted, what was its source? Money and drugs came off the tongue as trippingly as Lewis and Clark. Suppose Sheri had worked for this Pacheco, delivering drugs to upscale customers? Tooling around in her little sports car on real estate business was a perfect cover for such a sideline. And while Felix was away she had worked for herself.

Now Felix comes out of jail. He arranges to meet Sheri this morning at Mort's garage to collect the three weeks of receipts she's held for him while he was holed up on Rikers Island. She doesn't have the money—who knows, maybe the Bannermans had to pay the pool contractor, maybe she thinks the drug money's all hers—and an outraged Pacheco promptly sticks his knife in her.

I liked it. I didn't believe it for a minute, but I liked it. It took the heat off Mort Beaufoy. Totally. It was a typical story of the New York streets, instantly recognizable. Something like it happened every day of the week. If I threw this story off the sled the wolves would sniff and paw at it. There might not be a feeding frenzy, but the media would have to chew on it for days, maybe right up to the primary. So why didn't I have any real enthusiasm for it?

Because it didn't feel right. Sheri didn't give off the right emanations for the drug trade. "Drug dealer" wouldn't be one of your first fifty guesses for her on *What's My Line*. It was not impossible to believe, but it was not an easy sell. And there were bits and pieces that didn't fit. For instance, Pacheco lifting her dress so the knife wouldn't go through it; or, alternately, removing the dress entirely. That didn't come out of any drug trade lore I knew.

Then again, maybe I didn't know *Panamanian* drug lore. Maybe this was how the Panamanian underworld dealt with double-crossers. Something along the lines of "Fuck with me and you die, but your garment will never sully my knife." I would have to work on that, see if I could give it an origin in folklore and myth. But not until I let it marinate for a while.

I made the other phone call. While someone went looking for Hap Nordstrom I listened to the background sounds of a detective squad room. There were too many people in that room. They should have been out on the street chasing down Sheri's killer.

When Nordstrom came on he said, "Jock? I'll call you right back."

He rang me a minute later and there was no longer a hum of activity behind him; he had shut himself into an office. That was a good sign; he had something to tell me in private.

He said, "Listen, I apologize for this thing running away from me. I haven't forgotten I owe you a big one. I intend this case to square us."

I kept my mouth shut.

"I'm sorry about the leaks. I have no excuse, except that a U.S. senator is involved, so there's pressure."

"From the media."

"And your opposition. Who the hell is this Poppy Hancock?"

A load of gravel suddenly unloaded in my gut. "Herbert Turnbull's chainsaw operator."

"I don't doubt it. She's a terror." He lowered his voice. "And there's other factors I can't control—people up this way who aren't used to high-profile crime, who don't know how to keep their lips buttoned."

"Your partner?"

"It's not intentional. He's good, but he's green. I'm plugging the holes." Over the phone he sounded less funereal. "Jock, let me fill you in on where we stand right now. You're off the paper, so I know whatever I tell you stays strictly between us. We two *only*."

"Right. Shoot."

"And please, not too many questions. I've got to be on Staten Island before midnight."

"The bride is ovulating, huh?"

"And on call at the hospital. Okay. There won't be a full autopsy until at least tomorrow, but here's the early forensics.

All the blood is the victim's—at least it's all her type. She took a single sharp-impact thrust in the gut, probably from a long-bladed knife. Organs were punctured; if you have to know more precisely on that, wait for the autopsy. Bottom line is, she couldn't have lived more than a few minutes after taking the wound. The M.E. figures she was dead a couple of hours, more or less, when he got to the scene, which means she had to have been killed somewhere around the time she left Beaufoy's apartment. She was still alive at ten forty-six A.M."

"How do you know?"

"The cellular-phone record shows a call at that time from her to her boss, one Clifton Oliver. I caught him at home at six o'clock and he remembers getting the call. He says she had a question about a lease and they stayed on no more than a minute. That's what the phone record shows—a one-minute outgoing call at ten forty-six.

"Sheri's phone was picked up on two brief incoming calls after she had been dead for about two hours. We figure the super, LaPierre, picked up, probably without thinking. Not important anyway; people who phoned the woman after she was dead weren't likely to have killed her. I'll catch LaPierre tomorrow."

Was he putting me through one of his sly tests? "Hap, I told you. I took those calls."

"Jesus, you're right. That's in my notes. Sorry. You can see the kind of day I've had. We've been picking up every loose cannon in the north Bronx."

A thought struck me. "Didn't Sheri's boss tell you he spoke to me on her phone?"

"No, only that someone picked up when he called. He didn't tell me any more than he had to."

"That's his real estate training. Everything close to the vest. The second call—"

"—was from a client of Bannerman's in Mount Vernon. Hal Vector. His wife says they're looking for a house."

"Hap, his greeting was, 'Hi, Honeybuns.'"

"That could be interesting," he said slowly. "Or not. Was he being playful, or was it something more?"

"I couldn't tell, but if I were you I wouldn't ask him in front of his wife."

"I can't ask him anything until tomorrow. He's a C.P.A. with a giant accounting firm downtown, Cawber Latch Oberwalt, and he's gone out of town on an audit."

I suddenly remembered Scovil's tip. "Hap, do you know a boutique drug dealer named Felix Pacheco?"

"Felix the Pussycat. Very good, Jock, that's his territory and he made bail in time to have done the deed. But why? Anyway, he's been checked out. He was in a podiatrist's waiting room most of this morning; all he thought about at Rikers was having his feet pruned. Jock, if you keep interrupting I'll have to cut you off."

"Let's see. Prints on the car: there were none except for a thumb on a rear door handle."

"You'll find it belongs to one of the whizbang cops who were first on the scene. No other prints? None of the senator's on his own car?"

"Crime Scene didn't bother checking the steering wheel. The doors and the rear seat had been wiped clean. So much for prints; let me turn to the woman."

He was in a tearing hurry, all right. "There was recent vaginal penetration but she probably wasn't raped. Matching white silk underwear and sheer hose under that green dress were all undamaged. There were no bruises, lacerations, or other signs of a struggle. Nothing under the fingernails."

" 'Recent vaginal penetration.' You mean she'd been laid. Possibly by her husband."

"It still happens. There were traces of a lubricant used on some brands of condoms."

"So you won't have semen for a possible DNA match. Hap,

is the condom the contraceptive of choice for married couples?"

"I'm the last person you want to ask that question. But now I'm going to have to ask Bannerman if he's a user." The mournful Hap was breaking through. "There are things I do on this job . . ."

While that hung on the line there was a knock on my door. That had to be Manuel, the night bellman, a little early with the first editions of tomorrow's newspapers. I said, "One second, Hap, while I get my door."

"No, that's my cue to get off. Jock, this is a warning. I'm going to keep you advised, but don't screw with my case."

"Good night, Hap. Have a pleasant evening. And a productive one." But I had spoken the last sentence into a dead line.

Before I reached the door there was a second knock, more insistent. The usually polite Manuel was impatient tonight. I opened the door and Poppy Hancock swept past me into the room, trailing the heady scent I remembered like yesterday from that hotel elevator in Washington.

Poppy Hancock. She looked as good as ever in a dark, snug-fitting pantsuit. Better. Her bouncy black hair had bounced fetchingly out of control after a day of campaigning that had left her tired and maybe a bit more mature looking. She still reminded me of a high school cheerleader, but at a game that had gone into double overtime.

I said, "How did you get up here?" I deliberately chose the tone that worked with pizza delivery boys. "Nobody gets past the desk without being announced."

"That's what they told me when I dropped by half an hour ago. I'm staying nearby, a sublet on Fifty-fourth. Behind the Modern?" Naturally, one of the best damn locations in the city. "I asked to be called when you came in."

"You *asked* to be—? That's absolutely against the—"

"I know. And I'm not going to say who it was that betrayed you, except it isn't who you think. But his—or her—loyalty bent when a tiny sum was mentioned. At a slightly higher but still shabbily modest one it broke entirely. Disappointing, isn't it, how often we misplace our trust? Okay if I sit anywhere?"

She was surveying the room with distaste; none of my mud-colored furniture seemed to be beckoning. She sighed resignedly and sank into a bloated armchair. "I can't stay long. I've had a hell of a day and I've got an even messier one tomorrow." She murmured an afterthought. "I suppose you do too. . . ."

"Me? No, I'm going to work on my stamp collection. What do you want, Poppy?"

I didn't have a clue. And her pose of insouciance was making me clench my teeth. Usually if someone on the other side of any question comes to see me I figure I've got the edge. I had the feeling that with Poppy that was not necessarily the case.

She said, "I'm here to hammer out some ground rules. Why don't you sit down, Jock? You make me nervous. Or does your furniture scare you as much as it does me?"

I perched on the edge of the couch and suppressed a sneer. "I suppose you think the place needs a woman's touch."

"It needs a match. But let's not talk decorating. I've come with a quid pro quo."

There would doubtless be more quid than quo but I kept my mouth shut and waited for her offer. I might learn something.

We had been volleying, and she was poised for a return shot. When none came, it threw her timing. She took a moment, then put a new ball in play.

"I believe the voters are entitled to some substantive debate in this campaign," she began slowly. "I hope you agree."

She was reading my face. It was, I hoped, a blank page. "We owe it to them not to get bogged down in scandal and innuendo," she said, "not to wallow in allegations and outrageous charges. I say let's get on to the issues."

I had to say it. "I couldn't agree with you more." No outrageous charges? Where was she headed? You don't hire Poppy Hancock if there are going to be no outrageous charges.

"With that objective in mind," she continued, "and for the sake of the party—for God's sake, let's not lose sight of the party—I'd like to propose a couple of ground rules to push the Sheri Bannerman business into the background before it has a chance to run out of control. Stipulations that would free up the candidates to talk about the things on people's minds—gut issues, pocketbook issues, quality-of-life issues."

"Stipulations? Stipulations as to what, Poppy? Spell it out." This must be what it was like to cut through whale blubber with a butter knife.

"Okay, here's my proposal." She turned those marvelous eyes full on me. "Your side puts out a statement admitting that Senator Beaufoy had an intimate personal relationship with Sheri Bannerman. Phrase it any way you want, Jock. With your writing skills I'm sure you'll know how to make a plus of it— a frank admission from the senator that at the same time would be an example of his refreshing candor. I won't presume to tell you how to do your job."

This woman had more brass than Big Ben. "That's it? Senator Beaufoy confesses to cheating on his wife of forty-odd years?" My voice sounded to me amazingly calm. "What do we get in return?"

"Two things. One, Congressman Turnbull will never—not by indirection, by innuendo, by so much as a wink—refer to the liaison."

"He wouldn't have to. Beaufoy's mea culpa would hang over the campaign like an eight-day mushroom cloud. And even if that should start to blow away, your dirty-tricks guys would remind the electorate—"

"Jock, you have my solemn word—"

" 'You have my solemn word' doesn't compute for dirty-tricks guys. Come on, Poppy, you have something better than that up your sleeve." I was just curious enough to press. "What's the sweetener?"

"You must know that if Beaufoy doesn't 'fess up, we'll make the case for him. And our presentation won't be nearly as pleasant as if he did it himself."

"That's a given. You said you had two things. Let's have number two."

"I'll give it to you straight, but I don't know how sweet you'll find it."

Those violet flecks in her eyes were doing a slow dance. "If you don't agree to number one we'll go a step further. We'll make the case—none of this from Congressman Turnbull himself, you understand; he won't get down in the gutter—"

"No shit? I thought he lived there."

"Someone on our side, a middle-level aide, will float the idea that it may have been Beaufoy himself who killed the woman."

My blood stopped circulating. "You wouldn't dare. Not even you, Poppy."

"Why not? What makes it a no-no? You think people won't be speculating anyway? The police can't rule Beaufoy out. The question will be hanging in the air. Why not bring it down and put it on the table? Let people chew on it?"

"Because you'll only embarrass yourself if you try to spin an accusation like that out of thin air." I could barely control my anger. "The backfire will blow out your eardrums. There is nothing there. No hint of a case. Nothing to hold on to."

"There's enough. Do I have to tell you? Morton Beaufoy knew Sheri Bannerman was down in that garage. So far as we know he is the *only* person who knew that."

"The killer wiped all the fingerprints off the senator's car. You don't have to wipe your prints from your own car."

"It was his first murder. You expect him to be totally logical? Let me finish. Suppose they'd had a lover's quarrel and she was leaving him. Do you know how desperate old men get when young women abandon them?"

"No, Poppy. Tell me."

It lasted only a moment, but her cheeks flushed, actually flushed, and I had a sudden blinding insight into her own sexual history. The old congressman, her mentor?

She said coolly, "Beaufoy could have followed the woman down to the garage to plead with her to reconsider, possibly unaware that in his crazed state he'd grabbed a kitchen knife. Then, when his pleadings—his pitiful entreaties for her to come back to him—failed, the knife found its mark. It happens somewhere every day."

"Poppy, you're nuts. There's not a shred of evidence to support that yarn."

"Who needs evidence? We're not going to trial, only to the ballot box. To conclude, why did Beaufoy put the woman in his Buick? He planned to drive her somewhere after dark to dump the body. But, as we know, the plan aborted when a neighbor spotted the corpse in the car. Case closed."

"Too crude, Poppy, and too ugly. Even for you."

"I agree. But it won't come from me. Or Turnbull. Turnbull will denounce the middle-level aide who will make the charge, and demand that he apologize to Beaufoy. When the aide refuses, Turnbull will fire him. That way we get three days of news out of Beaufoy as possible murderer. How many days are there left to the campaign?"

She was cunning all right; I felt a little queasy. The only response was to bluster. I said, "What bullshit. Or Turnbull-shit, as I prefer to think of it. Which Morton Beaufoy will you guys be selling? The sick old man too feeble to serve in Congress? Or the randy stud who heaves bodies around like sacks of potatoes?"

"Both. Either. It doesn't matter. Some voters will go for one, some the other. We score points either way. You'll be foolish to turn down my proposal. Your man's in trouble. My route will cause him the least damage."

Her route led to the city dump. But it was in our interest to stall her as long as I could. I said, "As you well know, it's not up to me to make decisions on something like this. I'll pass your proposal along to Paul McClintoch and he and the candidate will deal with it."

"Beaufoy respects you. He'll want your input."

"If he asks, he'll get it." My tone was neutral.

"Jock, I think you're beginning to see that what I'm proposing isn't that outrageous, that it's at least worth considering."

"I said, If the senator wants my input, he'll get it."

She wouldn't stir the pot until she'd heard from me. If I could stall her for a couple of days, Hap Nordstrom might have a suspect in tow and I could tell Poppy what to do with her proposal.

She said, "So I'll hear from you tomorrow?"

"Or McClintoch. By the end of the day." I would have to be damned inventive to stall Poppy Hancock much beyond then.

"I won't keep you." She got to her feet. "Just between us, though, partisan politics totally aside, you know what I really think? I think Beaufoy did the dirty deed. Men do strange things when their hormones rage."

"You know what I think? It's as likely Herb Turnbull did the woman. Possibly with a butter knife stolen from one of his fund-raising dinners. Ambition also drives men to strange deeds."

She was walking to the door, and she wasn't going to dignify this last with an answer. "Good night, Jock."

"You're frowning," I couldn't resist saying. "That makes you the first woman who ever left here without wearing a smile of satisfaction."

She turned. "Next time you'll have to try harder. But, hey, we're still friends, right? No hard feelings?" She managed a smile and tilted her face up for a peck.

I wasn't going to let her jerk me around the way she had in that Washington hotel. I bent toward her lips, inhaled that magnificent scent, then dropped my head and bit her firmly on her smooth white neck.

Startled, she said, "Ow!" and pulled back.

I murmured, "You can spend all day tomorrow lying about how you got that hickey."

I knew I was one up. The best she could offer in response was, "Fuck you, Caprisi." And she was gone.

Manuel appeared ten minutes later with the morning papers. I looked him steadily in the eyes, but there was no guilt in them.

The dead honey-blonde in Senator Beaufoy's Buick made page one of the *Times*—page one of Section B, the Metro section. But it was on the front page of all four tabloids. It was the *News* that had found the inevitable high school yearbook photo of Sheri with the pasted-on smile, the cascades of hair, and the prediction that she was "Broadway bound." The *Ledger* featured a shot of Mort's Buick. Jerry Scovil hadn't had time to get the glossies, if they existed, from that downtown theater company; if they were any good the paper would spring for an extra edition in the morning.

The stories were about what I expected. The papers had gone to press before much was available beyond the bare bones, but there was no need to flesh those out with innuendo; a deadpan account of today's events in Riverdale was bad enough. An attractive young woman who had just left Senator Beaufoy's apartment, where the two of them had met alone, was found dead in his automobile. A story that could be written in crayons. Starting tomorrow, when the reporters dug in deep and the columnists and editorial writers checked in, things would get messy.

I slept no better than might be expected.

TUESDAY

10

At a quarter to nine in the morning the exterior of Mort Beaufoy's apartment house presented a couple of beehives of activity. I had expected to see TV remote trucks, and three of those were parked outside the garage. Two newsmen I recognized were preparing to do stand-ups; I supposed they were also hoping to lure the senator downstairs for a statement. Fat chance. Another reporter was sticking mikes into the faces of the building's residents as they drove up the ramp and out, on their way to work. The latter looked understandably resentful and put upon at the "How do you feel about the murder in your building?" questions, and they had little or less to say.

What I wasn't prepared for was the phalanx of men around the corner parading back and forth in front of the building's main entrance under the not too watchful eyes of a pair of cops. These picketers were a mixed bag, some in business suits and some looking as if they might be on their way to construction jobs. The theme that bound them together was expressed in the signs they carried: DON'T SELL DALMATIA SHORT; MANY CONQUERORS, NEVER CONQUERED; BEAUFOY, HONOR OUR PEOPLE; DALMATIA: RESTORE OUR ANCIENT NAME; and so on.

They were chanting, for the benefit of at least one television crew, "What do we want? Freedom! When do we want it? Now!" Where the hell was Dalmatia?

This was some kind of assault on the Senate Foreign Relations Committee. These people may have wanted to embarrass its chairman for a long time, and happened to be doing so this morning because they had just learned from the papers where Beaufoy was in residence. It was just as possible Hancock's people had orchestrated the demonstration sometime between yesterday and today and that nobody in this picket line gave a damn about Dalmatia. Somewhere on the Croatian coast, that was it. And didn't they already have a country, Croatia? The Balkans are as far beyond me as astrophysics.

I wasn't going to get involved; with all that was on my plate, an independent Dalmatia and its possibly three hundred advocates among voters in the state would have to wait their turn.

I parked in the street and entered the building for the first time through its tastefully low-key lobby: smoked glass, nubbly fabrics, dark, polished woods. The outer door was unlocked—I suppose because the super, LaPierre, was on deck polishing brass and vacuuming furniture. LaPierre, I hadn't noticed before, was a good-looking man with strong, deeply carved ebony features; he added class to the lobby, even in his Iron Boy overalls. He nodded when he recognized me, then shook his head sadly toward the front door.

I said, "This is quiet Riverdale? That crowd has to be driving you nuts." The chanting and shouting was filling this space that had been designed as a transitional zone of quiet between the bustle of the workplace and the tensions of home.

"The truth is, I have sympathy," LaPierre said. "And, you know, Senator Beaufoy will listen to these people. He is a man of compassion. He has been a great help to my own people in Haiti." He pronounced it in the three-syllable Haitian way, "Hah-ee-tee."

Then he said, "I should warn you, there are a great many

people up there in the senator's apartment. I suppose that has to do with the lady who was killed yesterday. They haven't caught her murderer?"

"Soon, I hope."

When I got out of the elevator on the fifth floor, the apartment door opposite opened and Ms. Kleiman, yesterday's near hysteric, peered out. She was wearing a furry pink robe that had seen better days. She looked completely normal now, a regular human being again, but she wore an expression of irritation on her thin, bony, sad face. She and Hap would have made a team.

"What *is* going on out there?" she asked. I couldn't tell if she remembered me.

"Dalmatians," I said, as if that would explain it all. "Nothing to do with"—I didn't want to set her off again—"yesterday's incident."

She shuddered anyway, and closed herself back in her apartment.

The taping of the TV spots proceeded smoothly in Mort's living room. The five-man production team had recently turned out a series of widely praised commercials for a local beer that took the form of unsolicited endorsements from a cross-section of New Yorkers. The TV ads were earthy and funny and seemingly impromptu, but of course they had been scripted down to the last dopey grin on the face of a Chinatown waiter. The team was pleased to be working now on something honest and useful. They believed in Mort Beaufoy, and it showed in their energy.

And Mort was right on the money. You wouldn't know there was a camera in the crowded living room. He was talking directly and without artifice to the people of New York about the subjects that had them concerned. They couldn't help but listen.

One reason he was so effective was that he didn't read the copy. The TelePrompTer had been unplugged and pushed into a corner. While the crew changed setups and lighting between shots, he would recline on his couch with the next spot and devour it whole. He was ready to go every time before the crew was. The makeup woman would give him a last minute touch-up and he would take his mark. Once the camera was rolling he might pause occasionally in mid-sentence to reach for the next phrase, or retract a word and replace it with another, but always to good effect. The performance was sincere and spontaneous. He succeeded in winning me over completely, and I had basically written this stuff.

Three takes were the most he needed on any of the first three spots. After the third he retreated to the bedroom to rest his back and make a costume change—professorial sweater and baggy pants to senatorial business suit. I grabbed the opportunity to pull Paul McClintoch into the kitchen, piled high with the crew's plastic coffee cups, for a hurried conference. In a few quick strokes I outlined what Poppy Hancock had pitched the night before and watched for his reaction.

It was, as usual, comfortingly bovine. "She really thought we'd go along with that?" he said, his eyebrows lifting almost not at all.

"She expects an answer."

"I'm not going to mention this to Mort. I think he's put yesterday out of his mind. Why lay this on him now?"

"What do I tell Hancock?"

"Let's see how long we can stall. If she decides to make good her threat, what the hell. There aren't ten people in this state who'd believe Mort Beaufoy is capable of murder. This will backfire."

I hesitated. "I agree, as far as the murder smear goes. But we'll be hurt by the sugar daddy allegation."

"That will come out anyway. If anyone can whip up heavy seas, it's Poppy Hancock. We'll just have to ride them out."

Poppy's momentary blush last night had stuck in my head. "Paul, do you know anything about Hancock's personal life? Boyfriends, liaisons . . . ?"

The question didn't surprise him. "Don't tell me your crotch is deserting to the opposition."

"I hope not. My pulse rate does go up when we meet but I like to think that's because the woman makes me so damn mad I want to strangle her."

"Okay, I'll chalk up your question to idle curiosity. This is something I happen to know only because I've been inside the beltway so long. Remember Charles Landmeer?"

"Congressman from Michigan. A brilliant politician. And one of the good guys."

"One of the best. He retired two years ago."

"Don't tell me he and Poppy . . . ?"

"It was a relationship so discreet that maybe it wasn't a relationship at all, maybe she just sat at his feet worshiping and learning. But if he wasn't putting it to her he should have had his head examined. She adored his mind, and, I think, everything appended thereto."

"He's married, isn't he? And a good forty years older?"

"Just about. The marriage is pro forma. While Landmeer was in Congress he made strategic public appearances with his wife, but they've been separated for many years."

I remembered what Poppy had said about young women who leave older men. "She dumped him, huh? I'll bet he took it hard."

"That I wouldn't know. But he should have seen it coming."

"Why?"

"He'd announced his retirement; he was a lame duck. For Hancock that would be worse than impotence. Anyway, I suppose he'd taught her everything he knew."

"Except right from wrong. The woman has the morals of a cruise missile."

"I note a tone of regret, Jock. Be careful."

We left the kitchen. Neither of us had mentioned my meeting with Krista Grolik. I think we were both too embarrassed.

Half an hour later McClintoch was on the phone conducting campaign business and I was huddled with the candidate in the bedroom reworking spot number six, the "fear of crime" spot. We were giving it more of a philosophical underpinning, to contrast with Turnbull's shrill cries of "Off with their heads." When we finished editing, Mort rose from his bed of pain and went to the window.

He said, "I know those television people down there are hollering for a statement from me on yesterday's tragedy. I want you to handle them. You've worked with these people as much as I have, and they're your peers. Put it however you think will make them back off."

I was relieved; I wasn't going to have to dissuade him from going down to face them, lance in hand, Don Quixote in medialand. And his vote of confidence gave me as good an opening as I would get to return to an awkward subject.

"Okay, I'll find something to say that'll hold them for now. But eventually you will have to face these guys. And a bunch more. And you must know the police are going to come back to you for at least one more go-round."

"John, you're making lazy circles. Come in for a landing. What's bothering you?"

"I don't want you facing questions you're not prepared to answer. Questions that can trip you up."

"Such as?"

"I hate bringing this up again. Yesterday you told me you didn't remember that Mrs. Bannerman was wearing a green dress."

"That again?" he said wearily.

I hung in. "Later you said it was because she probably wasn't wearing a green dress when she was here, that she may have spilled coffee on the dress she *was* wearing and changed, later, in her car."

He said nothing, merely looked at me calmly with his pale, watery eyes.

Embarrassed or not, I had to push on. "After I left you I visited the woman's husband."

He came alive with a look of concern. "That poor man. Is he bearing up? How is he taking the tragedy?"

"Okay, I guess." I waved this aside. Was this a time to worry about the husband? But how typically Mort Beaufoy. "The point is, he told me his wife was wearing the green dress when she left home yesterday morning. So that had to be the dress she had on when she was here. Mort, there was no spilled coffee on her dress. I saw it. No stains."

He was gazing at me steadily; his eyes looked like half-sucked butterscotch candies. Eventually he said, "None of that contradicts what I told you. Need I remind you again that I'm very bad at remembering what people are wearing? As for the spilled coffee, she may have spilled it on the table rather than on her dress. It was far from a memorable event."

"Agreed. But it becomes memorable if you can't field questions about the green dress."

"Who's going to ask them, John?"

"What do you mean? I told you, the press, the police . . ." I trailed off when I realized what was bothering me. I had already crossed the damn dress off my list of trouble spots. I wasn't worried about questions from the police or the press. I was worrying about questions I kept asking myself. Nagging questions. The truth, damn it, shall make you free.

Mort was saying, "You are obsessed by that green dress. But you are the only one I discussed it with, so there aren't likely to be questions on the arcane subject from anyone else. Are there?"

His answer, of course, was well reasoned, but it was less reassuring than unsettling. In any case, it became the final word on the subject. At that moment Mort's wife walked into the room with a small suitcase in each hand.

I had seen Clara Beaufoy in photographs and on the tube, but we had never met. She was at most half a dozen years younger than her husband, a tall, angular woman with thick, well-cut, gray hair and an intelligent face that spoke of social responsibility. I knew they had met when he was a newly tenured professor and she was a graduate student, and that after a brief teaching career of her own she had devoted herself to raising the children, serving as research assistant on his books, and stage-managing their personal lives.

She didn't give away much of herself now. She nodded briefly in my direction and dropped the bags before she turned to Mort and said in a neutral voice, "As instructed, here I am." He started to lift himself from the bed he had just sunk back down on, and she added, not unpleasantly, "For God's sake, Mort, don't get up on my account."

Mort made the introductions, Mrs. Beaufoy and I exchanged the briefest of pleasantries, and I got out as quickly as I could without seeming rude. I closed the door firmly behind me. None of the three of us wanted me in there.

The production crew had just finished preparations for the remainder of the shoot and they looked at me expectantly. I told them to relax. They were well ahead of schedule and didn't seem to mind waiting. The prospect of overtime may have strengthened their patience.

They waited. It was a good fifteen minutes before Mort came out from behind that closed door. He was in pain and walking carefully. Mrs. Beaufoy wasn't with him.

The last few spots didn't play quite as well as the earlier ones, everybody agreed, although nothing was said in front of the star. He fluffed his lines two or three times, and now the fluffs lacked charm. Some of his sureness was gone. Not surprising, was the consensus; he was clearly hurting and probably tired.

Before I slipped out to face the waiting reporters, I remembered to get the name of Beaufoy's orthopedist from McClintoch.

"You have a back problem?" he asked.

"No." I was writing it down. "This was a request from the police."

"God," he breathed placidly, "will this thing never end?"

All the years I was on the other side of the equation I thought of us as a vigorous press in a relentless search for the truth I prized—the first line of defense in a free and open society. Now I would have characterized the mob surrounding me as a flock of wheeling vultures. And like vultures, in the hours since I arrived this morning, the free press had attracted even more of its kind to the site of the hoped-for dead meat.

The first scavenger I spotted was the *Ledger*'s own Jerry Scovil, but I eventually recognized most of the others as they backed me against the lobby door. I noted that the Dalmatians—if they were Dalmatians—were gone. They had long since made their point, had their pictures taken, and gone off to work—or, more likely, to Turnbull headquarters to collect their crisp new twenties.

I waited till my ex-colleagues had staked out their camera and microphone territories and settled down before I made a brief statement to the effect that the senator sent his regrets, but on doctor's orders he would be housebound for another day or so. As their voices rose in complaint I added that he would have plenty to say on the issues at the appropriate time and would address all of their questions, but was there anything I could help them with until then?

Scovil got the first question by virtue of having the loudest voice. He said the issues could wait for the senator; he was here on the murder in the garage. He wanted to know more precisely about the relationship between Beaufoy and the dead blonde. The chorus behind him affirmed that that was what they all wanted to know.

I told Scovil he should stop using the word "relationship" unless he termed what happened between himself and whoever repaired his shoes a relationship. The senator was looking to buy an apartment, and this professional real estate salesperson had been looking to sell him one. The color of her hair was immaterial to the transaction. Next question.

The next question came from a beetle-browed youngish man toward the back of the crowd. I didn't recognize him. He wondered why the senator's wife wasn't present during this apartment-selecting process. I wondered where he had gotten hold of that piece of information.

I said, "Bud, you'll have to help me. Who are you and who are you with?"

The question surprised him. "Joe Bennis." Pause. "I'm a freelance."

"Okay, so where do you sell?"

"Different places." Pause. "This is for a spec magazine piece."

"Which won't come out until after the primary. If you sell it." I could smell him; the son of a bitch was a Turnbull plant. The others were already looking at him with suspicion. "Sorry, Joe, you're too low a priority for right now."

I looked for him a few minutes later; he seemed to have slunk off—I hoped with his tail between his legs. But of course I had to answer the question anyway; once for WCBS and once, in a slightly stickier form, for *Newsday*.

In essence I told them to save their questions for Mrs. Beaufoy, who was upstairs making lunch and baking her husband's favorite corn bread. She would be delighted to talk to them in a day or two, when she could take a breather from caring for the senator and dealing long distance with a house and office in Washington and the problems of children and grandchildren.

That brought another question, this one from the *Village Voice*. "Tell it straight, Jock. Just how sick is Beaufoy?"

"Are we on old news? He's not sick, Mike, he's got a structural problem stemming from the reality that man was not designed to walk on two legs but four. He's got a bad back, nothing more—a herniated disc and associated damage to the chassis—but he's improving every day."

"Improving how much?"

"He's not yet ready to wrestle alligators, but bring one around next week."

That's the way it went. They threw a lot of questions, most of them awkward to field, and a few, about the murder, unanswerable. With the latter I frankly admitted I didn't know—nobody did, that's why yesterday's crime was still unsolved. The full truth would have to wait for the successful conclusion of the criminal investigation; the senator was encouraged by the police to believe it was moving along rapidly. And I reminded them that the crime was only a day old.

Of course their most persistent questions had to do with variations on the theme of how come the body of the senator's business acquaintance ended up in his car shortly after she left his apartment. Every time I had to answer that one I used the word "Buick." I reminded them that at the time of the murder there were only three cars in the garage, and if the unknown killer decided to hide the body in a car there was a thirty-three percent chance the senator's Buick would be the unlucky winner.

I said I didn't want to teach this bunch their business, but they'd learn a lot more from Detective Sergeant Al Nordstrom than they would from me. Surely they remembered him from the case of the body in the rectory wall, which he broke in three days? I figured the windier I was, the less time they'd have for questions before the remote vans were called away to cover a fire in Queens, or whatever.

They hung in for a good twenty minutes. It seemed longer. It was a draining twenty minutes for me and a frustrating one for the media guys. They eventually dispersed without having been able to sink their teeth into anything new. I supposed that was a small victory for my side, but the depressing fact was, they'd be back.

Scovil caught up with me as I was unlocking my car door. I said, "Jerry, I don't have anything else to give you right now."

"No, I just wanted to thank you, Jock. For the lead about the glossies from that theater company. They're perfect. Just as you predicted, they say, A woman so fresh faced, so alive, so adorably fuckable, and she's dead; what a waste. We're running three two-column cuts."

Boy, did I feel good about being off the *Ledger*. I said, "Glad I could help. So, Jerry, if you run across anything that might do my side some good . . ."

"I gave you a tip, didn't I? The drug guy, Pacheco. There's a chance he could turn this whole story upside down. You didn't look him up?"

"Not yet. Did you?"

"It took me a while this morning but I found him."

"And . . . ?"

"The bastard hung up on me."

And Scovil called himself a reporter.

11

Until a generation ago, this west Bronx neighborhood a block or two off Mount Eden Avenue had been a bastion of middle-class values. The modest six-story apartment houses had been graced by dignity. That was then. The buildings were now well beyond the danger of being spoiled by graffiti; graffiti would have lifted some of them to relative respectability. Bricks were chipped or missing from building faces. Cornices were crumbling. Broken bottles, bent cans, and loose garbage clung to doorways like moss to the base of trees. At an abandoned synagogue, cinder blocks sealed off the windows and doors, turning the house of God into a military bunker. The only note of hope was an occasional geranium in a coffee can stuck defiantly on a sill or fire escape.

The city had given up, at least temporarily, on these war-torn streets. I had to drive warily to avoid potholes that could have been caused by shrapnel. A few years more of neglect, and nature would start to reclaim this turf. I could think of worse scenarios.

There was plenty of curbside parking. I pulled into a spot only a few yards from the address Hap Nordstrom had given me for Felix Pacheco. I had broken in on Hap during what sounded like a tactical meeting with his homicide task force, to lean on him for the information. Contacts beat legwork two to one.

As I climbed out of the car, a long, skinny kid, at most fifteen, loped over from where he had been sitting on a stoop, smoking. His body language reminded me of an elk whose territory is being challenged. He was trailed by a lesser kid, another smoker. By the time I locked the car door they were close enough for me to note that what they were smoking was cigarettes. I could deal with kids like these, they were practically mainstream.

But I had no doubt they were about to hit me up for a loan. The quickest way to adjust their attitude was to pick the subject for discussion. I said, "Hey, guys, your fathers know you didn't go to school today?"

The taller kid was spokesman for the pair. "He's got no father, mine's at work. How about yours?" He didn't wait for an answer. "Anyway, there's a teachers' conference. They let us out early." So much for that subject.

The kid could have been pulling my leg. Or not; his expression told me nothing, except that he wasn't backing off. The other kid was circling the car, peering in the windows. I didn't like that they were both wearing state-of-the-art sneakers. I guessed they hadn't earned the money for them by cutting the neighbors' grass.

I said to the spokesman, "Bet. Five dollars says while I'm gone someone will mess with my car, maybe break a lock."

The kid said, "I don't have no five dollars to bet."

"Yes you do." I took out a bill, slapped it in his palm, and started to walk away. A thought hit me and I turned back. "You didn't ask where I'm going."

"Because I know where you're going. Felix. Where else?"

* * *

The apartment marked PACHECO on the third floor of the building, which smelled equally of tropical spices and urban decay, had a door that looked like it had been put in by the tenant. It didn't resemble the others on the floor: it was a shiny steel unit snugly fitted into a pry-proof frame. A wise purchase. The front door lock downstairs was broken.

I pressed the Pacheco bell. From somewhere deep inside, mellow chimes sounded mealtime on a cruise ship. Not the sound I expected. About half a minute later the peephole opened and I was looking at a glassy blob through a sort of fishbowl.

I made my pitch to the blob: "Felix? Felix, you don't know me, we've never met, but if you can spare me about five minutes of your time—"

The blob had distended and contracted and now the peephole slid shut. There was a finality to the click.

No reporter worth his pay gives up after one lousy turndown. Jerry Scovil was not worth his pay. I was about to hit the chimes more insistently, if chimes can be made to sound insistent, and invoke in a vaguely ominous manner the name of Detective Sergeant Nordstrom, when the rattling of chains and the clicking of locks stopped me.

The door was opening. Even before I saw the man behind it he said, "Wrong, I do know you. You're Jock Caprisi, use to write for the *Ledger*."

Now the door swung wide, the occupant fully revealed as he finished his observation. "Good writer, stinking name. Jock. You think you would read a lady column-writer first name of Tampax?"

He knew me; good. And he was a wiseass; also good. Better that than the sullen, silent dealers I'd run up against in the past. Except for the accent, you would take him for a European type, possibly a German BMW salesman, only shorter. He was about forty, with sculptured hair just starting to go a distinguished gray. He had probably gotten the expensive haircut since getting out of the slammer, after leaving the podiatrist. A head to toe makeover.

He was wearing a white shirt of imported cotton with a long-point collar, a solid blue rep tie, black wing-tip shoes, and blue over-the-calf socks. I knew they were over-the-calf because he wasn't wearing trousers. He beckoned me inside with two fingers.

I had a few seconds to take in the place while he closed his steel door and fastened, chained, turned, or bolted his assorted security devices. I could never have imagined this apartment from the cracked tile hallway. We were in a foyer that opened into the living room. The hardwood floors, old but high quality, had been scraped and refinished. The walls looked recently painted, in a soft ivory. The furniture was new, decent reproductions of English campaign furniture; my host might have been an officer with Her Majesty's Rifles on temporary duty near the Khyber Pass. Everything here could be packed in an hour and loaded on an elephant.

The one jarring note was an ironing board set up in front of the softly playing campaign-type television set. It held an iron and a pair of trousers. Pacheco turned from his lock-up chores to follow my eye. "Have to catch up on my ironing," he said. "I been away a couple of weeks."

I had nothing to gain by playing let's pretend. Pleasantly but firmly I said, "You've been on Rikers Island."

"That's what I said, I been away. If you on Rikers, you away. Can't think of any place more." Unruffled, he was surveying me thoughtfully. "So what do you want to see me about, Jock Caprisi?"

"You don't think I'm here to make a purchase?"

"Nobody come here for that. I don't shit where I eat. Anyway, you're not a user." He had made a decision. "Please come in, be comfortable. You know what we say: 'My house is your house.' " He was sticking determinedly to English.

He led me into the living room, turned off the TV, and settled on the couch, a dapper little man but untrousered, with snug shoes. If he was having foot trouble I would have thought he'd wear slippers around the house. But maybe I had caught him getting ready to go out.

I sat in a campaign chair facing him. He said, "I'm not going to toss you to see if you're wearing a wire. I believe that's not your style."

"You've read my column?"

"Used to."

"I gave it up."

"I know, that's why I don't read it anymore. I read somewhere the reason is you went to work for old Beaufoy. The senator."

"True. That wasn't widely printed. You must follow politics. You going to vote for him?"

"Sure thing. He was good to my country. Panama. He hollered like hell."

"When was that?"

"When the U.S. troops went in. A thousand people died, maybe more, to catch that one little worm. The Pineapple."

"You didn't agree with the action."

"Beaufoy neither. He said it was not worth one U.S. life, not one Panamanian life, to catch the worm. You put the Pineapple out of business, someone else steps up to run it, and all you got is dead people. Plenty of them. Beaufoy was right."

"Aren't you in the same business as the Pineapple?"

"He was international. He spread the poison wholesale. I'm on the retail end. I know my customers. Grown-up people, quality people. They make their own choice. Like with cigarettes."

"Either way, just like the Pineapple, you're going to prison."

"I'm copping to a lesser. I've got a good lawyer, not one of these public defenders has too many cases. I'll go to the mountains for two years, at most thirty months."

"The mountains?"

"A joint in the Catskills where they got high unemployment and prison guard is steady work with a pension. So long as they got people to guard, you know?"

"You do your part for the economy."

"What the hell. I know what it's like to come out of nothing, to have nothing, and to make something of yourself. I have to put away myself for my social security; Uncle Sam won't do it for me. But while I'm upstate, to live costs me nothing. I like Ellenville. You been around there?"

"I haven't had the privilege."

"The air is good, the water is good. I feel bad for my customers is all."

"Why is that?" We could be moving productively.

"I think you must know my territory. My kind of people can't cruise dark street corners for a fix, meet their connection in a parking lot, wait for them in the doorway of a candy store. I make house calls, office calls. I wear suits from Saks Fifth Avenue, I carry a briefcase. Nobody ever questions me."

"What did your customers do while you were on Rikers?"

"Climbed the walls, is what they did."

"Nobody filled in for you, took over your client list?"

"What are you talking about, my friend? You think I run like a paperboy route? What I have is a custom service, a quality business. You got to know your customers, they got to know you. It takes years to build a client list like mine."

That was all he wanted to say on the subject. He said abruptly, "Jock Caprisi, I still don't know why you came here."

"I'm getting to that. And you'll thank me." I'd have to come up with something pretty soon. "But let me finish what I started. You say no one replaced you while you were away. Okay, what about a competitor muscling in? Somebody who heard you're out of action and you've got needy clients. So that person tries to fill their orders as a freelance. How long does your supplier take to—"

★ 134 ★

His hand shot out, palm toward me. "Hey, friend, I got nothing to say about my supplier. We don't discuss that. I'm going away for two years. I don't want the gig reduced because somebody offed me in the chow line."

"Felix, I don't want to know who your supplier is. I couldn't care less. My question is, if someone went into business on his own, a competitor, how long before he got a knife in the gut?"

"Tops? A week. I know where you're at, and it's not with no 'he.' You're talking about the blonde was killed yesterday in Beaufoy's garage. You want to make her a dealer got too big for her pants. I'm sorry, friend, I'd like to help your senator, take the heat off, but no way does this work. Number one, there is no knife in the gut from these people, it's two shots to the back of the neck. That's the way they do. And if you go around keep asking questions, you better watch the back of yours.

"Number two, nobody—I mean nobody I ever heard of — will put a woman in this business. Never happen. These big boys are old-fashion. Real old-fashion. So, bottom line, this blonde in the garage had nothing to do with the drug trade. Unless as a user. Sorry. So what was it you had to tell me I'm going to thank you for?"

"Right, that." I hadn't had time to prepare for that. I reached for anything at hand. "Felix, I figured if you turned out to be a right guy, answered some questions for me—which you did— it'd only be fair to warn you."

"Of what?" He was instantly wary.

I hated having to do this but I couldn't think of anything else. "I've been around the cops the last twenty-four hours. They've got a few theories about who killed the woman. One of them points at you."

"Why me?" The poise vanished. His mouth went slack and his eyes widened. He slid to the edge of the couch and pulled at an over-the-calf sock.

"For one, you were out of jail when the woman was killed."

"Me and two million people in the Bronx."

"Let me finish. The woman was killed with a knife, a weapon of passion, sometimes the weapon of choice for hot-tempered Latinos who believe they've been dishonored." I was getting into it now. "Sure, there's two million people loose in the Bronx. But in that particular part of it, how many Latinos? Were you up that way yesterday morning servicing clients?"

"You think I'm crazy? Right out of jail?" He was frightened, all right. "I phone a few regulars, told them where they could find a friend of mine, get a little help without they make a big stink."

"Okay. But you'd better be clear on where you were yesterday morning. All of it. Because you'll be asked."

He was looking sick. "I was at the foot doctor. And the hair stylist. And then I was home. How do you prove you are home? *Mierda.*"

We had apparently switched to Spanish. I got to my feet and started toward the door, comforting him with *"Vaya con Dios,* Felix. You'll be all right."

I shook his limp hand and waited for him to undo his door locks.

Pacheco didn't strike me as a killer, but I felt no guilt at having rattled his cage. If the strings Nordstrom was following ran out, it was more than possible he would put him on his list of suspects. Maybe he already had. I had done Felix a service by preparing him, I told myself.

From his front stoop I could see that my Honda was no more battle scarred than when I'd left it; the boys had won the bet, thank God.

But they hadn't expected me to return this soon. The bigger boy, the spokesman, was leaning innocently against the curb-side door, but his buddy was at the back of the car with a stub of pencil in one hand and a scrap of paper in the other. When he saw me he shoved both hands in his pockets and slowly drew them out empty.

Ignoring the spokesman, I walked up to the other boy and said, "What were you writing?"

He didn't answer. The spokesman said, "The phone number of some girl he likes. I gave it to him."

I said, "Why don't you let him speak for himself?"

"He's shy," the spokesman said. "He never says much, not even in the classroom."

I was still looking at the other boy. "Let me take a look at that paper." We were standing about a foot apart.

The spokesman said, "Hey, you want that girl's number? She's hot, but a little bit young for you. But you know, she might go for older." He was starting to amble our way.

The other boy stood his ground dumbly, not moving a muscle. I had seen a kid his age indicted for shooting a salesman who bumped him in the subway, but if this one was carrying a gun it was tucked someplace he wasn't going to reach easily. Anyway, he didn't look threatening, just sulky, and I had five inches and fifty pounds on him. The spokesman I figured for a talker.

So I went for it. I wrestled the shy one briefly and shoved my hand in his pocket, and came out with the scrap of paper. It had my license plate number on it.

I said, "Son, you need to work on your handwriting."

The spokesman said, "Yeah, that's right. I always tell him. Don't I, Luis?"

Luis still had nothing to say; he was not only sulky, he was slow. I could guess why I had been able to catch him red-handed. It had taken him the fifteen minutes I'd been with Felix to find a pencil.

I turned to the spokesman. "What were you going to do with this number?"

He looked at me in mock bewilderment. "I just told you. It's to call the girl. Hey, where's our five dollars we won?"

We were getting nowhere, and I was tempted not to give it to him, but what the hell, the car was intact. I handed over five singles, got in the car, and drove off, slaloming around the potholes, my license number deep in my pocket.

12

It was now well after two, more than twenty-five hours since Mort Beaufoy's neighbor spotted Sheri Bannerman's body in the back seat of his Buick. If the police didn't latch onto a likely suspect pretty soon, the trail would start to cool and the investigation would drag on, leaving questions that would thicken the air through primary day.

Already the all-news station on my car radio was broadcasting excerpts of another curbside news conference by Representative Turnbull that dripped with innuendo. The congressman, always the gentleman, deflected questions about senatorial hanky-panky with "That's not for me to say," "I suggest you ask the senator that one," and "You'll have to draw your own conclusions." At least there was no speculation about Senator Beaufoy as murder suspect.

Turnbull's performance turned my stomach. Or was it churning because I had eaten nothing since a petrified bagel at seven this morning? My mother believed I hadn't sat down to a proper meal since I left home, and she was about half right. It never bothered her that my father, on the road a lot and working weird hours, ate even worse than I did. She had decided a special providence watched over his stomach.

I found parking near a coffee shop on Fordham Road where the signs in the window announcing "Today's Specials" were browning and curled at the corners. I took my cellular phone inside. I could do some catching up while I ate.

I figured Paul McClintoch might be back at campaign headquarters from Mort's by now, so I tried there first while I worked on a western omelette and a cup of thin coffee. Paul walked in the office front door as a staffer was telling me he was expected any minute, and he took the call.

He had come directly from Mort's. On balance, he said, he thought the morning had gone well.

"What do you mean, 'on balance'?" I asked. I was trying to keep my voice down, but I couldn't blame the other diners for glaring at me over their sandwiches and newspapers.

"The spots went fine, I'm sure you'll agree, especially the first few. Two of them will be airing on local stations starting tonight. The problem, if there is a problem, is Clara Beaufoy."

"I'd never met her before and I barely said hello, so I couldn't tell much. Did she give you a hard time?"

"She didn't give me any kind of time, which isn't like her. A classy lady; we've always gotten along. I never saw her today, not even to say hello. I was on the kitchen phone when she arrived. She went straight back to the bedroom, and she never came out."

"Did Mort say anything was wrong?"

"Before I left I asked him if she was all right. He acted as though he couldn't imagine what would make me ask. When I pressed, he made a puckish comment about her planets being misaligned—Jupiter in the wrong house, or maybe out of town, he couldn't remember. Professorial humor. He was telling me she had things on her mind and not to make anything of it."

"Did he mention . . . ?" I was afraid to form the sentence.

"Getting their stories straight? He assured me if the media brought up the subject—why he met with the real estate woman about a new apartment when his wife was away—

Clara would back him to the hilt. He was only sorry the surprise element had gone out of his plan to make the apartment an anniversary gift."

Mort was continuing to hang on to that fable. I had to give him an A for stubbornness to go with his D in believability. His average was C-plus. I said, "Paul, is there anything I can do?"

Mildly he said, "Yeah. Make this problem go away. By first thing tomorrow morning."

I put in a call to Hap Nordstrom at his precinct house in the Bronx. If he was free to talk he might have something to tell me by now. I was riding his tail, I knew, but that wasn't necessarily bad. A voice in the detective squad room told me Sergeant Nordstrom was out. In hot pursuit, I prayed.

Over a second cup of what passed for coffee I checked in with the front desk at the Stanley. Andres, the day concierge, had two messages for me. "Paula" had phoned to remind me to call her "with an answer." No phone number. Poppy was maintaining her deniability in case I tried to blow the whistle on her blackmail effort. I took some small pleasure in picturing her sitting by her phone until it grew a fungus.

The second message was from Bryce Bannerman. Would I be free to attend his wife's funeral on Saturday? "Please" hung in the air. I could call him at home for details.

This was Tuesday. The poor bastard was going to have to wait another four days to bury his wife, because the coroner still had her corpse on a marble slab and was picking it over like it was a platter of antipasto.

Bannerman's call surprised me. And then on second thought, it didn't. I was the person he had shared his grief with when he learned of his wife's death. His emotions had been stripped bare in those first wrenching moments; he probably thought of me as a comfort and a pillar of strength, possibly a stand-in for his far-off family.

I polished off the omelette and called him. He picked up on

the second ring with a morose, "Yes, please?"

He perked up when I identified myself. And when I said of course I would come to Sheri's funeral he flooded me with gratitude. He rattled off the address of the church in Bronxville where the service would be held on Saturday, and the time.

And then he explained apologetically that the police were with him right now, asking more questions, and his partner, Hilton Bailes, had just walked in, so would I mind, please, if he got off the phone now? He hoped I would understand. This man was too sensitive to live.

I said, "Hold on a second, Bryce. Is Sergeant Nordstrom there?"

"Yes, he's been here about ten minutes."

"Could you put him on, please? Tell him I won't keep him long."

There was an exchange of voices off the mouthpiece and Bannerman came back on. "Hilly Bailes says to be sure to say hello. I understand you two had a nice chat down at the shop yesterday. Hilly's been a tower of strength ever since . . ." He suddenly became abject. "I'm sorry, Jock, Sergeant Nordstrom says he can't take the time to talk to you right now. I guess he's got his hands full. You know, supervising the hunt for Sheri's killer."

I hoped so. I couldn't blamed him for ducking me; I had become a swift pain in the ass. Or was he just plain worn out from his overtime duty at home trying to make an heir? Down the road I saw a tiny, sad-faced Nordstrom. Either way, he had given me the brush. I told Bannerman to remember me to Bailes and to keep his chin up; I'd see him Saturday.

What could Hap be after at Bannerman's? Was there new evidence implicating him? Or, more likely, was Hap pressing the grieving widower to produce an enemy of Sheri's where there was no enemy—basically treading water because he had no leads to follow? Busywork.

He was back where I had started my pursuit of the killer: if there is no rape or robbery, *cherchez* the victim's husband. There was no need for both of us to tread water. Let Hap handle the sweet, blindly adoring husband.

Could Hap have forgotten that Bannerman had an alibi? He had been with the pool contractor—Puller?—at the time his wife was killed. Had been with him, in fact, all day. It was a perfect alibi.

Perfect, yes, but believable? I was trying to put myself in Hap Nordstrom's head; something may have gotten his wind up. There was a way to check out Bannerman's alibi. I asked the waitress for the loan of her Bronx phone book.

I found Pools by Puller in Riverdale. A secretary picked up. She was sorry but Mr. Puller was out on a job site. When I asked her for the address she went instantly on the defensive. "May I ask what this is in regards to?"

"Of course. I promised Puller a binder before the banks close today. I'd like to put the check in his hands."

She spelled out the address and volunteered driving directions. It was a street in Yonkers, not that far over the New York City line.

Puller had gotten himself a plum of a contract. The site was at a motel still under construction; this pool was going to make the Bannermans' look like a sitz bath. I drove by slowly and took in the big picture. The work was being done well back on the property, and it was still in the early, first-you-dig-a-hole, phase. Three or four laborers were dragging around equipment back there, but the jumbo tractor shovel that would do the digging stood idle up front, not far from the sidewalk, its treads caked with mud and its big shovel jaw raised high.

I knew Puller was around somewhere—the Pools by Puller pickup that I had seen at Bannerman's house was parked behind the shovel—but I didn't see him. And he would have been easy to spot; I remembered a formidably big man.

I drove around the corner and parked. I needed time to think without attracting stares from the crew.

I had assumed Puller would be working at a private residence and that I'd try to approach him through its owners. That plan wouldn't work here. So far as I could see, there was no construction crew in the motel. At the moment, the only action was at the pool site.

I gave myself five minutes, but I couldn't come up with anything clever. I would have to improvise. In the past, the artless approach had sometimes worked best when I was trying to shake loose a piece of information. I locked the car and strolled back around the corner.

Still no Puller. I walked onto the property and stood in the shade of the raised shovel arm, surveying the pool area fifty yards away. Right now it wasn't much more than wooden stakes, rubble, and promise.

A kind of mournful whine caught my ear, metal rubbing against metal. I'm not sure what made me look up—to see that jut-jawed shovel straight overhead in free fall.

I had no consciousness of moving out of harm's way, but the next thing I was aware of was lying nose down on the turf with a mouth full of spiky weeds and the earth heaving under me. The steel shovel blade had hit the ground flat out less than a foot from where I had either rolled, dived, or sprung. A near miss, but a miss.

The earth stopped trembling and I started breathing. Whoever had secured that shovel arm should have been hung by his thumbs. I got to one knee and began to brush grass and earth from my hair and sleeves. Again I heard that faint whine. And now the shovel lifted six inches off the ground, a hulking beast on the prowl.

This time I guessed what could be coming. Still on my knees I scrambled forward from the steel teeth as the jaw made a roundhouse turn. I could feel something like its hot breath. If I hadn't moved beyond the perimeter of its swing the shovel would have batted me out to the sidewalk.

Until that swing I had given the machine the benefit of the doubt. But the question was now resolved: son of a bitch, this was no accident.

And the machine hadn't finished with me. As I got to my feet the far tread lurched and churned, wheeling the vehicle in my direction. Now the near tread kicked over and began laying a track that would roll directly into me. But this was no longer a contest. I could maneuver quicker than that lumbering monster. I scrambled easily to the side.

The operator didn't stop fast enough; the shovel was churning past me. When the cab came abreast I reached up and wrapped my arms around a dangling leg and pulled, dropping back on my full weight. The vehicle kept moving but I succeeded in keeping the operator from going with it. I had a firm hold on his jeans-clad leg, and the rest of him came loose and crashed down on my left arm as I fell.

It was good I didn't have to take his body across mine. He was Puller, and he had sixty pounds on me.

He also had an extra few inches and if this developed into an exchange of blows he would beat the shit out of me. The two of us horizontal was the closest to a level playing field I would get; to come out of this whole I had to disable him before he got his wind back from that hard fall and climbed to his feet. I yanked free, leaned over him, and put my shoulder behind two punches that made my knuckles ache—one to his jaw and one under his eye.

He was stunned, but it wasn't going to last. I jumped up and stood over him and placed a foot on his Adam's apple. If I pressed I'd kill him. He tried to snatch at my ankle but he was still partially winded from the fall. After a few seconds he

★ 145 ★

turned deep scarlet and let out a strained gargling sound. His arms dropped like logs to his sides.

I removed my foot and watched him feebly gasping for air. I wasn't sure what my next move ought to be. The engine was sounding louder, and I turned to see the big machine grinding its way toward us. Puller had put it in a tight circle when he was chasing me and it was bearing down heavily from my right side.

The near tread was going to roll right over Puller, who was sucking air, still too weak to move. He looked at the oncoming machine, then at me, plaintively. I grabbed his legs and dragged him out of the path of the tread.

By now a couple of the workers who had seen what was going on were running toward us. One jumped up on the runaway vehicle and the other came toward me waving a length of two-by-four.

Puller managed to gasp, "What the fuck do you think you're doing? Get the hell back to work."

If we hadn't become exactly chummy, at least we weren't punching each other out. We were joined in something of a bond now; I had, after all, kept his face from being stretched like a penny in an arcade machine.

We were sitting in Puller's pickup, explaining where each of us was coming from. I explained that I react violently when someone tries to kill me with a giant shovel. Puller said he was merely trying to scare me. The rest of his explanation was more complicated.

He claimed that some phony mob-controlled union had been pressuring him to sign a contract for his workforce. "Fucking extortionists," he called them. He had so far rejected their demands in several meetings and late-night phone calls that he described as ugly, but the pressure had only increased. He was bracing himself against some sort of strong-arm tactic and the waiting had made him jumpy. But again, he hadn't meant to harm me, only to get rid of me. Sure.

"You thought I was a union rep?"

" 'Amalgamated Natation Workers.' You ever hear such garbage? I thought you were casing the situation for some kind of sabotage. You drove by slowly, looking us over, and I recognized you from in front of Bryce Bannerman's house, that poor bastard. A shame about his wife, huh?"

"Yes, it is. So that's why you kept staring at me when we passed on Bannerman's front walk yesterday? You took me for an advance man for these muscle guys?"

"Now I realize you must be the detective who came to tell him his wife had been killed. Don't you cops check with each other? Some sergeant already caught me at my office this morning with a shitload of questions."

"Sergeant Nordstrom?"

"That's the one," he said irritably. "He your boss? I already answered his questions, so you're just wasting your time. And mine."

Should I set him straight? Hell, no. I never claimed to be a cop, and if he thought I was, that was his problem. He owed me for trying to put my lights out.

I said, "Nordstrom's NYPD. We're in Westchester now, he can't talk to you here. I can." All of this, amazingly, was true.

"So that's it," he said reasonably. "I see."

"Suppose you answer my questions. They could include a few new ones. And we'll forget about that attempted vehicular homicide just now. I'd rather not get into a lot of paperwork."

"I told you that was a misunderstanding."

"True. But here's a tip, Mac. It's illegal to drop a one-ton shovel on even a crooked union rep."

"My jaw hurts like hell," was his answer.

"So does my hand."

"You got questions, ask your damn questions. But keep it

short, will you? Those fuckers waiting for me back there get nineteen dollars an hour *without* some shyster union."

"Okay, short. You went to Bannerman's yesterday to discuss plans for finishing his pool?"

"We went over the specs, right. I told all that to Sergeant whoever the hell."

"What time did you get there?"

"The time? Who the hell remembers. I wasn't paying any attention to the time."

"No? I figure a man who pays his help nineteen dollars an hour always knows what time it is."

"Yesterday these palookas knew what they had to do," he said sulkily. "Today they don't know which end is up."

I hung in. "Okay, let's try it another way. Was it morning?"

He stared at me, rubbing his jaw where I'd hit him; he didn't seem to know what I was getting at. He said nothing.

I tried again. "I define morning as the period between breakfast and lunch."

"Jesus." Grudgingly, "Yeah, I went over sometime in the morning."

"Good, we're making progress. Not lightning progress, but, hey, it's your meter running. I ran into you when you were leaving Bannerman's. That was after four."

"So?"

"Did Bannerman leave the house during that period?"

Now Puller was running his fingernails along his jeans. A milder version of chalk on a blackboard. He said, "Twice, I think."

"Yes . . . ?"

"Jesus. Once to turn on the lawn sprinklers, once to turn them off."

"Otherwise you two were together all those hours? Deciding whether to trim the diving board in sunset pink plastic or Mediterranean blue?"

"There were a shitload of details. You'd be surprised how

many. Bannerman is involved professionally in interior design. He has strong ideas. So do I. We argued."

"For five or six hours? The Lincoln-Douglas debates didn't run that long."

"I wasn't paying—"

"Right, I'm sorry. You weren't paying attention to the time."

"We took a break for lunch."

"You went out?"

"We were in the kitchen with the plans. Bannerman made sandwiches. You want to know what was in them? Did I ask for mayo? Jesus."

The defensive edge had drained out of his voice. "You have to understand, the points we were discussing involve options over and above the contract price. There was a tug-of-war over money."

"So Bannerman was never really out of your sight."

"He went to the can. I went to the can. Oh, yeah, he cut out a few times to make business calls. To his partner, he said."

"Cut out to where?"

"He's got a home office somewhere in the back of the house."

"What's the longest he was gone? Back there in his home office."

"Christ, you're worse than Sergeant Whoever. I don't know. Ten minutes. Twenty. I wouldn't even guess—"

"Right. Not your strong point, time."

I had consumed about five dollars' worth of his at his workers' rates. I thanked him for it and he scrambled out of the truck without so much as a goodbye, rubbing his bruised face and growling that he had to "get these mothers moving their asses."

I watched him make a beeline for his crew at the work site, a big man with exaggerated shoulders and narrow hips, a comic-strip stud. He had never once looked me in the eye.

There was obviously something here I hadn't been able to get hold of. What I needed was a serious one-on-one with Bryce Bannerman. But there was no way he'd sit still for that before he buried his wife on Saturday. And by Saturday my candidate could be in the toilet.

13

I waited till I drove out of the neighborhood and then I checked in by phone one last time with the senator. If he wanted to see me it would be better to find that out before I got on the parkway for the city. I had run up a lot of mileage on Mort's behalf, but it had gone mostly in spinning my wheels. I would get back to what I had been hired for—to advise him on his image.

He was delighted to hear my voice. "I don't know what magic you worked when you talked to the media this morning, dear boy, but they seem well satisfied. I haven't been bothered since. Not a call. I am beginning to feel unloved."

"Don't drop your guard," I said. "The situation remains highly fluid. As soon as the pack smells fresh blood they'll attack again. By the way, did you ever hear from the Dalmatians who were picketing out front?"

"No, thank God. Because I can't think of a single comforting remark I might have made to them. In any case, did they represent Free Dalmatia or Herb Turnbull?"

"Who knows?" At the moment there were no flies on Mort Beaufoy. "Mort, I'm in the area. Is there anything I can do for you?"

"Today? I can't see what. Take the evening off. With my blessing. Buy your lady a romantic dinner. You do, I trust, have a passionate involvement?"

"At the moment, Senator, only with your cause."

"That's good too." He was in an up mood. Or was he forcing one? "We're not doing the local anchors tonight. McClintoch arranged for me to take call-ins from radio stations upstate. I'll be sticking with the themes we laid out. And I expect to scintillate," he added dryly.

"Is there any way I can coax you into taking a few small jabs at your opponent?"

"No, let him poke his own eye out." He paused, and lowered his voice. The ebullience was gone. "Come to think of it, you can advise me on one small matter."

"Shoot."

"The murdered woman. Mrs. Bannerman. I feel simply wretched. If the poor woman hadn't been visiting me—"

I cut him off. "Not your fault, Mort. Someone was out to kill her. He'd have found her somewhere."

"I don't believe anyone was out to kill her. She had the misfortune of being in my garage when a mugger appeared."

I had no answer to that.

"Her funeral is on Saturday. I understand it might be a bit awkward, but do you think it would be entirely inappropriate for me to attend?"

"With Mrs. Beaufoy?"

"Clara has heavy responsibilities in Silver Spring. She'll be back there by then. She'll be here only a day or two more to answer whatever questions might arise."

It was Looney Tunes time again. I said, "The funeral is an absolute negative, Mort. That photo op would make even the *Times*. I understand your concern for the dead woman, but it has to remain at arm's length. Let the flowers speak for you."

That was a near miss. I loved my candidate, but he had to be watched every minute. There were no givens with Mort Beaufoy.

Despite Mort's blessing, five o'clock was too early to knock off work a week before the primary. I wasn't doing enough for the old man, not enough that counted. Was there some mopping up I could do around here before I went back to town? I ran through my mental checklist. Had I crossed all my *t*'s and dotted every *i*?

A single uncrossed *t* floated into my consciousness. It was more in the area of sleuth than media consultant, but in the end they served the same urgent purpose.

On my mind was Clifton Oliver. It still bothered me that this dandy, with his carefully tended mustache, his hundred-dollar necktie, and his perfectly cut British trousers and vest—a man who was at least as much style as substance—had left his office yesterday without his suit jacket. If it had been mine, I might simply have forgotten it; I had been chased down the street often enough by waiters or barbers holding my jacket aloft, sometimes along with my necktie.

Clifton Oliver didn't make that kind of mistake. What he wore or didn't wear was a matter of deliberate choice for that moment. He must have come to the office yesterday morning dressed in the full suit. Logic suggested there was a chance he came in today wearing the trousers of that suit, intending to complete the outfit at the office and go home in it. If so—or even, if not—did I have a shot at finding out why he chose to leave the jacket there yesterday?

I was maybe ten minutes from Clifton Oliver Realty's spiffily restored Victorian house. Whoever of the staff was on hand would be leaving for home, or for appointments with clients coming from work. Yesterday Oliver was the last to go.

* * *

It looked as if the others were already gone. When I entered the building the desks in the big front office were deserted. The only occupants of the room were a couple in their thirties, who sat on chairs against the wall, worriedly studying a packet of photographs of houses for sale. They didn't look up when I came in.

I could hear Oliver's voice, though not his words, coming from his office. I drifted back that way and took up a position just outside his open doorway. The room was crowded. I guessed that some of these people were the same salespeople I had seen here yesterday. They were facing Oliver, who was standing behind his desk, and all I got of them was their backs.

I did recognize Jared Phillips by the ponytail lying on his neck. He had his arms around two women—comfortingly, I supposed, since I saw tissues raised to dab at eyes. One woman was older and one was a youngish redhead, almost surely the attractive redhead of yesterday. The others were all women, at least one or two more than I remembered from yesterday. This must have been the entire staff, gathered for an announcement by the boss. He was in the middle of it as I tuned in.

". . . but none of you will miss her more than I, believe that or not. She was a superb saleswoman, and I trust not one of you will take offense when I say nobody worked harder or more conscientiously for this office than Sheri."

There were sober murmurs of agreement as Oliver continued. "But put all of that aside. When we dig down to the bedrock of life, how important is hard work, in and of itself? What I will remember Sheri for, what I suspect all of you will cherish her for, is this: she was the soul of this office, its shining light. There was never a day, so far as I can remember, when she . . ."

I could tell there would be another yard and a half of this, and I tuned out in favor of an inventory of Cliff Oliver's wardrobe. At first I couldn't see his trousers past the staff heads. I saw shirtsleeves, gold cufflinked again, and a necktie that had cost possibly as much as my shoes. And the mustache that would have taken a ribbon at a dog show.

As if at my command, two heads parted and the trousers revealed themselves. I had missed the boat. Oliver wasn't wearing the pants he had on yesterday; rather, a dark blue pair.

And then I spotted a sculpted wooden hanger hooked on a file cabinet; it held a flannel jacket in a soft gray. I looked for a second hanger, one that would be holding the tweed jacket he hadn't worn home yesterday. There wasn't one. Yesterday, I now remembered, there were no hangers here at all. Where was the tweed jacket? And why? And could I be obsessed about this because I had nothing better to do?

When I tuned Oliver back in he was saying, ". . . so I'll match the total of whatever amount the staff decides to contribute. Diane, will you inform the two who aren't here today?" So this wasn't the entire sales staff.

Diane was the redhead. "I'll try to reach them both right away," she said through a catch in her voice.

Oliver said, "Oliver Realty was Sheri's second home. Our flowers should reflect that. They should make a real statement at her funeral. Are we agreed?" The staff murmured their agreement, and he said, "Thank you. That about does it. And God bless you all."

The meeting was breaking up. As the women filed from the office, Jared Phillips called out over their mournful chatter, "What about the police, Cliff? Are they getting anyplace with catching Sheri's attacker?"

"I heard from the officer in charge last night. He said he'd let me know as soon as they know something. Soon, he expected." I thought, Don't stand on one foot, Cliff.

When Oliver's office cleared and I acknowledged a nod of recognition from Phillips as he went by, I stuck my head in.

"Cliff, can you spare me a couple of minutes?"

"Caprisi." He was understandably surprised to see me. And not overjoyed. But he managed a hearty, "Yes, of course. Give me a few minutes to take care of the Mastersons. They have an appointment."

The Mastersons were the couple inspecting the photographs. Oliver beckoned them into his office with a salesman's smile, and I took the seat at Sheri's desk. Bryce Bannerman, the unknowing widower to be, still smiled out at me from his silver frame. I supposed they were waiting, out of respect, till after the funeral to clear Sheri's desk.

Phillips swiveled in his chair to face me, his ponytail doing a slow pendulum move. He said, "You can't be too careful about school districts."

"Excuse me?"

"I'm sorry. Aren't you looking to buy?"

"Oh, right. There are no children. Yet." I had a flash image: me leading a trembling tot by his or her moist hand to the first day of school. It gave me a warm, not unpleasant tingle in the pit of my stomach.

"You don't ever want to buy," Phillips was advising me mechanically, "without projecting the neighborhood at least a dozen years down the road. Schools, taxes, assessments, quality of community life."

"I suppose you're right. Thanks, I hadn't thought of that. Damn shame about Sheri Bannerman."

He blinked and ducked his head. "Yes, we did all love her."

"You have any idea who might have wanted to kill her?"

"Nobody who knew her. It had to be a mugging, pure and simple. If you don't mind, I'm still too upset to talk about Sheri. I can't believe she's gone."

"I'm sorry." That seemed to be that; Phillips was shoving things into a briefcase. I said, "Do you guys have a john I can use?"

He directed me to the staff bathroom, upstairs, and I left to find it. This was a free shot for me to nose around. With any luck the absent jacket was somewhere on the premises.

The narrow stairs sagged underfoot. The upstairs hallway was shabby and smelled of mildew. The wallpaper—old, but not old enough to be quaint; my parents' house had a similar paper—was both fading and peeling. Clearly this was crew quarters, and unlike the impeccably restored main floor not a dime had been spent up here.

Phillips had said the first door on the left was the bathroom. I inspected that room first, just in case. The walls were covered in tile the color of badly stained teeth. The room was clean but depressing. Two huge mounds of paper towels at the sink made me wonder whether real estate salespeople, like restaurant workers, were required to wash their hands before leaving the rest room. I certainly hoped so, considering all the handshaking they did. I closed the door as I left.

There were three other doors off the hallway, and I knew I could take the time to peer into those rooms without having to look back over my shoulder. Anyone coming up those groaning stairs would signal his arrival.

The first room was smallish, probably once a child's bedroom. The floor was piled haphazardly with rolls of floor plans, and the walls were lined with metal file cabinets—twenty-something years of Oliver Realty done-deals. A quick glance was all it took: there was no jacket here.

The second room was slightly larger, and just about bare, nothing in it but a single file cabinet. This was probably for overflow from room number one; it would take a few more years, even if business picked up, before it started looking cluttered.

Room number three, at the back of the house, was large and gabled. More promising. It was serving as a utility space, really as a surrogate attic. It looked as though everything Cliff Oliver couldn't think what to do with for the past twenty years had been shoved in here. I went in and closed the door behind me.

A swaybacked office sofa had been retired to this room to expire in dignity. Movers' boxes were piled to overflowing with discarded office lamps, worn seat cushions, and assorted junk. Old chairs were nested, whether or not they fit into each other. A clunky wooden desk, scarred and chipped, was half hidden behind the boxes. Framed pictures of sold-out real estate developments leaned against whatever would take them.

My eye went to the window, double-hung and half open. A wooden chair stood in front of it, strongly backlit by a low sun; I could guess the reason for the chair's bulky silhouette. I moved into the room and to one side, closing the door behind me. I had guessed right: a jacket was draped over the back of the chair.

As I drew closer I saw that it was *the* jacket, Cliff Oliver's British tweed jacket. I made my way to it through the junk. I didn't know exactly what to expect—stains? rips?—but it seemed to be okay, an expensive jacket but an innocent one. I ran my hands down the lapels, felt in each of the pockets. Nothing.

And then it struck me. Why would the jacket be hung in front of an open window except to *dry*? I felt down the back and shoulders. Gorgeous material. I ran my spread palms along the front and then up the sleeves. Yes, the right elbow was slightly damp. Oliver had washed something out of it yesterday and left it here overnight. He must have washed like hell to leave it still damp a day later.

Could he scrub tweed thoroughly enough to remove all traces of whatever—paint, lipstick, blood? A crime lab could tell. But by the time I reached Hap Nordstrom and he obtained a search warrant by fooling some judge into believing he had a legal reason to ask for one, the jacket would be long gone.

One thing was certain: I was not going to walk Oliver's jacket past his entire staff and out the front door. Was there another option? I leaned out the window and looked down. A service alley ran parallel to the rear of the house and past other back yards to a side street. Two covered trash bins sat flush against Cliff Oliver's shingled rear wall.

I took the jacket from the back of the chair and held it out the window. Could a well-made English garment survive a two-story fall undamaged? Testing . . .

It landed with a muffled thud across one of the trash cans and slid halfway down one side, confirming what I already knew—good English cloth drapes beautifully. I pulled my head inside the window and froze. A click across the room had announced that the door was opening.

Luckily, I was on the door's blind side. As it swung wide I ducked behind the sofa and glided silently along it in a deep crouch to what looked like a secure hiding place under the desk.

Had somebody been sent to look for me? Not likely; I hadn't been upstairs five minutes. I wondered whether it would have been better to stay near the window, look casual, and say I had come back here to enjoy the air and take in the view, such as it was. Not if this was Cliff Oliver come upstairs to fetch his jacket.

It wasn't Oliver; I heard the door close, and the staccato click of heels on hardwood floor told me whoever was in the room with me was a woman. She was walking briskly toward the window. I angled myself to get a shot between two packing boxes.

Perfectly framed in that narrow area was the redhead, Diane. She had her hands on the chair that had held the jacket. I felt a rising alarm that wiped out the pain my cramped quarters were inflicting on my legs.

But Diane didn't seem to notice that the jacket was missing; she wasn't looking for a jacket, only the chair. She turned it toward her and placed on the seat what looked like a makeup travel-case. She snapped that open, and arched her back and with a couple of deft gestures reached behind her, zipped down her gray cotton dress, and stepped out of it. Chrysalis to butterfly, she was now clad in a one-piece lilac undergarment trimmed in lace. Nice figure.

Next she pulled what looked like a black silk scarf from the makeup case and dropped it over her head. It turned into a skimpy sleeveless dress that made the most of her good shoulders and long, slim arms. She took a moment to fold the gray dress carefully and place it in the case.

Someone must have told her the bathroom was in use; that's why she had changed in here. She snapped the case shut and disappeared with it from my window of opportunity, her heels clicking sharply again as she walked to the door and left the room. I scrambled out from under that desk and unbent my cramped back and legs.

It was my good fortune that Oliver was still huddled with the Mastersons when I got downstairs; I wouldn't have to make a feeble excuse to him for having dropped by. I told Phillips I would catch Cliff in a day or two, I had to leave for another appointment. Before he could launch the sales pitch I read in his eyes I beat a hasty retreat.

The desk closest to the front door was Diane's. As I went by she was layering on lipstick with the kind of brush someone else might use to paint the back fence. She relaxed her mouth into a warm good-night smile and winked a dewy eyelash.

"Have a good evening," I said. You and some extremely fortunate man.

I walked at a fair clip to the near corner of the block and made a right and then another, to enter the alley that ran behind what turned out to be four other buildings before it passed

Oliver's. Oliver's trash cans were in clear sight—but not his jacket. I assumed it had slid off the cans and was lying on the ground behind them.

I hurried to the cans and made a quick search. No jacket. No damn jacket anywhere in sight and no place for one to hide. I couldn't believe this. That jacket was too heavy to have blown away, and anyway there was no wind, not so much as a mild breeze.

Had some gut alarm, some psychic signal, caused Oliver to dump the Mastersons and scurry around to the back of his building to retrieve his missing jacket? Highly unlikely.

And then I saw it—anyway, *a* jacket. It hadn't blown away, but it had almost certainly *walked* away. Or shuffled away. Emerging from the shadows at the far end of the alley, a bent figure wearing baggy pants and a jacket too big for him glanced back at me over his shoulder, wheeled to his right, and galloped toward the street. I didn't make the track team at Penn and I hadn't run in years, but I was confident I could catch a frail elderly man who very possibly had not eaten today. I loped after him.

The street had pedestrians, traffic, shops. If the old guy had continued to run he would have drawn attention to himself, so he had slowed to a brisk, stiff-legged walk with a little bob in it—Walter Brennan in any one of a dozen loveable geezer roles on an all-movie cable channel. This frail gent would make better use of the jacket than Cliff Oliver, but there was a U.S. Senate race at stake. I closed on him relentlessly.

We each had to dodge traffic at the first intersection, and a twins' baby carriage on the next block. But I had narrowed the gap. I caught up with him just before the second intersection, at the entrance to a florist's, and spun him around by a bony shoulder.

He was weatherworn, all right, and his nose was a battleground, but he projected a seedy dignity and his feral eyes blazed righteously through crimson rims. We were attracting a few stares, so I eased him into the space between the two deep windows of the shop.

I said, "Excuse me, friend. That's my jacket."

He looked me over, calmer now. "No way, sonny. You're no forty-four portly."

"That makes two of us."

"Here's the difference, pal. I found it." His voice was gravel with a little sand mixed in. "It's my jacket. That's the law, you can look it up. Or do we call a cop?"

"There's no need for that," I said quickly. "How much would a jacket set you back at the Salvation Army?" I looked at his trousers. "A complete suit. One that fits."

"In material like this? Good British tweed? Probably made in London by a Jermyn Street tailor?" He was a better judge of clothing than I was. He held the jacket open to look at the label, and confirmed, "Yep, made in London."

What was I getting into? "For the sake of argument," I said grudgingly, "without making any kind of commitment, what are we talking about here?"

He was surveying me again, calculating what the traffic would bear. He scratched his dirty beard and pursed his cracked lips. My heart went out to him; a dozen layers under that scruff he had been somebody.

Finally he said, "Ten bucks . . . ?"

I gave him twenty. He snatched it, slid out of the jacket, and took off down the street; I hoped he would go for clothes before he went for booze.

Only when I picked the jacket off the ground did I see the thin woman looking at me from just inside the shop. She held a vase in one hand and a clutch of mums in the other. She said, grimly disapproving, "Did you take that jacket from that old man? What in the world did you have in mind?"

I recognized her then; Beaufoy's neighbor, who discovered Sheri's body. I was reminded of when I was a kid and did something I didn't want my mother to hear about; some one of her friends was always on hand to witness my perfidy.

I said, "It's all right, Ms. Kleiman. Nothing to be concerned about." She was expecting more. "It would take a lot of explaining."

"It would have to," she said, and spun on her heels. "My God, what you see out here."

I think I preferred her hysterical.

14

Octavio handed me three messages when I walked into the Stanley lobby at a little past six-thirty. I put them in my pocket and said, "Octavio, have we ever talked about unannounced visitors?"

"You don't want them. You told me that last year when I started, you don't have to tell me again. Anyway, it's the house rule. Is that jacket for the cleaner's?"

"No, it's not." Oliver's jacket was folded over my arm.

"Because if you're not satisfied with the cleaner we've been using, I can—"

"The cleaner's fine. About unannounced visitors. I had one last night."

"I'm sorry, I didn't know. Sometimes the lobby is crowded, sometimes someone covers while I'm busy. I'm sorry we're not perfect here at the Stanley, Mr. Caprisi. We do our best."

"Okay, okay. It's just a reminder." I could see that Octavio was prepared to debate the subject, but I didn't want to miss the top of the network news shows and I left him.

Waiting for the elevator I shuffled through the messages. "Paula" had called again and would be in touch. I would have to instruct the switchboard that I was out to "Paula." Sergeant

Nordstrom asked me to call; that sounded promising. And "Mr. McClintoch called: He's at the office."

It had been another troubling day, and I would have liked to feel, at least this once when I opened my door, that it was good to be home. But this was the Stanley, my suite was still my suite, and today felt no better than usual.

I turned on the TV. While it warmed up I called Lupe at the switchboard and gave her my instructions about calls from "Paula." Then I surfed the three network channels.

The New York senatorial primary campaign, "of increasing national interest now that it appears to be developing into a horse race," was the third story on NBC. No progress had been reported by the police in the murder of the dead woman with whom Senator Beaufoy had met shortly before her body was discovered in his car.

Beaufoy's media representative, John Caprisi, was shown in a pair of sound bites filmed this morning outside Beaufoy's New York residence. They weren't bad except for Caprisi's looking as though he needed a shave. "Needed a shave" often translates to the viewing public as sinister; I would have to watch that. The NBC reporter concluded that the dead woman was so far no more than a small black cloud on Beaufoy's horizon, but that "political observers" warned it was a cloud that could grow to darken his sky.

I caught a shorter piece on ABC five minutes later. No sound bites from the media rep this time, but there was one from Detective Sergeant Alfred Nordstrom, who admitted that the police were pursuing several leads, "one of which might prove promising." Or not. There went another big fat nothing.

An ABC camera had caught Representative Herbert Turnbull leaving a fund-raising luncheon at the Sheraton. The snake looked even more spineless than usual. He made a show of trying to duck the reporter's query about the Bannerman murder, but he managed to be looking directly into the camera when he said, "That is a matter you had best take up with the senator—should he at some point in time be able to get out of his sickbed."

So much for the news. Whoever picked up my call at Nordstrom's squad room said the sergeant would have to get back to me. I played it safe and identified myself only as someone "returning his call to the Hotel Stanley."

I caught McClintoch at campaign headquarters with his mouth full of ham and cheese sandwich; the poor bastard probably couldn't remember his last hot meal. He had called to remind me to meet him again at Beaufoy's tomorrow morning so the three of us could go over the draft of the major speech the senator was to give at a monster rally upstate on Sunday. The draft was a staff team effort; my job would be to give it style and bite. I was hoping Beaufoy would loosen my muzzle for this one. Turnbull's sickbed reference had ticked me off again.

I was barely off with McClintoch when the phone rang again. It was Nordstrom calling back. He sounded in a hurry. "I promised to keep you informed. I thought you'd want to know. I have an update on your lead—the call to Sheri's phone. Hal Vector is still out of town."

Who the hell was Hal Vector? Right, the "Honeybuns" caller. I said, "Didn't you tell me his wife said he'd be back today?"

"They talked this morning and it turns out he's had to stay in Pittsburgh another day."

"Because he heard the police are asking questions?"

"She says it's business. Jock, I'm on top of it. I'll get to him eventually."

Sure, what's the hurry? "So what else is happening?" I said.

"Don't press me. There are good people on this homicide. Believe me, we're following every lead, no matter how remote or improbable. You think we're moving too slowly, but this is a weird case. It doesn't fall into a recognizable pattern." And then, as though it wasn't a change of subject, he said, "Jock, did you get me the name of the doctor who put the senator in the hospital?"

"You'll have it tomorrow. Are you still on that?"

"You weren't listening. 'We're following every lead, no matter how remote or improbable.' And stop worrying. You know we'll break this case."

But when? I could sense he was pulling away, and I let him go. The lead detective on this murder case was shutting down for the day because his wife's thermometer was calling.

I had wanted to tell Hap about Oliver's jacket, but what was the use? Whether I grabbed the jacket or Hap did, it was inadmissable evidence in every court in the land. Before I did anything else about the jacket I would have to find out what Oliver had removed from that damp elbow. If it turned out to be egg yolk or grape jelly I could put the jacket out of my mind, except for getting it back to Oliver.

I called a lab I had used once at the paper to challenge the police on the identity of a car in a hit-and-run accident. (I had the wrong drunk, but so did the cops; the guilty driver eventually turned himself in.) The lab had closed for the day. I hung the jacket in a closet. There was nothing more I could do for Mort Beaufoy until tomorrow.

This was Tuesday. Tuesdays were usually Barney Lupescu's turn to cook for the ladder company in the ancient firehouse two blocks south. Barney was a much-decorated smoke eater; equally important, he was the best home-style cook in Manhattan. If he was making his famous stuffed cabbage, I wanted in. My few bucks in the pool would buy me a superb dinner with friends. Whenever I began to brood about what was wrong with New York I would make myself think about the firemen, and that would set me thinking about all the other things that were right with this city.

I was reaching for the phone to call Barney when it rang. It was Octavio, on the desk. "There's a Felix Pacheco here wants to see you. With another gentleman." Almost as a challenge he added, "You want them?"

"Thanks, Octavio. Send them up."

This sounded promising. My visit to Pacheco today must have kicked in his thought processes and he had come up with a lead for me, something that might be of help to Senator Beaufoy, a champion of Pacheco's people. It was possible Felix would want some small favor in return, and who could blame him?

I opened the door to the knock and tried immediately to close it: neither of this pair was Felix Pacheco. Two against one, they shouldered their way in and slammed the door—two inner-city Latinos about twenty years old who had almost outgrown their dark suits, the suits they wore only to funerals and special occasions like this visit to a midtown hotel.

"Who the hell are you? Where's Felix?" I demanded.

"He couldn't come," the bigger one said politely; he had a scar, old but still lively, that ran down his neck from ear to Adam's apple.

"Then who—"

"Why don't you just listen," the shorter one said, "and let us ask the questions." He was going to be fat before he was thirty. He looked around contemptuously and added, "This is where you live, huh?"

This was too much. I could take criticism of the place from friends, family, and the women I dated but not from a punk who wouldn't be able to button his jacket if his life depended on it. I said, "Yes, this is where I live. What about it?"

The shorter one made no further comment, but allowed himself a brief smirk. Scar said, "Sit down, we got to talk."

With that the punks made the mistake of sinking into the couch. The cushions ballooning up around them made them look like they were wearing water wings. They were still plenty threatening—loosey-goosey and unreadable. You wouldn't know for sure whether they intended to hit you up for a few bucks or put the traditional two bullets in the back of your neck. Even more unsettling, they may not have known themselves which way they would go until the moment arrived.

I had kept up an outraged front, but I could feel my palms beginning to sweat. I purposefully chose to sit on the arm of a chair, a foot higher than they were. I said, "You're not from Felix."

"From the neighborhood," Scar said, and then I understood. The kid who wrote down my license plate number this afternoon wasn't as dumb as he appeared; he remembered it. This pair had been sent to check on Felix Pacheco's visitor. By Felix's supplier, I assumed. What had I walked into?

"You have questions, ask them," I said; I was hoping to get some leverage out of my perch looming over them. "This is not a convenient time for me. You caught me on my way out the door. What do you want?"

"Don't be in such a hurry," Scar said, reasonably. And then he used a line he had probably had success with before. "People in a hurry end up in accidents. You want to get in an accident?"

It was a no-win question and I didn't answer it. He didn't like that; his scar glowed briefly, a coal fanned to life. He asked it again. "You want to get in an accident?"

"Nobody wants to get in an accident," I said. "Not even you. Am I right?"

These two had probably started strong-arming in grade school, shaking down classmates for quarters, but they were still learning the upscale end of the business, and Scar didn't have a ready reply to my answering his question with another. He changed directions. "People think they can go where they want, stick their nose anyplace. That's what you think? You can go anyplace you want, it's a free country?"

"Not entirely. There are certain limits," I said. "We have to respect each other's privacy."

"Bullshit," he said, and that seemed to end the possibility

of a debate on the Fourth Amendment. "What were you doing up at where Pacheco lives?"

"What do you think I was doing?"

The short one said, "Hey, we ask the questions, remember?" He had caught on to my technique.

I said, "It was personal. It had nothing to do with your business. Tell that to your boss."

"Who said anything about a business?" Scar said. "I don't have no boss. Leave bosses out of this." He was as skittish on the subject as Felix was.

I said, "If you did have a boss, and I was in the same business as him, is this the way I would live?"

That they understood; if I was dealing drugs I could surely do better than this dump. I had scored a point.

But they had only been testing me. The short one said, "We know who you are, we know what you do. Now I'm going to tell you something. What you did today was a mistake. You was nosing around Pacheco for information. For the newspaper."

"I don't work for the paper anymore."

"We know that, man," he flared. "To *sell* to the paper. Or the police. Because you got no job now."

"I work for Senator Beaufoy."

"What's that, a six-week gig?" He wasn't so dumb either.

I said, "I'm not interested in Pacheco's business. If he has one. If I was, you think Pacheco would be stupid enough to talk about it?"

"No, he won't do that."

"So what are we talking about here?"

Scar said, "Teaching you a lesson, man."

"What do you mean, a lesson?"

"You know, so you don't forget. To keep your nose out of where it don't belong. You know what I mean?" He was looking at my legs. I crossed them. "That's right, like break your legs. Maybe one is enough."

★ 170 ★

Jesus Christ, he wasn't kidding. "Wait a minute. For visiting Pacheco? To talk about something that has nothing to do with whatever it is you do or don't do?"

Scar said, "Except, everything does. And we got our instructions." He was looking at the card table. "What you got over there?"

"My computer. And my printer. My tools for writing, how I make a living."

The two looked at each other, seemed to come to an agreement. The short one said, "We gonna leave it up to you. Your leg, whichever one, or your tools how you make a living."

Jesus Christ. I said, "There's stuff stored in that computer I need—reference material, man, a million pieces of information."

"So you want the leg?"

"No, I don't want the leg. Wait a minute, will you? What if I promise never to go near Pacheco again?"

The short one nodded. "You won't, after the lesson."

Scar said, "I think you want us to do the computer. We do the computer, the printer, we pull out the phone, and we leave. Okay?"

"Will you wait a second?" My voice had gone tight. "You've already scared the shit out of me. You've made your point. You don't have to do anything else."

The short one said, "We got instructions."

They stood up and the couch cushions sighed back toward normal. Scar pulled back his jacket. They had come prepared; he drew a hammer out of his belt. "This won't take long. You was going out, in a hurry, right?"

He walked to the card table, hammer cocked. The short one followed him. Jesus Christ, I couldn't believe this.

A light rap on the door brought them up short. Scar mouthed, "Who's that?" and I shrugged back, "Who knows?"

He mimed for me to keep my mouth shut or the hammer would shut it for me, did I understand? I understood.

None of us stirred, and after an interval the rap came again—louder, and repeated insistently. More a pounding than a rap. Then we waited through another long interval. Don't go away, I prayed.

And now an impatient voice came through the door. "Caprisi, I know you're in there, you son of a bitch." Poppy Hancock.

The short one glared at the door, Scar at me. He had the hammer at the ready, next to his ear. Poppy was saying, "Jock, open the damn door."

I could see my visitors' minds working. A moment later their eyes met in agreement: this business had become more trouble than it was worth. Scar leaned over and breathed in my ear, "You be nice, we be nice." He stuck the hammer back in his belt and pulled the jacket over it.

I called brightly, "Coming, Poppy." Like in a sitcom.

I went to the door. I opened it and stood on the jamb, so she couldn't get past me; just in case. She was looking better than ever today, glowing with health. Or was I just glad to see her? The air was being pumped back into my balloon.

I said, "Sorry, I was in the john."

My visitors edged past me with a hurried " 'Scuse me, Miss," and "Good-bye, lady," and walked swiftly toward the stairs. Poppy looked after them curiously. Scar's hammer was showing. She murmured, "Who are they?"

I let her walk past me into the room, and closed the door. "The boys?" They were none of her business. "They came to fix my computer."

"Not your wagon?" It was Poppy's ability to size people up that made her so good at politics.

She wasted no more time on small talk. She sank uninvited into a wing chair and said, "Jock, how long did you think you could go without taking my calls? You owe me an answer."

I was almost back to fighting strength. "To what?" I asked innocently.

"Don't play games. If there's no deal, if the senator is not going to own up to a relationship with the dead woman, we're ready to go to stage two. At once. If you think we've been nasty up to now, you ain't seen nothin'."

There was no way I could continue to dodge her. I said, "Poppy, do I have to spell it out for you, the consummate pro? There is no sting like voter backlash. Once you guys start implying that Beaufoy is guilty of murder and you can't back up the charge, you put yourselves in seriously deep shit."

She smiled a tight, superior smile that made me want to wrap my hands around that supple neck and squeeze. She looked like the cat that had swallowed a cageful of canaries. She let me hang for a long moment before she said, "I take it we have no deal?"

"Damn straight."

She uncrossed her legs with a slight rustling of nylon. "So that ends the meeting. Don't say I didn't try." She got to her feet. "There was only the one item on my agenda."

"Wait a minute, I've got a couple," I said. She looked at me expectantly. "For one, I'll thank you to stop sending your two-bit ringers to our press briefings. The one this morning—"

"—was terrible, I hear. You won't see him again."

"What about the Dalmatians? Are you planning to sic them on us again?"

"I heard about the Dalmatians. Do you really think we were behind that demonstration?"

"Weren't you?"

"Would I waste my limited resources that way?" I must have looked blank. She added, "Do you know how many of the sixty-two counties in this state have a measurable population from the Dalmatian coast?"

"No, and please don't tell me." I didn't even know there

were sixty-two counties in the state. "Okay, I'll give you the Dalmatians. How about Turnbull's relentless, totally scurrilous references to Beaufoy's health? To say nothing of some below-the-belt leaflets I've seen on that subject. With phantom sponsors, by the way—untraceable. Illegal, I believe. There is nothing, for Chrissakes, seriously wrong with—"

"No? So produce your doctors."

"We may do that."

"Good. And we'll produce ours." She started for the door. "Look, I hate to pull myself away from your cozy nest but I'd rather not risk another predatory assault like last night's."

I realized now that the devil-may-care scarf at her throat was there to cover the hickey I'd inflicted. I said, "I'm sorry about that. It was an irresistible urge. It won't happen again."

"Apology accepted. Good night, Jock."

I was right the first time, she had never looked better. I suppose that was part of the reason I ventured, "Just when we've gotten business out of the way and we can be civil, you're leaving?" Was she in a hurry to throw the switch on her dirty-tricks engine? "What's your rush?"

"It's nothing personal. I've had a long day. I'm ready to wrap it up."

"You haven't had dinner, right?" She didn't answer, and I pushed. "I was just about to phone for a reservation at a favorite place of mine. It's right here in the neighborhood. How are you on stuffed cabbage?"

"What is it, Jock, are you angling for the Romanian bloc?" Her vote counter didn't stop for a minute. "Thanks for asking, but I'd better pass. I don't think it would be wise for us to be seen together."

"No last names. And believe me, nobody you've ever known goes to this place. Real home-style cooking. You'll love it."

She looked at her watch. Very slowly she said, "Can we do it in an hour?"

Apparently the go-ahead signal to her dirty-tricks department could wait an hour. In an hour I might possibly shake loose whatever it was she had up her sleeve about Beaufoy's connection to the murder. I called Lupescu at the ladder company.

Dinner at the firehouse was over by nine-thirty, but Poppy and I didn't make our exit until a fire call dispersed our tablemates at a little after ten. Time no longer seemed a problem for Poppy. She had slipped away once to make a three-minute phone call, and that may have released the hounds of Hell. Whatever, she wasn't talking.

It was still a pleasant early fall evening when we got outside. I said I'd walk her the six or eight blocks to the apartment house where she told me she had a sublet.

"Thanks, but that really isn't necessary," she said. We were turning the corner.

"Why not? Think of it as the proper windup of a date."

"Because it isn't." She was fussing with her handbag. "A date. Here's the seven bucks I owe you for my share of the meal."

I avoided her outstretched hand, "My treat. One day you'll suggest a place for dinner."

"Fine. That'll be dutch too." She shoved the money in my jacket pocket. "But thanks." Her tone softened. "They're a nice bunch of guys." Without further discussion we continued walking.

The dinner couldn't have gone better. Lupescu had outdone himself, and the men of the ladder company, separately and as a unit, had fallen hopelessly in love with Poppy, whom I had introduced as "my friend Paula." They responded to her the way they say the Philharmonic did to Bernstein. The horns never sounded mellower, the violins soared. Five minutes into the meal Poppy knew every man's name.

She seemed even more at ease with their nicknames, which

took another two. In the hour that followed she learned as much about each of these smoke eaters as it had taken me days to extract when I followed them around to research the Sunday piece that was my introduction to the company.

The fire bells sounded as we were picking at the last of the coffee cake. For a minute I half-believed the boys were going to let some tenement burn to the ground rather than desert their fair Paula. The firehouse hound, a Dalmatian—he should have been picketing this morning—spent the entire meal with his snout in her lap; he was living the fantasy of every man in the room.

We walked much of the way to Poppy's street in a silence that wasn't in the least uncomfortable. Once we got east of Sixth there were few headlights and fewer pedestrians. The midtown streets seemed less brutal in the glow that spilled from restaurants and shop windows. Quieter, too.

I was trying to figure out how to open Poppy up a bit. What did she know that might persuade a measurable number of voters that Beaufoy was Sheri's murderer? I couldn't begin to guess what she might have in her dirty-tricks bag.

There was no way to introduce the subject. The way to extract secrets, of course, would have been during pillow talk—the whispered confidences of two very strange bedfellows politics had made. The image sent a surge of warmth through me. But there was as much chance of that coming to pass as of Poppy confiding that Herbert Turnbull had put the knife in Sheri.

When we were less than a block from her place, Poppy did begin to talk. "You know something? At the risk of repeating myself, I had a very good time."

"Me too. Lupescu is an artist."

"Oh, sure, the cabbage rolls sang," she said impatiently. "But suppose they hadn't? I'd still have to thank you for a terrific evening. And I've just figured out what made it work— aside from those straight-ahead firefighters."

It was the first time I had ever heard her talk without an attitude or an agenda. I sensed a compliment coming. "So tell me," I urged.

"It was the no-alcohol dinner."

I was only slightly let down. "Poppy, you know the guys are not allowed to drink."

"Of course I know. There's no booze or beer in a firehouse. Those big dumb plastic jugs of Pepsi and Sprite on the table alongside Lupescu's stuffed cabbage . . ."

She squeezed my arm, either in affection or to hold my attention. "Jock, it was family time. No showing off, no pretension. What you saw was what you got. *In vino veritas?* Baloney. Alcohol is a mask." She released the arm.

"I forgot. You did once tell me drinking was the world's number one time-waster. Half a cut, I remember, above stock car racing." I knew what I was doing.

"No, stock car racing is a close third. Mindless sex is second."

Gingerly I said, "So are you in a meaningful relationship, or what?"

She smiled. "You're no longer with that rag, but you're still a reporter. Right, Jock?"

"The habit dies hard."

She hesitated only a second. "My meaningful relationship ended a while ago. After six years."

"I'm sorry."

"It wouldn't have worked. He was older." Beat. "Quite a bit older."

Thirty-something years, if I remembered correctly. "I'm sorry about that too."

"About his age? Don't be. Women have a secret they usually don't share with young men. Older men make marvelous lovers."

I said, "It's a comfort to know I have something to look forward to."

We had stopped in front of her building and the doorman was sizing us up. No matter. The slight tingle of electricity had gone out of the air.

She slipped long, cool fingers into mine and squeezed. "Good night, Jock." She unsqueezed. "You know, I'm going to hate myself in the morning."

I held on to the hand. "Wait a second. You only say that if you invite the man upstairs."

"Not only then. You're a good guy, and I'll hate myself because of what I'm going to do to your candidate in the morning."

"So don't do it."

Her face registered total disbelief. "You've got to be kidding."

She brushed her cheek, warm and velvety, against mine, and ducked into the building.

I would almost have sworn the fat doorman was looking at me pityingly.

I put in a seven A.M. wakeup call with the switchboard, and spent a troubled night. Of all the dreams that tumbled through my head, one stuck out, the only one in color.

Someone—Mort Beaufoy?—was coming at Sheri Bannerman with a knife while I stood by, unable to help. We all three knew that whoever wielded the knife wasn't allowed to stab Sheri through her green dress, so maybe, just maybe, she was safe. And then I watched, horrified, as slowly, deliberately, almost defiantly, she pulled the dress up over her head.

Triumphantly, it turned out. Underneath she was wearing a one-piece lilac undergarment trimmed in lace. We all knew the would-be killer wasn't allowed to stab her through that either. For some reason the knife had to plunge into a bare midriff.

Sheri threw back her head and laughed.

★ 178 ★

WEDNESDAY

15

I punched my way across the radio dial, AM and FM, all the way up the Henry Hudson Parkway. Nothing. Whatever charge Poppy had loaded against us hadn't gone off by the time I arrived at Mort Beaufoy's apartment house at a little after nine in the morning.

There was no police crime scene tape across the garage ramp but I decided to park in the street anyway. With both the press and the Dalmatians gone there was plenty of room at the curb. And I had had it with Mort's garage. A single police car was stationed at the street corner, where it commanded both the garage and the building's front entrance. A uniformed cop lazed against the car door. This Riverdale street had just about returned to its customary drowse.

The super, LaPierre, was out front with a trash bag, gathering up the torn signs, Styrofoam coffee cups, and assorted litter left after yesterday's mob scene. The mess was not of the building's doing, but LaPierre didn't seem resentful. When he saw me he put down the bag and followed me into the lobby.

"Mr. Caprisi," he said, "do you have a moment? Will it be all right to show you something? To ask your advice?"

I told him if it didn't take too long, because I was expected at the senator's. I said I didn't know he knew my name.

"Oh, yes," he said. "All the New York papers show up in my trash." Uh-huh.

He led me through the back of the lobby to the service area. He said, "That detective told me to keep my eye open for a briefcase the police couldn't find."

"The black dispatch case the dead woman left home with. It wasn't in her car. You found it?"

"I don't know. I'm not sure this is what the detective described to me." He was twirling the combination lock on a metal utility closet. "The building's trash cans went out Monday morning for garbage collection. I usually bring them in the same afternoon. But with the dead woman on Monday, and all that happened out front yesterday, I didn't bring them in until last night. And I found this in one of them."

He had taken out a small, soft-sided black bag that he was holding by two corners. He turned it this way and that with thick, blunt fingers that handled it delicately. "It's black, yes," he said, "but I don't know . . ."

"No, this wouldn't be it," I said. "This is the kind of bag doctors carried when they used to make house calls. The dead woman's was flat, bigger, with hard sides. What they call a dispatch case."

"Yes, that's why I wondered . . ." he said. He was as disappointed as I was.

"You were right to save this. It's odd that it happened to be thrown out at this time. . . ."

"The garbage truck came collecting early Monday morning. So this bag could have been put in that trash can even before the woman was killed."

"Or any time after until last night. Are there any doctors in the building?"

"We had one. He moved out a year ago. Anyway, you can see, the bag looks like new."

"Did you look inside?"

"I shook it." He shook it for me. "It sounds like it's empty. I was afraid to open it. Because of fingerprints." He was still holding it by the corners.

"You're a good citizen, Mr. LaPierre."

"Not yet. But I have my first papers."

I said, "Let's open it. But carefully."

LaPierre was right. The bag was empty. It had a faint smell, benign but distinctive, that I couldn't quite identify.

LaPierre was saying, "So what do you think I should do with it?"

"Save it for the police. I'll let Sergeant Nordstrom know you have it."

He nodded, relieved to be sharing the responsibility. He put the bag back in the closet with care. "A shame we had that tragedy here," he said. "To cause all that trouble for the senator. Our finest tenant."

"Is he?"

"And Mrs. Beaufoy. Twice we have had to delay painting their apartment. Do they complain? Never."

"You're painting the Beaufoy apartment?"

"Early next month."

"You didn't hear that they may be moving?"

"I saw that on television. I was surprised. Usually when the tenants are planning to move they don't want all the trouble of the painters. But of course, sometimes the building is the last to find out."

It was Clara Beaufoy who opened the door to me at Apartment 5A. She nodded coolly. "Yes, Mr. Caprisi," was the extent of her greeting. She was dressed to go out, and the suitcases she had arrived with sat next to the door.

"Are you leaving us?" I asked.

"That's exactly what I'm doing. Someone has to tend to the home fires."

"Will you be back for the primary?"

"No." She read my look. "I've done what I was asked to come here for. My husband and I sat for a series of phone interviews with radio stations yesterday. Our mutual interest in buying a new apartment came up more than once. That should have put the subject to rest."

"Should have?"

"There is no rest for the weary. A detective called on us last night to ask questions. About my precise whereabouts when that woman was killed. I had to explain more than once that I was several hours to the south. I'm beginning to understand the meaning of the term 'police harassment.' "

"They're talking to everyone in the building."

"They had already grilled Mort to a turn. I can't imagine what more we two could contribute. Last night's officer skirted the edges of a subject he didn't have the nerve to confront head on—the state of my marriage. Mort and I have been in politics eighteen years but that was a first."

"You mustn't take it personally. The police are just doing their job."

"I told him if his marriage was as sound after forty-odd years he could count himself lucky. At least he had the decency to be embarrassed. But not as much as I. You come from tabloid journalism, Mr. Caprisi, so let me explain. In my part of New England we don't discuss the state of our marriage other than with our spouse, and often not even then."

"I can see you're letting them get to you. I'd take my cue from the senator. He doesn't let any of this bother him."

"He is amazing, isn't he? I stand in awe." Some of the starch had gone out of her. It came back as she called to the bedroom, "Mort, Mr. Caprisi has arrived."

She didn't wait for an answer. She picked up her bags, and I opened the door for her. She said, "Don't let him stand on his feet too long. The weight of the world is killing that back. Good-bye."

I watched her march out to the elevator. I could almost hear the waves pounding against the rocky coast of Maine.

McClintoch showed up a few minutes later. He, Mort, and I spent the better part of three hours picking apart the draft of the big speech, now slated for delivery in Syracuse on Sunday.

Mrs. Beaufoy was right; Mort did look a little the worse for wear today. We kept urging him to take breaks but he refused, and he plugged away as hard as Paul and I. He pointed out that he had better get used to the pace because beginning tomorrow, according to our campaign calendar, he was slated to start circulating among the voters. He could hardly wait.

"You don't win elections with front porch campaigns," he said. "And Morgenstern tells me it will be safe to go out by tomorrow, as long as I don't overdo it."

I had been waiting for this opening. "That's your orthopedist?"

He nodded. "Cyrus Morgenstern, at New York Medical. They don't come any better."

We finally did get Mort to retire to the bedroom for a brief lie-down, and I put in a call from the kitchen to Hap Nordstrom's squad room. While I was dialing I guiltily remembered another chore: I had forgotten to take Clifton Oliver's jacket to a lab for analysis. I would have to do that today. Without fail.

Nordstrom was out—hot on the trail of our murderer, I prayed, as always. I left word for him to call me at this number; I had some information he had asked for. Then I briefed McClintoch on my meeting with Poppy Hancock. Anyway, the parts that concerned him: how she had cornered me on her ultimatum, forcing me to reject it, and then repeated her threat to destroy our candidate. Not in some theoretical future but today. Had Paul heard any rumors about an impending bombshell from the Turnbull camp?

He said, "I've heard nothing, but rumors like those would go to the media before they reached us."

Mort was up, and we went back to work. It wasn't long before we knew something was stirring in the media. Mort had turned off the speaker on his answering machine, but it began beeping and blinking a new message every couple of minutes. We dutifully refrained from punching Playback; we were determined to finish our rewrite before we had to face whatever was waiting out there.

At a minute or two before noon, McClintoch looked at his watch and declared we had done whatever could be done by committee; it would be up to Jock to take the draft home and buff it to a soft shine. I knew what McClintoch was aiming for: the twelve o'clock local news on Channel Two. He turned the TV on.

The primary campaign was the leadoff item, and it delivered a right enough bombshell. The *New York Ledger* was claiming in a late-edition exclusive report by Jerry Scovil that on the morning of the Bannerman murder a reliable witness heard Senator Beaufoy in a loud argument with a woman. The witness had requested anonymity so as not to be besieged by the press, but Scovil was in possession of a tape of this person's "vivid" testimony. While waiting for the elevator, the witness had heard angry sounds pour through the door of the Beaufoy apartment—ugly, bitter sounds that spoke of a major confrontation between two people who were more than casual acquaintances.

Now Herbert Turnbull's campaign manager, Poppy Hancock, appeared on the screen, caught by a Channel Two camera at a Long Island shopping mall where Representative Turnbull had gone to greet voters.

Paul said in that calm voice that became eerily more so in crisis, "Perfect. Here comes Hancock to connect the dots."

Turnbull had previously refused to comment on this "disturbing new development," but Ms. Hancock was ready with a few words. She trusted that Mr. Beaufoy would now face up to some questions the voters needed answered before they could make up their minds, questions that had been hanging in the air too long. Maybe the press had been too timid to ask them, but surely that would not be true of the police. In all fairness to the electorate, it was time the senator spoke up—frankly and fully.

Poppy was fetchingly dressed in a sweater and a short straight skirt that did justice to her shapely legs. There was no scarf at her neck today. I hadn't bit the bitch nearly hard enough.

On our side of the screen the silence of deep space hung over us as the Channel Two report ground on relentlessly with reactions to the news from ordinary citizens on a midtown street. Neither Paul nor I had so much as stolen a glance at Mort, who lay on the couch at our back.

Meanwhile, a Con Ed worker crawled out of a hole to say he thought the senator should withdraw from the race, "at least until this business is cleared up." Sure, when—next spring?

A businesswoman with a briefcase observed, "Let's not convict the senator in the court of public opinion." So far so good. She went on, "But the media circus is distracting us from the issues. I wish the senator would find a way to bring it to an end." I supposed confessing to the murder would do that; she was no help. The segment was wrapped up by a passerby who said only, "The whole affair is thoroughly disgusting." I didn't chalk her up for our side either.

The news moved on to a City Hall story. Paul turned the TV off. Neither he nor I spoke; we were waiting for Beaufoy to break the ice. When he did, it was with the first burst of emotion I had ever seen from him.

"That's the most damnable lie I've ever heard," he exploded. I liked that he had an explosion in him. "Nothing remotely like that could possibly have happened. Neither Ms. Bannerman nor I ever raised our voices above the conversational. We had no reason to. Is this what politics has finally descended to? Is there no safe haven for a man in public life? What in God's name has happened to civilized discourse? Who was it who made this scurvy accusation?"

"Let's see if we can find out," I said. "One of the messages on your machine may be a callback from Sergeant Nordstrom." I took the precaution of going into the kitchen to make the call.

I caught Hap over a sandwich at his desk. Yes, he had called me. What was the information I said I had for him?

I dropped my voice to give him Dr. Cyrus Morgenstern of New York Medical, then raised it again to ask him what the hell that piece in the *Ledger* was all about.

"Still reading the tabs, huh, Jock? Don't you know better than to believe everything you see in the *Ledger*?"

"You mean this is a fake?"

"I mean it's too early to get your nuts in a knot. We'll check it out. In due course."

To Hap it was a lead, one of many. So what if it cost Beaufoy the election? That was not his department. And then I remembered that he had voted for Beaufoy. Twice.

"Hap, who is the witness with big ears, the source of this so-called exclusive?"

"Don't ask me. Talk to the man who got it."

"You think I can shake this out of Jerry Scovil?"

"It isn't Scovil's story. Some freelance interviewed the witness."

"You mean this is secondhand?"

"Scovil has the tape. He got it from the freelance."

"This smells all the way to the Canadian border. Who's the freelance?"

"This didn't come from me, okay? His name is Joe Bennis."

I should have guessed. "I know that fraud. He tried to screw up my media briefing yesterday. He's on Turnbull's payroll, for Chrissake. And he suckered Jerry Scovil?"

"I'm sorry. But there is a tape of the interview."

"Come on, Hap. What's the name of this witness who heard the big fight?"

"She was promised anonymity."

"She's a she. We're making progress."

"She doesn't want the press all over her."

"I'm not the press anymore. And this smear can kill the senator in the primary. Come the general election, if you still like him you better bring a pencil to the voting booth."

He put his hand over the phone while someone asked him a question I couldn't hear. I heard his answer, faintly: "Give me a minute, will you? To finish my goddam sandwich?"

He was back on. But not speaking. It would be just my luck for him to pass his irritation on to me.

I said, "Hap . . . ?"

The words came out grudgingly. "It's Helen Kleiman. You know, the nervous Nellie who found Bannerman's body."

She lived right down the hall; I could confront her in a minute. That was good. But she was close enough to the Beaufoy apartment to have reasonably heard whatever there was to hear. That could be bad.

16

I needed a serious talk with the nervous Ms. Kleiman and I didn't know how to go about it without unstringing her. We were now, after all, in an awkward adversarial situation.

It went easier than I expected, maybe because I didn't have to unnerve her by ringing her doorbell and nosing into her life. Luck was on my side. She had gone down to the lobby for her mail and I caught her in the fifth-floor hallway as she stepped out of the elevator.

She was the same depressed woman with the bony face I remembered from each of our encounters—not the mask of tragedy, exactly, more the *skull* of tragedy—but she acknowledged me without animosity when I called her name.

"Much quieter out there today," she said. "A relief after yesterday. That dreadful shouting and jostling. I thought my head would split."

I was getting the impression she had no idea she had kicked off a new scandal, that she hadn't listened to the news, hadn't bought a paper, had possibly forgotten all about her talk with Joe Bennis. If that was so, it was another piece of luck for me.

"Keep your fingers crossed," I said, tuning in to her wavelength. "The snoops may have deserted us to chase down other streets. Let's hope so." She had her mail in one hand and was opening her door with the other. "Do you have a minute, Ms. Kleiman?"

The question startled her; but I suspected many things startled her. She stood at her open door, her keys swinging from bony fingers, her mouth a slit. "Here . . . ?" She looked around the empty hallway.

I said, "Wherever . . ."

She hesitated long enough for it to become a big thing. Eventually she surprised me. "You might as well come in." The decision made, she swung the door wide and I followed her through it.

I said, "Have I caught you at a bad time?" She didn't answer; possibly all times were bad for her.

It was a large studio apartment, pleasantly cluttered with homey furniture and doodads. The decorating looked like it had been done years ago; everything was well settled, except, of course, the flowers. There were two big bunches of those— definitely not arrangements. Probably whatever hadn't sold at the shop.

"Please ignore the mess," she said.

"Is this a mess?" I was working hard to be agreeable. "You ought to see my place."

"A man's mess is considered a charming eccentricity." It was a sour observation. "Sit anywhere." Now that I was in, she seemed resigned to her role as hostess.

I picked a chair next to one of the flower bunches. I touched a big, bright pink flower. "I always forget. What do they call these?" The truth is, the only flowers I can name for sure are daisies, roses, and chrysanthemums.

"Gerbera. From Africa, originally. They do make a bold statement, don't you think?"

"Definitely. You're a lucky woman. I can't think of a pleas-

★ 191 ★

anter place to spend the day than a flower shop. Did you study horticulture?"

She waved a dismissal. "No, I'm a late-Sixties flower child. I went to seed and made it pay." Tight smile; she had said it before. "By the way, a flower shop's not nearly so pleasant a place when you have to deal with bills and such. I'm a co-owner."

"Is that why you're able to go to work so late?"

"My partner takes the mornings three days a week. That's one of the pluses."

"It wasn't one the other day. I'm sure you'd have preferred Monday to have been one of your early days."

Her eyes widened and she shuddered. "The day of the murder," she gasped. "Yes, I'd have missed that. Horrible."

"You were badly shaken."

"I was a mess."

"You kept repeating, 'The green dress, the green dress.' "

"Did I? I've blocked all that out."

"I'm not surprised. But was there something about a green dress you might have found particularly upsetting?"

"I can't imagine. Except . . ."

"Yes?"

She was embarrassed to say it, then decided, Why not? "Does this make sense? The only dead people I'd seen until then were laid out in coffins. People in coffins aren't usually dressed in green. What was it you wanted to talk to me about?" She hadn't missed a beat.

"You know I work for the senator."

She nodded. "Did he send you here?"

"No, it was my own idea. But you've upset him."

She went bolt upright in her chair. "How did I do that?"

"You gave an interview to a journalist—"

"Oh, God, no. You know about that? He said it was background. 'Not for attribution,' he said." Her face was in a knot.

"I knew I shouldn't have talked to that man. But he kept hanging around the shop, pressing me. He was interfering with business. I just wanted to get rid of him."

"You're free to talk to anyone you please. You don't have to apologize for that. What disturbs the senator is the falsity of what you said."

"What do you mean, that I lied?" Her jaw quivered. "I didn't lie, I assure you. How did you hear about that interview? That man swore my name wouldn't even appear in the book."

"There's a book?"

"He's writing a book. It won't be out for another year, so I thought—"

"Ms. Kleiman, I can assure you there'll be no book. I know the man you talked to. Joe Bennis?"

She nodded slowly.

"He was using you."

"For what?"

"To promote the senator's opponent."

"Herbert Turnbull?" She made a face.

"Yes. And whatever you told him, before the day is over you'll have to go over it all again with the police. So you'd better get your story straight. You couldn't possibly have heard the senator in an argument the morning of the murder."

"An angry argument. Very. Mrs. Beaufoy was especially upset."

"Wait a minute. The senator was arguing with his *wife?*"

"Yes. And not for the first time."

What was going on? "Ms. Kleiman, Mrs. Beaufoy wasn't in New York the morning of the murder. She had gone back to Washington the afternoon before. Sunday."

Her slit of a mouth dropped open. "Then that must have been when I heard them. Sunday morning. I never said the day, when I first mentioned the argument."

"Bennis suggested Monday?"

"I suppose. After all, what difference did it make? But yes, come to think of it, it *was* Sunday morning; it was a day I wasn't going to work."

"And it was Mrs. Beaufoy you heard arguing with the senator?"

"No question, I know that voice. Very down east."

I took a moment to regroup, and I spelled it out slowly. "So you heard the senator and his wife arguing on Sunday morning. Not the senator and Mrs. Bannerman on Monday morning."

"Oh, my God, is that the way it came out? He said—that reporter?—he was doing a chapter on the personal pressures a politician has to deal with. He was looking for color—background material. After we talked awhile—gossiped really—he turned on his tape machine and asked some questions that went back over the ground we'd already covered. As a reminder to himself, he said, because he hadn't taken notes. He assured me there'd be no names in the book. Anyway, not mine, not the senator's."

"Don't you see why he did that? Turned the tape machine on *after* he found out what you knew?"

She shook her head sadly.

"That way he could frame his questions to get the answers on the tape he wanted. You were manipulated, Ms. Kleiman."

"Can I have been that dumb?" Her voice had grown small. "The way you tell it, I may very well have been. But this is so ugly. It's crude and obvious. Rudimentary, don't you agree?"

"It is. Politics isn't like airplane design or computer science. It doesn't advance in sophistication year by year. It operates under the same rules that governed it when Lincoln was denounced as a tool of the devil."

Her distress had increased. "Without mentioning my name—because I'd die—surely there's a way to repair this damage. To get the truth out."

"Probably. The question is, how long will it take to catch

up with the lie? The truth is never as interesting."

"Remember, *I* didn't lie." She was moving to protect her flanks. "*You* said it correctly—I was manipulated."

I was pissed. This was not the time to sort it out, but I knew the truth wasn't going to be much better for our team than the lie. The senator in a big fight with his wife the day before the murder? Terrific.

I said, "What I don't understand, Ms. Kleiman, is why you told that reporter anything at all about Senator Beaufoy that could do him harm. Do you have something against the senator?"

Her jaw quivered again. "Certainly not."

"Or Mrs. Beaufoy?"

"I hardly know the woman. We've talked a few times. In the elevator, at the mailboxes. They're perfectly decent neighbors."

"I'm sure you've heard that they're thinking of moving."

"It will never happen," she said dismissively. "Would you like a cup of coffee?"

"Thanks, but only if you don't have to make it." She was feeling guilty and looking to make amends. I held on to the opportunity. "Why won't it happen?"

She moved to the kitchen alcove and began fussing with cups and milk. She was too nervous not to be moving. She said, "Clara Beaufoy loves the building, loves the location. I told you, I don't really know the Beaufoys. But when you live alone and you have a limited social life you pick up more than the average neighbor." She was piling things on a tray. "Clara Beaufoy gets both votes in that family."

We were easing into new territory; it was gossip time. I said, "I'm new to the senator's staff. I'm still feeling my way. What do they fight about? Other women?"

"I doubt it. I'd guess that bad back has him in a lot of pain."

"Sure. Lately."

I hoped that would stir something up but she didn't respond. I took a hard look at her as she brought over the tray with what was left of the coffee in her drip machine. Put a little flesh on that face, take off a few years, and she probably hadn't been bad looking.

So I made another try. "He never made a move on you?"

It was her first laugh—small and pinched, but a laugh. "No, but don't use me as a litmus test."

"You're selling yourself short."

"Thank you, but I'm past all that. Ten years with the wrong man cured me. And when you give up on men, they give up on you." It was flat and matter-of-fact, clear-eyed acceptance. "I take my comfort from more reliable sources—music, books, flowers."

"You're no help, Ms. Kleiman."

She looked startled. It didn't take much to startle her. "What do you mean?"

I said, "I've been thinking it's time for me to plunge into the commitment pool—find a good woman, start a family. You are not encouraging."

"There are better role models for commitment than me," she said. And then, deliberately shifting the focus, "And for marriage than the Beaufoys'. Theirs is used up. They are decent people, so they've found a way to make do. But the marriage? Used up. That's all I was trying to say to that reporter. Not that Beaufoy isn't a good senator. What's the one got to do with the other?"

If only the voters saw it that way.

17 It was early afternoon and by now Jerry Scovil's exclusive take on the Bannerman murder would have spread as relentlessly as athlete's foot. A few old-fashioned news outlets might still be holding back on the story pending independent verification, but most would not be able to resist repeating it. They would take care to cover themselves by naming the *Ledger* as the story's source, but that would slow its spread only slightly. How many people pay attention to the source of a news story?

For our side the worst course would have been to ignore Scovil's attack. We had to try, at least, to limit the damage. With McClintoch at my shoulder in Mort's kitchen I dictated a statement over the phone to campaign headquarters for immediate release. It called the *Ledger* story "a shameful fabrication of the opposition's dirty-tricks department," and went on to say that no less could be expected from Turnbull and his campaign manager, Poppy Hancock; their success as mudslingers and distorters of the truth, separately and together, was their main claim to fame.

Mort was still badly rattled, and as angry as I'd ever seen him. But he stuck to his principles; he refused to get down in the dirt on this issue, exactly as he had refused on all others. "I won't give Turnbull the satisfaction," he said.

So the release went out over McClintoch's name. We didn't expect it to do much good; the media would see it as a predictable knee-jerk response to Scovil's story. But our denial would be on the record.

I wasn't going to settle for merely stepping on the serpent's tail; I had a chance to take a whack at the head. It was likely Scovil was at the *Ledger* right now, working on the followup to his exclusive story. If he was, he would probably be in a foul mood. Because he had nothing to follow up with. He would have to rework what he had already written, throwing up smoke to cover that he had no new facts.

I waited till I was alone in the kitchen to make the call. I was right on both counts. Scovil was at his desk at the *Ledger* and he came on the line with a snarl. "What is it, Caprisi? You caught me at a bad time."

"Jerry, you don't know what a bad time is."

"The hell is that supposed to mean? I'm in no mood for cryptic."

I knew he wouldn't hang up on me; I had already given him one good lead on this story. I said, "You know that Joe Bennis is on Turnbull's payroll."

He came back with a sour homage to Claude Rains in *Casablanca.* "I'm shocked to hear that, Caprisi. Shocked. I thought he was with *Modern Bride.*"

I stuck to my script. "You're relying on Bennis's tape. A dubious item with no corroboration."

"Have you forgotten? This is the *Ledger.* Story first, corroboration second."

"You can be hung out to dry, Jerry. Bennis didn't allow you access to the witness who gave the interview. But I had a long talk with her."

"You did?" He was genuinely surprised and a touch hum-bled. "How'd you get to her? Who is she? Bennis said he was 'shielding his source.' "

"Bennis wouldn't shield his mother from a spring shower. He didn't give up the source, because you'd find out what I did—the interview was a sham. Bennis played the woman like a fish on a line. She never heard an argument, heated or otherwise, between the senator and the Bannerman woman."

Silence. Then, probing, "Jock, you're not exactly a neutral source."

"We can go back and forth on this all day. Neither of us has the time. Why don't you record the rest of this call?"

"Why, what are you—"

"Do as I say. Go on, roll your tape."

There was nothing from his end, then a grudging, "Yeah, okay. We're on the record. So?"

"Listen carefully. Jerry, if Joe Bennis is right about his interview with the senator's neighbor and I'm wrong, I hereby promise to give you an exclusive interview announcing my resignation from the campaign because of my growing doubts about the senator's ethics. Good enough?"

The silence from the other end felt good.

That maneuver wouldn't kill the story either. But until Scovil found out whether I was right or wrong about Bennis's interview with Ms. Kleiman, he would have to play out his theme with caution. His second-day story would be low key, the word "alleged" would figure in it relentlessly, and Scovil might even persuade his bosses to push it to the back of the paper among the discount furniture ads.

I had done all I could about Scovil. But before heading back to Manhattan there was one more good deed I could perform in Riverdale. The coroner was still holding Sheri Bannerman's body. I assumed Bryce would be grieving for his wife at home until the funeral, but by now he would have heard the news of the supposed passionate argument between Sheri and the senator. Bryce had enough real pain to deal with. I would stop by and at least put this one to rest.

Mort was in improving spirits when I left him. Some of that may have had to do with the dawning realization that his wife was on her way out of town. I wasn't going to get anywhere near that subject. I also knew he was finally plugging in to the mounting excitement of the campaign. He was slated to speak at a street rally tomorrow, and that had him keyed up.

"Between my hospital stay and confinement to the apartment I've taken on a prison pallor," he said, walking me to the door. "A nice shade of battleship gray, if I may amble into a new metaphor. I am ready to be launched—to confront the foe, that miserable wretch. To put myself in harm's way. And about time, wouldn't you say?"

What did he think he was in now if not harm's way? I wanted him to fire off a few salvos at the harmer. It wasn't going to happen. Mort was too nice a guy to be in politics and I suppose I loved him for that, but God, he was a trial. I gave him a thumbs-up and got out of there.

Between Beaufoy's apartment and the Bannerman house the all-news radio station had not a word to say about the campaign. I couldn't take much comfort from that. The drive took only seven minutes, less than half the eighteen-minute news cycle. Who knew what lies about us were being broadcast during the other eleven?

The first thing to hit me when I turned onto Bannerman's street was the Pools by Puller pickup in Bryce's driveway. I looked toward the back of the property. Three or four men were at work near the pool apron. Mac Puller loomed over them, shouting and pointing, lifting this, dragging that, riding herd. His crews earned their nineteen dollars an hour.

I was surprised to see work going on. The sounds no doubt carried into the house, where they would remind the grieving widower of the pool his wife would never see. And then I thought, hey, the job is contracted for, Puller is on a schedule, life goes on. In the end the pool might prove a comfort to Bannerman. Solitary laps in the embracing water could help in the healing.

I parked behind the pickup and walked up the path toward the front door. Puller spotted me and moved rapidly in my direction. His shouted "Yo!" sounded not a whole lot different from the tone he used with his employees. I hoped he wasn't planning to get physical. Toe to toe he could more than likely beat me to putty.

He turned out to be cordial enough. Even though, as he got close, I saw that the side of his face where I hit him had turned the color of an *Arizona Highways* sunset.

"You looking for Bannerman, he's not here," he called.

"No?" It had never occurred to me that he wouldn't be home. "Where'd he go?"

By now Puller had caught up with me and his voice dropped to the conversational. "He went back to work. Downtown to the antique shop."

"I figured he'd wait until after the funeral."

"He needed a couple of hours, he said, to straighten out some things."

"Now? Was there some sort of emergency?"

"I doubt it. He said going downtown beat hanging around the house feeling sorry for himself. It made sense to me."

"What kind of shape is he in?"

"He'll live."

This guy had a heart of poured concrete. I said, "When I saw him he was taking it hard."

"Yeah, well . . ."

He had been watching his crew out of the corner of his eye. Now he whirled to face them. "Yo! I stop work don't mean you stop work. Jesus!" They scuttled like roaches.

He turned back to me and his voice dropped forty decibels. "You never know with couples. I've seen a lot of it. A wife dies, a husband dies, the one left pulls a long face, cries buckets, goes into a funk—I get the full treatment from the survivor every time. Sometimes it's for real, sometimes it's for show. Because it's expected."

"That's what you think about Bryce? He's for show?"

"Hey, I wasn't talking about him, about any one particular person. I meant, looking in from the outside you never know." He worked his jaw cautiously. "This still hurts like hell. Where you kicked me?"

"That was my fist. If it's any comfort, that still hurts too. That what you told your wife about your face? Someone kicked you?"

"I don't have a wife. I won't ever have to pull no fucking long face if she dies." He glanced back over his shoulder. "Excuse me. I got to kick some ass."

Nineteen dollars an hour.

On my way back to town I picked up from the radio one new and depressing news item about the campaign. WCBS had just released the results of an overnight CBS/*Times* telephone poll. Of three hundred and sixty-one people who intended to vote in the New York primary, a bare hundred and eighty-nine said they would vote for Senator Beaufoy. Considering the margin of error, that lead over Representative Turnbull was "statistically meaningless." The calls had been made before Jerry Scovil's exclusive story broke in the *Ledger*. The next sampling would drop Mort below fifty percent. Meaningfully below.

The clerk who had been nearly out of sight at the top of a ladder the last time I visited Bannerman & Bailes was this time up front and on duty—an angular young man with unruly hair and trifocal eyeglasses. He looked as if he knew his antiques. Or should. He was standing in the bright light near the shop window, in scholarly discussion with an elderly customer about a Fabergé egg they were passing back and forth between them as carefully as they might a hen's egg.

Bryce was nowhere in sight but I had to wait no more than thirty seconds for the clerk to detach himself from the customer and bound toward me wearing a friendly grin and cradling the egg in his hands. I had the feeling that these days two customers in the shop was a special event.

The smile faded when I revealed that I wasn't a customer, just looking for Mr. Bannerman.

"Oh. He's in a meeting at the moment. Are you sure I can't help you?"

"I'm a friend. It's to pay my condolences."

"Oh. Yes. Of course. He's in the office with Mr. Bailes. Why don't I see if—"

"I know the way," I said, and swiveled rapidly rearward through the clutter before the clerk could object.

I had forgotten how deep the shop was. When I got within a few yards of the office door I heard angry voices, and then scuffling feet, furniture scraping the floor, bumping sounds. I considered whether I might learn the most by pressing my ear to the door. Then, the hell with it, I flung it open without knocking.

The two partners were lurching and bumping around the crowded office, each with a firm grip on an arm of the other. The contents of shelves rattled. An etching on the wall swung like a pendulum. Hilton Bailes was grasping the silver letter opener I saw the last time I was here. This time he held it like a dagger. His lank, swept-back blond hair had come loose from its lacquer and was hanging across his lean face. He looked like a prize Afghan hound, an angry one. Bannerman's haggard face was flushed with the effort of the struggle. He looked, for him, almost fierce; there was not a "please" in sight.

I kicked the door closed and managed to work myself partway between the careening bodies. Using my elbows as a wedge and moving with the traffic flow, I was able to push the two men far enough apart to allow me to hack away at the gripped wrists. The three of us were performing a folk dance of unknown origin. Meanwhile I was shouting, "What is this? Cut it. Will you two cut it?"

Both combatants suddenly realized how out of hand things had gotten. They stopped struggling and released each other. The letter opener clattered to the floor.

"What the hell is going on?" I demanded.

"It's a personal argument," Bailes spit out.

"Over a letter opener?" I was picking it up.

"Antique. Late Italian renaissance." He was calming himself by assuming a selling mode. "A Cellini influence is very much in evidence."

Bryce was still breathing hard. "Bullshit," he gasped. "This crazy bastard tried to open me like an invoice."

"Don't dramatize," Bailes snarled; his anger had flamed again. "You know something, Bryce? You're lower than a rat's ass."

He looked at me, looked at Bannerman, and pasted his hair back in place with both hands. By that time he had made his decision.

"Screw you, Bannerman," he snarled. "Now and forever." He stormed out of the room, the yachtsman in heavy seas.

I had been dense, but there was no longer any mistaking what had gone on here. When the dust settled I looked Bannerman in the eye. "Do I say it or do you?"

Bryce stared at me forlornly, but his mouth was clamped shut.

I said, "I walked in on a lovers' quarrel."

"Ex," he said grimly.

When Bannerman and I made our way forward through the shop a few minutes later, I was braced for another confrontation between the partners, but Hilly Bailes wisely kept out of sight. The only sound when we left was the bell that dinged as I opened the front door.

We had no trouble finding a place in the neighborhood where we could sit and talk. Lunch hour in the nearest pub had thinned to a few stragglers, and it was too early for the afternoon drinkers. We found a booth toward the back. The lighting was dim, conducive, I hoped, to confession.

I ordered a beer and Bryce a double cognac. He looked ghastly, something like an air-crash survivor, and he had to bite his lip to keep it from trembling. He downed a fair amount of the brandy as soon as he was able to wrap his hands around it. Meanwhile I was explaining that the *Ledger* story—he had heard it on the radio—was completely without merit; his wife had definitely not been overheard in a passionate argument with the senator, or anybody else.

Giving Bannerman this reassurance was my original purpose for looking him up, but now it was no more than an icebreaker. What I was after now was the Bannerman & Bailes story. I would have to tiptoe my way into that.

And all the while I was making sure Bryce understood that the *Ledger* had lied about Sheri and Beaufoy, I was wondering, Does he really care what might have happened between them? Or for that matter, between Sheri and anybody else?

When I was finished he said, "Jock, I appreciate your coming to tell me that. It does relieve my mind. It reduces the nightmare. Please, it was thoughtful of you." He seemed sincere.

I didn't have to introduce the delicate question of his relationship with Bailes. He knocked back much of the rest of his cognac and did it himself. "You knew about Hilly Bailes and me?"

"Not really," I admitted. "Maybe I should have. When I talked to Bailes the other day, before he knew Sheri was dead, he bad-mouthed the two of you. But especially Sheri. Viciously. He was steamed because—what?—you had dumped him and gone back to your wife?"

"No, that's not it." He was turning his glass with nervous fingers, round and round, a poor lost soul picking his way through the wilderness under a heavy load. "Look, you might as well hear it all." But then he shut his mouth and fixed his gaze on the farthest wall.

He was going to unburden himself, but in his own time; when the load finally became unbearable. I had no intention of getting in the way of the process. I sipped my beer. He finished his cognac. I mimed to the waiter for another round. We had time to burn; it was still five and a half days to the primary. Yeah.

When he was good and ready, Bryce cleared his throat and began. "Hilton Bailes and I met during our freshman year in college." He had warned me; I was going to get it all.

"We roomed in different dorms and we didn't have any classes together, but we managed to find each other and lock on almost from the first. Not as lovers; that didn't happen for nearly two years. But we found we had a great deal in common—aesthetic judgments, musical tastes, pet hates. Please, a million things. And where our experiences had taken different tracks, we took pleasure in teaching each other what we knew. Did you know Hilly was an accomplished sailor?"

"No kidding?"

"A year or two after graduation we each came into a small inheritance, just about enough to start the business. It went well. Very well. We were as compatible as partners as we were friends and lovers."

"You lived together?"

"No. We decided that would be more togetherness than we

could handle. Because we spent so much time in the shop. Maybe it was a mistake."

"Why a mistake?" The new drinks had come but Bryce didn't touch his. He didn't seem to need it; talking was easing his tensions.

"If Hilly and I had shared a home Sheri probably wouldn't have happened. But we didn't, and she happened. This beautiful young actress breezed into my life and decided she was in love with me. She was really something. Please. I was flattered, I was confused, I was stupid."

"Did she know—"

"She found out soon enough. About Hilly and me. She thought, foolish girl, she could still make it work for us. She would save me. And I thought, even more foolishly, I'd give it a try. She was a force of nature, my Baby." He took the first sip of his new cognac. "So we got married."

"And it didn't work."

"It worked. Please, Jock, it did work. Everything but the sex. In her way Sheri really did love me and in my way I came to adore her. We found a great deal to admire in each other. And once we put aside the sex there were no tensions, no disappointments, except for Sheri's frustrations in her career. Jock, she was a damn good actress. She never got her chance. And now . . ."

He took a pull of the brandy and stared at a spot over my shoulder. "We got along beautifully in so many ways. There was a core of tenderness. We were thoughtful, we were protective."

"Like brother and sister."

His eyes came back to me. "Better. I've got a sister. Sheri and I were there for each other in all the ways that counted. When the economy buckled and the business started to slide— Bannerman and Bailes—things became hairy. We had expenses. I was scared. Sheri's reaction? She plunged into her real estate work more ferociously than ever. She brought in remarkably good money. We were able to live as well as we ever had."

"But you and Hilly Bailes had become lovers again?"

If he found the question awkward it didn't show. "Except for a year or so it had never really stopped."

I pushed it. "And you and Sheri weren't sleeping together?"

"Not in years."

I pushed it further. "What about her sex life?"

"I never asked and she never spoke about it. It was the one wall between us. But since sex wasn't part of what Sheri and I had together it wasn't much of a wall. I suppose . . . I guess . . . surely she must have had a lover. Lovers. Please, I devoutly hope so. I tried not to think about that."

He was thinking about it now, and he looked distressed. I said, "And you and Bailes. When did you end that relationship?"

"Over a month ago."

His pained look was fading, the embarrassed one returning. "Yes, he did think I'd gone back to some sort of sexual thing with Sheri. He still does. That must be why he was so bitchy to you about her."

I watched him drain his brandy; he seemed to need it again. I said, "Okay, you didn't break with Hilly because of Sheri. So what did cause the break?"

He looked me straight in the eye. "It was over Mac."

"Mac . . . ?"

Was I supposed to know? I tried repeating the name in a voice somewhere between knowing it and prompting him to enlighten me. "Mac . . ."

"It's never happened to me before. I went head over heels." He read my stare. "Mac Puller."

I had to speak very slowly to make my mouth form the words. "Your pool contractor? Pools by Puller? The palooka who at this very moment is prowling your backyard kicking ass?" I couldn't help laying it in.

"Please, he's a fantastic man. Mac—"

"Hold it. Give me a second."

I was trying to pull the concept together. I said, "The day Sheri was killed, when you and Puller spent what I thought was entirely too many hours working out the color of your diving board trim or whatever the hell decorating decisions had to be made, what you were actually doing was . . . ?" I let the question hang unspoken.

It roused the first smile I had seen from Bryce, a shy smile of remembrance. He said, "We did spend part of that time on pool plans. . . ."

"But you two were really together all those hours? One way and another?"

Softly, "Oh, yes, we were very much together."

I leaned forward. He was drifting, and I wanted his full attention. "Bryce, I have to tell you, when you described that day to me—how you and Puller spent it—it didn't smell right. And if that's the way it hit me, it must have stunk to high heaven to the police. Puller could have provided you with an alibi just by telling the truth, a foolproof alibi that made sense. Why didn't he do that?"

"Mac keeps a very low profile," he said earnestly. "He says if the guys who build his pools at so much an hour—"

"Nineteen dollars."

"If they knew he was gay he'd never get any work out of them."

"I can see that."

We were winding down. Before I let him go maybe I could shake one more piece of the puzzle out of him. I said, "Can I ask you one last question? About a possible boyfriend Sheri may have had?"

"Let me hear it."

"Can she have had a lover who was rich enough to shower her with money?"

"A rich lover? Why not? But would she have let herself become financially dependent on him? Never. Please. Baby was too proud, too self-reliant. She was your classic independent woman."

Through his pain he was taking pride in that.

18

"If you're not satisfied, we'll find you another dry cleaner, Mr. Caprisi. But you have to tell us. We don't know if you don't tell us."

Andres, the Stanley's day concierge, was plucking at the garment I was carrying folded over my arm, Clifton Oliver's tweed jacket. I had gone back to the Stanley for the sole purpose of picking up the jacket to take to the lab I knew on Second Avenue. I had stopped at the desk on my way out to check for messages.

I said, "This is not for cleaning, Andres. I'm taking it to lend to my brother."

He murmured darkly, "You never said you had a brother."

I said, "You want to give me my messages?"

There were three. "Sergeant Nordstrom, but he'll be out." "Paula will try you again." "Felix from the Bronx. He straightened everything out but don't come to visit him again. Ever." I was in agreement with that course of action. Total.

I couldn't guess what Poppy Hancock wanted. We had wrapped up our business last night. And suppose we hadn't? Where had she found the nerve to try to contact me after this morning's repulsive stunt? The woman had the hide of a bull elephant.

Not literally; her actual hide, the little of it that had come under my hand, was velvety smooth. Warm to the touch. And extraordinarily responsive.

I had first met Rod Weiss my first year on the *Ledger,* when he was a civilian forensics specialist with the NYPD. Now middle-aged, with a drooping, brush mustache and a back curved from bending over too many slides, he was, I hoped, making better money at Bridger Laboratories than he had as a civil servant. My previous visit to Bridger was before his arrival there, and I was surprised to see him.

Along with his own look of surprise, he greeted me with, "Hey, Caprisi, your candidate's not doing so great, huh?"

"Nice to see you too, Rod. My candidate's doing fine. He's exactly where we want him at this point. Where we can watch the momentum build."

It was bullshit and Weiss paid no attention to it. He said, "Can you believe it, people are actually beginning to speculate that maybe Beaufoy killed the blonde? I'm not one of them, but you know the reasoning. An older man sticks a knife in a woman to prove himself. Penetration by a rigid object. It speaks for itself."

"Rod, I won't validate Turnbull's bad-mouthing by debating it. But I will remind you that the senator is barely out of a hospital bed."

"A man challenged on his virility has the strength of ten."

"Or not."

I wasn't going to get sucked into a back-and-forth on this. I turned abruptly to the business at hand. I showed him the sleeve—damp at the elbow yesterday, now dry—and asked if he could find out what, if anything, had been washed out of it.

He bent close over the sleeve and fingered it intently for a good thirty seconds. I wondered what was going through his head. When he looked up he said, "Hell of a good material."

"I already knew that. But what—"

He tossed the jacket on a counter. "I doubt anything can be coaxed out of this elbow but Highland wool and German dyes. But give me an hour." His tone was not encouraging.

I knew what to do with the hour. Three blocks up the avenue was Cawber Latch Oberwalt, Certified Public Accountants, business home of the elusive Hal Vector, he of the "Honey-buns" call to Sheri. I had looked up the address soon after Hap Nordstrom briefed me on Vector, and tucked it in my wallet. It tingled a reminder of hoped-for possibilities every time I reached for a bill, much like the legendary condom that resides in the wallet of the horny high school boy. Vector was supposed to be on an audit in Pittsburgh that was taking longer than expected. I wondered.

Cawber Latch Oberwalt occupied the nineteenth through twenty-first floors of a new office building designed on the principal, How little can we spend per square foot on this shoe box? CLO's large reception room on twenty was no-frills, but neat. The business weeklies were fanned out on coffee tables like cold cuts. I presented myself at the reception desk, presided over by a sleepy-eyed young woman, bottom of the pecking order, who was on the phone.

"Soon as my relief shows, Lisa. Meet you in the coffee room." She hung up and looked at me without interest.

I went for broke. "Hal Vector, please."

That opened her eyes. She looked startled. Or guilty. She glanced down at a clipboard, then up. "May I ask who's calling?" She was rattled. "I'm sorry, he's out of town."

I leaned on the desk to get my face close to hers, and said softly, with a smile, hoping to rattle her further, "Then what's the difference who's calling?"

She recovered well enough. "I'm sure he'll want to get back to you."

"Alfred Blaine. Waters and Sons." I straightened up. Vector was in the building, I would bet on it. "Okay if I use your phone? It's a local call."

"Of course. Any of those. Dial nine."

I sat down on the leatherette couch furthest from her. I pulled the phone on the coffee table toward me. There were four digits on the label. I punched another four at random.

"Fenton."

"I'm sorry." I spoke directly into the phone in a voice too low to carry to the desk. "I was looking for Hal Vector."

"Well, you ain't got him." An older man, very sure of himself.

"His extension is . . . ?"

"Why don't you look in the—" Then, resignedly, "Okay, just a sec. . . ." He took longer than that, but he did come back. "Twenty-one twelve."

The receptionist was looking at me. Or maybe past me, watching for her relief. I thanked Fenton and punched up 2112. It rang five times before a voice said, warily, "Yes?"

"Mr. Vector, could you tell me your room number?"

"Twenty-one twelve." Beat. "Who is this?"

"Mail room, sir. Sorry, I'm new."

"You must be. Phone numbers and room numbers are the same."

"Yes, sir." If that wasn't the "Honeybuns" voice I would eat a gross of honey buns.

Having confirmed that my tabloid blood still flowed freely, I hung up. Of course I had used the gimmick before. Vector had instructed the reception desk to say he was out of town; he would have given the same instruction to the switchboard. The trick was to bypass the operator by making an inside call. A five-finger exercise.

I had to wait only three or four minutes for the receptionist's relief. She appeared through the door behind me, one of two to the offices. I held on to the franchise by keeping the phone tucked under my chin as though waiting for my party. Meanwhile I leafed through a back copy of *Business Week*. I was reminded again how badly I managed my finances. How would I ever send kids through college? Then again, what kids?

A minute or two after the changing of the guard at the receptionist's desk a visitor appeared from the elevator and presented himself to the desk. I hung up and headed for the door to the offices.

"Sir?" the new receptionist called.

"Mr Fenton's expecting me," I said. "That's all right, I know the way."

The interoffice staircase was just inside the door, and I climbed to the twenty-first floor. The nearest door was 2160. The offices ran in a U around a central well for services and clerical help. I picked up a few nods and smiles but no hostile looks as I made my way around the U to Room 2112. There was no sound of conversation from the other side of the closed door. I opened it without knocking, stepped in quickly, and closed it behind me.

He was in his shirtsleeves, a thin, bleached-out man, almost albino, about forty. He was working with a computer at a desk layered with papers. He looked up at me, startled, with pale, frightened eyes. He suspected that whatever this was about, it wasn't going to be good.

"Who are you?" he asked, not unreasonably.

"Jock Caprisi. I used to have a column in the *Ledger*?"

"How did you get in here? I don't read the *Ledger*, never have. I'll thank you to—"

"I'll bet Honeybuns read it."

"—get out of my office." He had hesitated hardly at all. "Or do I have to call security?"

"Do I have to call your wife and tell her you're not in Pittsburgh? I'd hate like hell to do that. She'd hate like hell to hear it. Where are you staying, Hal, the club?" It was a good-sized office; he could afford a club.

"What do you want, Mr. Caprice?" He had stood up. I didn't think it was out of courtesy.

"Caprisi." If only briefly, I had seen "Honeybuns" register on his face; its judicious use might allow me to lead him around like a show dog. "You were the last person to telephone Sheri Bannerman the day she was killed."

He had had time to compose himself. "Was I? I suppose that's in a phone record. Yes, my call went through, she picked up, but for whatever reason, she never spoke. What difference whether I was her first call of the day or her last? Ms. Bannerman was finding me a house. We spoke once or twice a week."

" 'Ms. Bannerman'? What happened to 'Honeybuns'? I was the one who picked up your call that morning."

By now he was fully prepared. "Is that why you're here? Because of what I happened to call her? I sometimes call my secretary Sugarplum."

"You didn't say it like someone buying a house. Not nearly."

"Okay, I used to tease her. A bit sexist, I suppose. Is that a problem for you? Take it to the Human Rights Commission." Maybe I wasn't going to lead him around like a show dog.

I said, "You're my first C.P.A. with a pixie sense of humor. What kind of clients do you have?"

"Mostly soft-goods manufacturers. Come to think of it, none of your damn business."

"True. All of this is really police business. I suppose you'd rather talk to them. You want me to call the detective in charge? He'll be glad to hear you're back from Pittsburgh."

That knocked some of the wind out of him. He said, "What do you want? And why?"

"The truth. Not to print it, not to tell it to someone who'll get you in trouble with the cops or your wife. I have a totally different agenda."

"Mine is to be left the hell alone. Okay?"

"I can do that. Then what? Are you going to put down roots in 'Pittsburgh'? How long do you think you can keep ducking the police?"

He stared at me with those colorless eyes. Then he left the desk and walked to one of his three windows. He looked out at the roof across the avenue. And then his narrow shoulders sagged and I knew he was mine.

He turned to me and said quietly, "I hope until they solve this murder. Once they do, there won't be any reason for them to talk to me. Good enough?"

He was backlit by the afternoon sun. I had to squint to see his expression. It was far from serene.

I said, "You and Sheri were having an affair?"

He turned back to the window. It took him a long time to say it. "Yes, we were having an affair."

"Since when?"

"You want dates? I don't know. Months, not years."

"How did it start?"

"How do you think?" He was still facing out the window. "She drove me around Westchester showing houses. My wife was mostly home with the kids. We've got a baby. One thing led to another. It happens, you know?"

"She was a good-looking woman."

"Damn right. And aggressive."

"Did she ever mention having enemies? Talk about things that were bothering her? Or people?"

"Never. We didn't have time for that kind of talk. I had a family waiting. And a job. So did she. She was supposed to be showing properties. Mostly we grabbed an hour here, an hour there. You know what I mean?" His voice was flat, emotionless.

I was coming up empty and I pressed. "Isn't there anything

★ 217 ★

at all you can tell me that might explain why she was murdered?"

He had at last turned back to face me. "I'm sorry. It was an affair. For both of us. A fling. It gave us both pleasure but it never got beneath the surface. I saw her at most once a week. I'm pretty sure she was seeing somebody else."

I opened my mouth to ask and he said, "No, I wouldn't have the least idea who. Or even if."

"Then what makes you think—"

"I don't know. You sense that kind of thing or you don't. I did." I detected a little color in his face now, but only in his pointy chin. His white lips were firmly closed again.

It had taken some ingenuity to get in here, and I was learning nothing from Mr. Chatterbox. "What about the affair? How did you manage it? Where did you meet?"

"Where else? Motels. Afternoons. Here and there around the county. Never the same one twice. It was not as romantic as we would have liked."

He was still keeping a tight rein on his emotions. He started to frame a sentence, then thought better of it. Instead he said, "Look, I don't want to talk about this. It's too soon. Maybe one day, but not now, okay?" He was scared stiff—for his wife and for his job. He had given me all I was going to get.

I said, "Hal, you have my word. Your secret's safe with me."

"Thanks. I appreciate that." It was going to be hard for him to get back to his spreadsheets. He said, "Tell me something. You think the police are close to breaking this thing?"

He looked wretched. Why not give him hope? "Pretty close, I'd say. Good luck."

I closed the door on my way out. Sheri Bannerman and an anemic C.P.A.? It was not what I would have figured.

Rod Weiss handed me Cliff Oliver's jacket with an "I told you so" look.

"I can at least tell you one positive thing about this sleeve," he said. "It's cleaner than the rest of the jacket. I'm sorry. Someone wanted to get a stain out of there real bad. And he succeeded."

"You see an 'Out, damned spot' scenario?" I was looking for any encouragement he could give me.

"Yeah, most people feel about telltale blood the way Lady MacBeth did. They'll work like hell to get rid of it. On the other hand some people get just as worked up about orange marmalade on their good jacket. Who do we bill for this, the *Ledger*?"

"Don't you know I've severed all ties with the *Ledger*? Send the bill to Reelect Senator Beaufoy headquarters here in Manhattan."

Weiss groaned. "You mean when Beaufoy loses, the lab gets to stand in line with the other creditors?"

I didn't need that either.

19 Back at the Stanley I was still a few minutes early for the evening news. I filled the gap with a call to Hap Nordstrom's squad room in the Bronx.

He picked up on the first ring and I went on the offensive. "I thought you were going to call me."

I went on the offensive because I was feeling a shade guilty about having poked into, around, and under Nordstrom's investigation these past few days. Not very guilty. No reporter worth his salt sits around waiting for handouts from the police on a hot crime story. Anyway, nothing I had done was going to slow the police pursuit of Sheri's killer. Hap had not even been anywhere in evidence during my prowls.

Was he still on the case? I had this flash image: Sergeant Nordstrom is in bed on Staten Island trying to make a baby on the city's time while Poppy Hancock dangles Mort Beaufoy out a window by a nylon cord.

I didn't give him a chance to reply to my opening. I said, "Hap, where the hell have you been?"

"Where do you think I've been?" he snapped. "Riding herd on the task force. Believe it or not, it's a hefty one. We're checking out everyone who ever touched Sheri Bannerman's life. So far we've come up empty. But, Jock, none of this goes at warp speed."

No kidding. "What about Mort's doctor? Did he clear him?" I wanted that load off my mind.

"Let me shut the door." He was back on in a moment. "I don't know why I keep briefing you." His tone was good natured. "You're off the paper and can't do me any good."

"You never know."

"Doctor Morgenstern confirmed Beaufoy's back condition."

"No surprise there." But I breathed easier.

"I asked him how active a person could be with a back like the senator's. He said, 'I would advise extreme caution.' I said, 'I'm not asking what you'd *advise*. I'd like to know what's possible.' He said, 'That depends on the incentive.' When I pressed him to be more specific, he fell back on doctor-patient confidentiality. I don't think you can make that into a campaign slogan."

In the end, not terrific news. And Hap, I knew, *liked* the senator. He said, "As for Sheri Bannerman. She was well liked—by her friends, her coworkers in real estate, her customers, her family out west, her acting buddies. I understand she was a lousy actress, so it's unlikely she was stabbed by a jealous colleague. And no, Jock, the few parts she got in that downtown company were too small to outrage audiences to the point of murder."

"I don't have a task force, but I would have guessed all of the above."

"I do have one small piece of news."

Maybe he had saved the best for last. "Let's have it."

"And then I have to run."

"You two are still trying . . . ?"

"Not tonight. Gerta's temperature has dropped." He turned huffy. "There's other things in our life, you know? Here's your nugget. Are you sitting?" He didn't wait for an answer. "Bryce Bannerman is gay."

"Don't tell me." My taxpayer dollars at work.

"He and his business partner, Hilton Bailes, are longtime lovers."

"Who'd figure? What does this mean for the case?"

"When I know you'll know. Or shortly thereafter."

"Hap, I need a heavy."

"Hang in there. We're working on a theory."

"Yes . . . ?"

"It has to do with Sheri's dress—why the knife didn't go through it. I can't say any more just yet."

And to make sure I didn't press further he mumbled, "Gotta go."

Bullshit. He didn't have a theory, he was kicking up dust. He and his task force didn't know any more than I did.

Hap's timing was perfect. As he rang off, the local news shows were starting. I surfed.

I could have stayed with any channel. They all ran the same story in the first, second, or third slot—the *Ledger's* exclusive report of that passionate argument between Senator Beaufoy and Sheri Bannerman the morning of her murder.

Jerry Scovil still hadn't been heard from with a follow-up piece. If he was going to skin back on his story he was taking his sweet time, probably on instructions from management to hold off. The *Ledger* hadn't had its name spoken so often since its clear beat years ago on the story of the Central Park horse that returned to the stable with an empty saddle but a booted foot in each stirrup. The *Ledger's* page-one headline read PARK MADMAN GOES "HEADLESS HORSEMAN" ONE BETTER. Washington Irving, the paper's "founder," must have smiled down benignly on that one from some Sleepy Hollow paradise.

Each channel followed its recap of the *Ledger* story with commentary by one or another political pundit. The sages issued the required caution not to "rush to judgment" on Beaufoy, but if I heard the phrase "appearance of impropriety" spoken mournfully one more time I would throw up. I almost did that anyway when Poppy Hancock came on. The charismatic campaign manager got sixty seconds on ABC when she was "cornered" by a determined reporter after her candidate, wearing a shit-eating grin, waved the man off with an "absolutely no comment. I mean it."

Ms. Hancock's position was that it no longer mattered what the senator had done or not done. It no longer mattered what a witness may or may not have overheard. (This was Poppy covering her admirable ass on whether Bennis's tape had the facts right.) It no longer mattered that the senator's doctor said a man with his back condition was still capable of great physical exertion. (How she got that I couldn't even guess. Another Hancock coup.) All that mattered now was this, according to Ms. Hancock: the dread possibility existed that the state of New York might be represented in the greatest deliberative body in the world by a man with a dark cloud hanging over him.

Truth is, that didn't matter either. What mattered was that Poppy was wearing a red silk dress and speaking her piece beneath the lazily turning blades of a helicopter at the Albany airport. The considerable breeze thus pressed the fabric into her belly button and whipped it fetchingly against her thighs. It didn't matter what Poppy said; at this moment half the voters would have shouted "Right on!" if she called for a sharp rise in taxes.

I was so mad I could barely see straight enough to punch up the numbers. A perky female voice said, "Turnbull for Senator headquarters. When he wins, we all win." Not half bad.

I asked for Poppy Hancock, and the next female voice said, "Ms. Hancock's office."

I asked for her again, and this time a booming male voice

came on with a challenging, "Yes? Who is this?"

I said, "Her brother." I had suddenly remembered siblings—brothers? sisters?—from my research for the magazine piece two years ago.

"From Michigan?" The threat had gone out of the voice. "You missed her by ten minutes. Does she know you're in town?"

"No, and I've got a plane to Flint in an hour. Damn. Is there a number where she can be reached?"

Warily, "I can't give you her cellular number but she should be home in a few minutes. If you know that number . . ." A faint whiff of suspicion had reappeared.

"No problem, I'll call her at the Fifty-fourth Street apartment . . ."

"Right." I could feel the suspicion dissolve.

". . . if you're sure that's where she went . . . ?"

"Definitely. To change. We're just down from Albany and Saratoga. I'm scheduled to pick her up at seven-thirty. The candidate is speaking in Queens tonight."

"I know. I hear the campaign's going great guns." I thought I would choke. "We're all rooting for you guys back home. Oh, and to whom am I speaking?"

"Poppy's assistant. Ray Gallagher. She hasn't mentioned me?"

"Only to say they don't come any better."

The lobby on Fifty-fourth Street, with its free-flowing terrazzo floor and bursts of tropical greenery around a foaming waterfall, could have been the waiting room of a successful dental practice in Caracas. Instead of last season's fashion magazines I was presented with the inevitable sign "All visitors must be announced."

I was ready for it. I told the stone-faced concierge I was here to pick up Ms. Hancock. At his still expectant eyebrows I added, "Ray Gallagher."

He phoned upstairs, then reported, "Ms. Hancock says you're much too early, she's not nearly ready, but if you like you may go up to wait. It's Fourteen-A."

"I know."

It gave me a lick of pleasure to see the look of pure shock on Poppy's face when she opened the door. She was wrapped in a terry cloth robe, her usually bouncy hair was wet and lank, and she was wearing no makeup. All of those tests she passed with flying colors, but that didn't make me any less angry.

I brushed past her before she could decide what to say, and walked into a living room furnished in golds and rich browns—warm, tasteful, expensive. The walls were hung with Watteau-like oils under pinpoint lights.

"Hell of a nice room," I said.

"It's a sublet," she said coldly. "Not necessarily my taste."

"Oh, I know. Your style would be more operating room modern. Slab table, work light, instrument rack. And a bucket to catch the blood."

Her jaw was set firmly. "You went to a hell of a lot of trouble to get in here, Jock. All you had to do was call."

"Once a tab reporter, always a tab reporter. We don't call, we insinuate ourselves."

She pulled the tie of her robe tight. "Look, Caprisi, the other Ray Gallagher is coming to pick me up in half an hour and I've got to look fetching for the voters in Forest Hills. So tell me fast what your problem is and get out."

"It's not my problem, it's yours." The words tumbled out. "You don't seem to understand that you've painted yourself into a corner with your sleazy lies, your total lack of ethics—"

"I'll talk ethics anytime you want—except during a political campaign and when my hair is wet. What lies? Point to a lie."

"Forget the professional lies. I expect you to lie through your eyeballs for Turnbull or whoever you're turning tricks for. You lied to me personally—you to me."

"When was that?"

"You gave me your word you weren't going to use that creep Joe Bennis again."

"Oh no—I said you wouldn't *see* him again. And you haven't, have you?"

"Just his handiwork. Very clever. But it's his handiwork, that famous taped interview, that will nail you to the wall if you don't publicly disavow it."

"The CBS poll lit a fire under your team, huh? You're running scared, and you're pissed."

I *was* pissed. And I didn't give a damn if it showed. "Poppy, you as good as called a United States Senator with eighteen productive years in—your words—'the greatest deliberative body in the world' a murderer. You implied that this scholar, teacher, author of major legislation, champion of world peace, Nobel Prize candidate, is a fucking knife-wielding killer. That is way outside even the outrageous bounds of political name-calling."

"Keep your pants on, he hasn't won the Nobel Prize yet. And Jock, I never said he did the deed. Not actually. But if he did, he won't be the first hero who was driven over the edge by misplaced passion. What the voters do with the facts is their business. All I did was lay them out."

"You laid out what's in Bennis's tape. A total fabrication."

"Says who?"

"You never talked to the woman Bennis interviewed. Why should you? The tape delivered what you wanted. I did. She denied to me everything that's on that tape. Everything. She was had."

An unaccustomed flicker of doubt passed across Poppy's

face. But just a flicker. "Bennis made the tape. What's this got to do with me?"

"Your barrage of innuendo about Beaufoy since the murder, beginning with your smirking allegation of a sexual involvement and culminating in this damnable blood libel, is going to end by blowing you out of the water."

In a cool, measured voice she said, "I will look into your charge that I've got the senator all wrong. If it turns out that's the case, there will be a sincere statement of regret from me." Beat. "Probably less than a week after the primary."

The bitch. "No good, Poppy. Turnbull has been 'no comment' from the first. He's made you point-man on this search-and-destroy. When the truth comes out—and it will soon enough, because the police are about to nab the killer and Jerry Scovil is going to disown his *Ledger* story—you're the one who'll take the fall for the low blows you've delivered. Remember that quaint expression from Watergate? I thought of it last night. You'll be left to 'twist slowly, slowly in the wind.' After this, a candidate who hired you to run his campaign would be taking a poison pill. Unless you protect yourself now with a firm disclaimer on the senator's character and behavior."

She had been staring icily, unblinking. Now her features slowly softened and her violet-flecked eyes took on a sparkle. "Why, Jock Caprisi," she almost gasped, "I know you're looking to score points for your man, but I could almost believe you're also showing concern for my good name."

That assessment brought me up short. I wasn't sure why my pitch had come out as it did. I had been looking for anything that would make her back off enough to ease the pressure on Beaufoy at a time when the tide was turning against him. Could there also have been an element of concern for Poppy in what I said? Did I actually give a damn?

What the hell, I figured, give it a shot. I said, "Of course I'm concerned for you. Campaigns come and go, but you've only got the one name to live with." Was that too straight-ahead earnest? I bent it with, "The two, actually. Paula and Poppy."

Those violet flecks had never seemed so luminous. "My goodness," she murmured. And again, "My goodness." And then, almost regretfully, "It's probably a carload of horseshit, but you do make it sound sincere."

She had drifted toward me and now she cupped my ears with her hands and brushed her lips against mine for a moment, in a gesture, I supposed, of gratitude. The aroma I remembered from our previous meetings clung to her. She was straight from the shower, so it couldn't be perfume. I had always suspected it was too subtle for any concoction, that it had to be nothing more than pure essence of sexual woman.

I put one hand around her head, and her thick, wet hair trickled water along my fingers. I drew her to my lips, and this time hers locked on deliciously. My other hand undid the bathrobe tie and slipped inside the robe and around to the warm, velvety curves of her still damp back, and down to the reverse curve of her behind. Sheer heaven.

She unlocked her lips and pulled back. In a firm voice betrayed by a husky, breathy overlay she said, "You have to let go, Jock. Ray Gallagher will be here to pick me up in twenty minutes."

"No he won't."

I buried the words in her neck. "I figured on taking you to Queens myself while I set our record straight. I called Ray from my car phone and said my plane was late and I'd drive you to the rally on my way to the airport."

"Your plane? Who are you supposed to be?"

"Your brother."

"Oh, my God. This is even dirtier than I thought." Her smooth buns twitched under my hand. "Look, Jock—"

I cut short the debate with an attention-getting gesture of affection.

It was extraordinary sex. Almost no words were spoken, none were needed. We were completely in tune with each other—dolphins at play, geese on a heady flight, whales sounding; and soon beyond any metaphor that had a chance of communicating the exhilaration, the deep sense of joy.

We had come to something like a halt only twice, and even then, only briefly. The first time was for Poppy to phone Ray Gallagher in Queens to tell him she wouldn't be showing up after all because of "a slight gastrointestinal flare-up." She was sure she'd be back to normal by morning, and would he stand in for her with the candidate? Gallagher said no problem, and did she at least enjoy the brief visit with her brother? She assured him she did. Very much so.

She hung up guiltily; this was the first time in ten years, she said, that she had shirked a political responsibility. . . . And then she returned joyfully to the fray. It hadn't been an idle boast when she told me more than once she didn't believe in casual sex. She was a major player. So what were we two up to, I wondered.

That issue was further confused later, the second time we came up for air. Lying back on the pillow and staring at the ceiling, Poppy said soberly, "You may very well be right, Jock. About my painting myself into a corner."

Hope surged. We were sharing the pillow and I took advantage of that. I leaned closer, gathered a handful of that wonderfully thick hair, and whispered directly into her warm ear, "So you'll issue some sort of clarification . . . ? To the effect that there was never any attempt by your camp to impugn the integrity of Senator Beaufoy . . . ?"

She turned her head, putting us nose to nose. "The hell I will," she murmured sweetly. "What we're doing works. I'll just have to cross my fingers and take the heat. If I couldn't take the heat I'd have gotten out of politics long ago and gone into the kitchen."

And with that she rolled on top of me. Whatever her relationship had been with that elderly congressman from Michigan, my hat was off to him.

She was asleep, and I was fighting it, when I pulled my clothes on. I couldn't read my watch but I suspected it would surely be light enough to do so if I waited another few minutes.

It had been a night. Nothing would have pleased me more right then than to crawl back in bed and curl up next to Poppy's naked, nourishing body and sack out. A strange business. I had every reason to despise this woman and in most ways I did. But in the course of that blissful night I felt in some way as though I had come home.

I pushed the feeling aside and forced myself to get out of there. This was going to be a big day, Mort's first in public, and he would be facing questions. I managed to leave the apartment without waking Paula. Poppy.

It was late, all right. When I crossed the lobby I noticed that the waterfall had been turned off.

THURSDAY

20

I bought an early *Ledger* at an all-night newsstand and climbed into bed with it at the Stanley after removing only my shoes. Even that small effort took an exercise of will.

The page-three story on the campaign focused on how close the race was with only five days remaining till the primary. Two new polls projected a Turnbull win if his steadily rising share of the voters was not reversed—an unlikely occurrence, both agreed. Paul McClintoch, poor bastard, was quoted to the effect that the Beaufoy camp was well satisfied with the present state of voter preference. He interpreted the numbers as indicating that Turnbull had "peaked." With Beaufoy at last taking to the hustings, the final few days would see a gradual turnaround. Sure, and I was king of Romania.

The article was credited to Barbara Murillo, a general assignment reporter, and it made no mention of the Bannerman murder. I turned every inky page of the *Ledger* until I was back among the ads placed by personal injury lawyers. There was no story by Jerry Scovil, nothing at all on the scandalous revelation by the senator's neighbor. McClintoch's assessment might be right after all: Poppy's final shot hadn't blown us out of the water; maybe Turnbull *had* peaked. I tossed the paper aside, rolled over, and fell into a deep, untroubled sleep.

I managed to pull myself out of bed at nine. While I showered I dripped a quart of strong coffee to go with an English muffin I found in the fridge. It was as dense as a hockey puck. I was scheduled to meet the senator, McClintoch, and a bunch of staff people at a monster rally at noon in the garment district.

Until it was time to leave for that I made myself useful. I called someone I knew at every news organization I could think of and assured them that the Jerry Scovil exclusive they had reported was pure horseshit, a fact that would soon be independently confirmed. I laid the same line on each of them: "You notice there's no Scovil in the *Ledger* today? He's on his way to Nome to interview the dogs in next winter's Iditarod."

All the while, Poppy lingered pleasurably; in my loins, understandably, and (I despised myself for this) in my heart.

Staff work had been good. When I showed up at ten after twelve, a large lunchtime crowd was gathered on Seventh Avenue. They backed up for a satisfying block north and south of a temporary platform on Thirty-eighth Street that was festooned with bunting and banners.

I knew McClintoch would be holding off Beaufoy until the last minute, to reduce the strain on his back. A warm-up speaker, the state party chairman, was more or less holding the crowd's attention with a stem-winder pending the senator's arrival. Behind him, the platform was in disarray as the candidates for lesser offices jockeyed for positions that would make them most accessible to the television cameras.

When Mort did finally show up in a rental limousine (were the police holding his Buick?) he stepped out of it, carefully, and gave his characteristic tight wave, hand close to chest. A warming cheer rolled up and down the avenue.

I was hanging back among the television-remote vans to make nice with the media people, but I watched Mort slowly lead his group, a mixed bag of ethnic movers and shakers, as they threaded their way to the platform. They looked for all the world like a slow freight-train. Every time Mort stopped en route to shake a hand the train would lurch and bump to a halt.

Krista Grolik, the recipient of Mort's desert island fantasy, was stationed near the platform, handing out leaflets with the volunteers. When Mort spotted her he made a short detour to embrace her. Apparently it had been some time since they had seen each other; they were enjoying the impromptu reunion.

The committee didn't make the senator wait. As soon as he mounted the platform, the party chairman put a hasty button on his speech and introduced the candidate. He was met with thunderous applause. He looked out over the sea of bobbing heads, beaming, then stopped the applause with hand gestures. To make sure it wasn't renewed he leaned in to the mike and began speaking.

The crowd had energized him. He seemed younger up there on the platform, almost spry. His voice had a sparkle to it.

"You've probably heard some rumors about my health," he said. "Well, here I am." There was brisk applause. "If I felt any better I'd have to be checked for substance abuse." This brought a ripple of laughter and more applause. He cut it short with, "Most of you are on your lunch break, and good representation in Washington may not be your most pressing hunger at the moment. So let's get to the meat."

He was off and running. And in rare form. He spoke to them as one intelligent adult to another, and they listened with respect. He talked about the state of the world, the state of the economy, and what people of goodwill might do about both. He talked about health care reform and his ideas for attracting new business to the state. He made no promises, and he never mentioned his opponent. He didn't ask for the vote of those present, only for their thoughtful consideration of the matters he discussed. I was reminded, after all that had happened these past few days, of why I had always been drawn to him as a politician.

The crowd took it all in. There was almost no restless shuffling. He had them. It was a superb performance. No, "performance" was the wrong word. It was a superb display of character.

And he did it in well under twenty minutes. By then I could tell by the way he used the lectern to take pressure off his back that he was beginning to tire, so I was relieved to hear him launch what sounded like a wrap. I guessed that he would be off in another two minutes.

And right about then some milling and jostling began halfway back in the crowd, both to the north and the south. Seconds later huge banners suddenly unfurled, a man at each end holding them aloft with a pole and snapping them taut. The TV crews swung their cameras to catch the messages: MORT—GET YOUR HOUSE IN ORDER; THANK GOD THE DEAD DON'T VOTE; SOMETHING'S ROTTEN IN THE STATE OF NEW YORK; and SHAME, SHAME, SHAME.

Bystanders and Beaufoy volunteers sprang to action, angrily wrestling the banners away from those who held them. The banners were all soon down and being trampled underfoot. But not soon enough. The cameras had zoomed in on the banners and so had the senator. For an instant his head dropped to his chest and he sagged against the lectern as though his knees had buckled. For that instant he was a hundred years old.

He rallied quickly and pulled himself erect, but in the effort he lost his train of thought. I had hoped he would dismiss the disturbance with his usual tart wit. It didn't happen. When he found his voice, it held a telltale tremble. He said, "That wasn't necessary. Not at all. None of that was part of civilized discourse. I think enough has been said here today. And done here. I won't keep you. Thank you for listening, thank you for coming, thank you for voting next Tuesday."

The crowd wasn't prepared for that abrupt finish. The applause was sporadic, uncertain. The senator turned carefully from the lectern, still holding it with one hand, waving gamely with the other. When he felt himself steady he gestured well-meaning aides to stand back, and walked unassisted off the platform toward the waiting car. En route, volunteers shook his hand and spoke words of encouragement. The faithful Krista Grolik, too far back to reach him, waved and blew a kiss. She was smiling, but her eyes glistened with tears.

The schedule called for me to ride up to the Waldorf with Mort for a press conference. Two cops cleared a path for me and I pushed through to the limo. I heaved myself in the open door and sat down beside the candidate. He was ash gray and almost catatonic.

That bitch Hancock.

It was shortly after one P.M. when we reached the hotel. Mort's press conference, his first since well before he went into the hospital, was scheduled for two. There was every expectation that it would be brutal. The purpose of this gap in the schedule was to give the candidate an hour to lie down and relieve the pressure on his back before he met the media. With that objective a small guest room had been reserved a few floors above the, I think, Marie Antoinette Suite. Maybe that wasn't its exact name, but it was the room where the beheading was to take place.

Mort had been dead silent on the drive uptown, and he was dead silent on the elevator ride that he and I took alone to the eighth floor. Not until he was safely in the room and stretched out on the single bed, and I had dragged over the one easily moveable chair and sat next to him, did he finally allow himself a single, "Jesus."

"Your back must be killing you," I offered supportively.

"My back, dear boy, is the least of it. I have had a relatively easy time in public life. And I've been in seclusion so long of late, I've forgotten what's out there. I suppose I can expect more of what I was just exposed to."

"It will get worse. Yes, you've been in an isolation chamber. Welcome back to the wonderful world of politics."

"Politics? In my tame political past I have accepted being called a liar, a buffoon, an incompetent, and a horse's ass." He shuddered. "But this . . . This . . ."

"Wait'll the boys and girls downstairs get hold of you." He had better understand what lay ahead.

Mournfully he said, "I thought you had found a way to shut off the most vicious ad hominem attacks."

"So did I. It may take somewhat longer to turn things around."

"Surely there's something we can do right now to ease the pressure."

"Yeah. We can come up with Sheri Bannerman's murderer."

He sighed. "Every so often I find myself yearning for the university life. Backbiting as that can be."

He had never seemed so vulnerable. Was there a way to leverage that to our advantage? "About finding that killer," I prodded. "The police are stalled. They need a fresh lead, something to shake them off dead center. It will have to come from a new direction."

I waited, but he didn't take the bait. When he finally spoke, it was to say, "I'm going to try to catch a few minutes' sleep."

I felt let down. "Good," I said, "so am I. I had a lousy night." Poppy suddenly loomed large in my thoughts. My mouth tasted of ashes.

I draped myself across the abbreviated couch on the other side of the room. There was no way I was going to fall asleep—any more, I was sure, than Mort. Both our minds were on over-drive. If there had ever been a chance to open a crack in Mort's dubious account of the morning of Sheri's murder and reach in to the truth, this was it. I ran my mind over everything I had poked my nose into these past three days. Had I learned anything I could use against Mort in his present unguarded state?

One possibility presented itself. I came back to the odd disclosure that had lain undigested in my gut since yesterday: Hal Vector, the bleached-out accountant, as Sheri's secret lover. They were about as unlikely a couple as I could imagine.

Something had been going on between them—Vector's guilty reaction when I found him made that clear. I'd backed him into a corner with what I knew and he'd been obliged to make some sort of shameful admission. Among the choices open to him, did he pick not the truth but the lie that best preserved his dignity?

If he did, I would have to face up to an assessment of Sheri I'd avoided making before because of Mort. Did I have the guts to confront him with it now?

I called softly, "Mort, you awake?"

"Of course I'm awake."

I swung my feet to the floor, crossed the room, and sat again in the chair beside the bed, like a doctor on a house call. It was now or never.

"Mort, I've been meaning to ask." I was careful not to make it sound like an accusation or a judgment. "Was Sheri Bannerman a hooker?"

"A hooker?" It was another word he spoke as if for the first time.

"A call girl, if you prefer. I'm asking if she was selling you an apartment or renting you her body."

"What would make you ask that?" He continued to lie flat on the bedspread. His voice was calm enough, but muscles were working in his face.

I said, "She was making a lot of money—too much to come

from real estate. From what I saw of her I don't doubt she could command high prices for sex. The day before she came to your apartment you had a loud argument with Mrs. Beaufoy. You were practically flat on your back, but you were packing her off to Washington. She may have wondered why."

He took a moment. Quietly he said, "Sheri Bannerman did sell real estate, you know."

"That too. But you don't really need any, do you?"

"John, you are trying to knit a garment out of a very small ball of yarn."

"Try this on. I met a man yesterday, an accountant who lives up your way. My guess is, he's one of Sheri's regular clients. If the police get to him—and they will in the next day or two—that fact will come out."

I leaned closer. "And once the cops have one client, once they establish what Sheri was into, they'll start building a list." I let that sink in. "But not if they catch her murderer first. That would end the investigation."

"She came to see me that morning," he said in a small voice. "Does it matter why? The poor woman left my apartment. She was killed elsewhere. What possible help could I be in the solution of her murder?"

"I wish I could tell you. Maybe none. But there's a puzzle here with pieces to be fit together. And you are very possibly holding one of them."

He shifted his body as though to improve his position. It was a stalling tactic. He was preparing himself for confession. I waited.

"I never dreamed there might be anything remotely resembling a 'client list,' " he said plaintively. "She said this was something she did only occasionally, when real estate was soft. I would never have been so indiscreet. So irresponsible." He spat, "So stupid."

The floodgates were opening. I said, "Then it was sex she came to you for."

Small voice. "It's not that simple, John. It was the fantasy. Don't you have fantasies?"

"Everybody has fantasies," I said reassuringly. I thought of Krista Grolik's story. "Some more graphic than others."

He hadn't heard me; his voice overlapped mine. "Those endless weeks at New York Medical," he was mumbling. "Immobile much of the time, a prisoner of that hospital bed."

His voice remained small; he was looking at the ceiling, telling it more to himself than to me. "The hospital was my world. I inhaled them when they leaned over me to adjust the pillows or fix the bed covers. I heard their clothing rustle as they went by in the hall."

Had I lost the thread of his narrative? I said, "Hold it. Are you talking about the nurses?"

He was still in a more or less private place. He said, "Their laughter—wicked laughter, it seemed to me—floated to me from the nurses' station. But mostly I was drawn to the uniforms—white, virginal. They beckoned—mockingly, in my view. Yes, the nurses. Forbidden fruit."

He turned to look at me now; he was back at the Waldorf. "In my drugged and weakened condition, that made them seem double-charged sexually. Dear boy, how much of my view came from medication, how much from my pain and imprisonment, I can't say. But, yes, I was in something of a state."

I thought of the nurses I had seen when I covered stories in hospitals. They wore white, usually, but it was often pants and loose shirts. No great turn-on.

I said, "And that's how your nurses at New York Medical dressed, in traditional white uniforms?"

"Not often enough, sad to say. And never that wisp of a white cap I remembered from my youth, perched just so on the head. Informality has made regrettable inroads. But that's how I saw them in my mind's eye. In my fantasy."

He turned from me to the window that looked out on Park Avenue. "And that is what I asked of Sheri. I wanted the

★ 241 ★

idea—in the Greek sense of the word—of the nurse. Immaculate white uniform, crisp cap, white stockings and shoes."

"And carrying the little black bag doctors use—used?—on house calls?" Now I knew the smell I hadn't recognized when the super showed me the bag; it was the smell of new.

"That's very good, John. How did you guess? The picture-perfect visiting nurse."

"And Sheri went along with all of it?"

"Except for the stockings. She said they'd be too time-consuming, since she would be changing in her car."

"Why not in your apartment?"

"The illusion wouldn't work for me unless when I opened my front door I saw the finished nurse standing there. Respectable. Inviolable.

"Sheri understood. 'It's a good part,' she told me, a challenge to her as an actress. She was eager to play it. Did you know that her ambition had been for a stage career? I gathered that her success had been somewhat limited, but she rose to this single occasion. Most admirably. She had shopped carefully to create the character—'Nurse Bannerman,' her one shot at a leading role, I suppose—and she dressed nearly to perfection. During the visit, unfortunately, the little cap fell off. It seemed hard to keep secured."

No doubt; those caps weren't designed for acrobatics. I said, "She left the cap behind, didn't she?" I had suddenly remembered the strangely creased linen napkin Mort fumbled with when I first went to his apartment that day.

"Again, very good, John." His embarrassment at having to describe the escapade was easing; maybe because I seemed to be taking it as no big deal. "I didn't see the cap until you rang my doorbell. What could I do then? In my embarrassment I hastily deconstructed it—it was all tucks and folds—and treated it as a crumpled accessory to my coffee service."

I said, "Sheri, her costume, the house call—the adventure must have set you back."

He nodded. "I respected her for knowing her worth. She was well beyond my means, but worth every penny. That hour was a once in a lifetime peccadillo. Now there's a word I've always wanted to be associated with."

"You'd never before . . . ?"

"Cheated? Never. Fantasized? Often. It was in the hospital that I came to believe it was time to act on one. If not then, never. And it would have been never if a party stalwart who paid a call on me there hadn't left me Sheri's business card. She visited the next day, we laid out the ground rules, and I paid her considerable fee in full. At the time, my wife was out on errands." He added thoughtfully, "They may have passed in the corridor when Sheri left."

"That wouldn't have been good."

"I'll never know for certain. . . ." He banished the thought and said, "If not for the tragic, unrelated, and unpredictable aftermath, the Nurse Sheri experience would have been one to warm the rapidly cooling bones of my declining years."

He seemed loose enough now for me to ask: "With your back, Mort, how were you able to manage . . . ?"

He looked dismayed. "Dear boy, you misunderstand. There was no actual . . . coupling. Not only my back, but my scruples, strange as they may seem, prevented that. What transpired was some imaginative game-playing. Certain liberties were taken, yes. The forbidden fruit was nibbled. One or two minor transgressions occurred. That was the sum of it."

"And she left you as she had arrived? Dressed as a nurse?"

"Yes. That is why when you told me hours later there was a dead woman in my car who was wearing a green dress I didn't relate it to Sheri. I never saw her in a green dress. She must have changed down in the garage. Only to be stabbed."

Was that the sequence of events? Not likely. I didn't need to remind myself that the knife hadn't penetrated that green dress. But this was not the time to work on that puzzle. Or to make moral judgments. I had a candidate to prepare for a meeting with the press.

On a radar screen that registers illicit sexual traffic by politicians, Mort's lone "peccadillo" would have been a barely discernible blip. But that blip would still be enough, if detected by an adversarial press, to outweigh all the graft, corruption, incompetence, and old-fashioned avarice of Herbert Turnbull, and tilt the election in his direction. Welcome to the wonderful world of politics.

"We've got about half an hour," I said. "We'd better go over what you're going to say to the vultures downstairs."

He said, "John, you just pulled a painful confession out of me with the excuse that it would help resolve this mess. Will it? Does it do us any good?"

"First things first," I said. "But I think it may."

The press conference ended in a draw. Mort scored high when he was able to point to his record, outline some proposals for the year or two ahead, and gently remind those present of the clout his eighteen years in the Senate gave the state. He won grudging respect for his continued refusal to get down in the mud with his opponent. And he was given another big plus: Jerry Scovil was not in attendance.

He broke even on the question of his health. He was here, wasn't he? And he demonstrated with every answer that he was mentally sharp. But after half an hour he was starting to look like a coon hound at the end of a long night's hunt. The cameras were no doubt picking that up, and the pictures on tonight's news broadcasts would show it. He assured the gathering often enough—too often?—that he was on the mend. Probably half of them believed it.

Where he did less than break even was on the key issue of Sheri Bannerman, his relationship with her and questions about her unsolved murder. Mort stuck to his original story: he knew Ms. Bannerman only as a real estate salesperson; everything pertaining to her tragic death was as much a mystery to him as it was to them. He made sure to stress that there was not a word of truth in a published report of a passionate argument between him and the deceased. He noted that the author of that article was not among those present.

But the Sheri questions were relentless and often cruel; some of them were asked two or three times in slightly different forms. Overall, Mort was no more than moderately convincing on Sheri. Raging anger should have been his response to some of the pushier questions. He addressed them all with the same statesmanlike calm.

The final question of the session was especially nasty, and it brought the meeting to a dark close. Someone asked if the senator would comment on a rumor widely circulating— several of those present had heard it—that the police were ready to make an arrest in the Bannerman murder but were holding off until after the primary.

"Why would they do that?" Mort asked in all innocence.

"I don't know, Senator," replied the questioner, a newsmagazine man. "The theory is, they don't want to make a move that could affect the outcome of the election. Do you have a take on that?"

Mort's mouth was tight. "I'm not going to speculate on what goes on in the minds of the police." And then, "People, I'd like to stay longer, but you'll have to excuse me. My trainers are signaling that I've got to run. It's a big state and I still have miles to cover. Thank you all for coming."

Ignoring a volley of shouted questions, he turned and marched out of the room through a door conveniently near his back. He left hanging in the air this sour aroma: the arrest that would most affect the election would be Morton Beaufoy's.

McClintoch had shown up to accompany the senator to

21 I weighed various strategies on the drive to Yonkers. I decided finally to leave Oliver's jacket in the car. I was looking for dialogue, not confrontation.

I had arrived once again near quitting time at Clifton Oliver Realty and I walked in on the usual end-of-the-day bustle. The redhead, Diane, wearing a pleated miniskirt and looking, as usual, very good, glanced up from locking her desk to flash a warm smile and a "Hi." One of the other saleswomen brushed quickly past me on her way out the door. Others were on the phone or hastily finishing paperwork.

Jared Phillips was hanging up his phone. When he saw me he masked a *You again?* look and nodded a cool greeting. He glanced at his phone console and said, "Cliff's on the phone. Anything I can do for you?"

"I think not. I can wait."

He yanked his ponytail and shot me an appraising look. "You're not really house hunting, are you?"

"What makes you say that?"

"I'm not sure. . . . But I'm right, right?"

"Don't I fit the profile of the home buyer?"

"Maybe that's it."

I pressed. "You wouldn't take me for the father of two and a third children?"

He said pleasantly, "Actually . . . no. Or likely ever will be." That gave me a chill. He glanced at his phone console. "He's off now."

Cliff Oliver was in country squire dress today, an elbow-patched houndstooth check jacket and a carelessly knotted silk scarf tucked into a body-hugging shirt. That was as far down as I could see; he didn't bother to stand up behind his desk.

I said, "If you have a minute, Cliff, I may have some news for you."

"A minute's about it," he said; he was not happy to see me again and he was not going to hide it. "I've got to pick up Kelly and my wife. Somewhere a caterer is waiting."

"Your daughter's wedding. That's moving right along, is it?" Let's get that out of the way.

"A hundred and ninety people. For a sitdown dinner in a goddam tent. Did you know it is cheaper to buy a restaurant than to host a sitdown dinner in a rented tent on your own lawn?" He didn't wait for an answer. "What is this news you have for me, Mr. Caprisi?" I was no longer Jock.

I closed the door and pulled up a chair opposite his desk. I was going to take more than a minute of his time. "Are you missing a tweed jacket?"

He turned the color of tile grout. "I've been looking for that jacket for two days." He decided anger was the way to go. "What the hell is going on? Do you have the jacket?"

"I do."

"Where did you get it?" By now a new color, dangerously close to eggplant, was flooding his face. "You've got a goddam nerve. You must have removed it from these premises."

"Take it easy, Cliff. I wouldn't make accusations against someone who rescued what appears to be a very good jacket."

I let that sink in before I went on. "Last time I left here I happened to glance into your alley on my way to my car and I saw this perfectly good jacket draped across a trash can." His eyes were attempting to bore holes in me. "At that moment a homeless man walking by scooped it up and put it on."

He looked more relieved than dismayed. He said, "Didn't you just say you had the jacket?"

"Will you wait a second? A moment later I thought, Hold on, that jacket matches the tweed trousers and vest Cliff Oliver was wearing the day we met. Maybe it blew out of that open window on the second floor; I'd better check with Cliff. So I bought it back from the old guy."

"Am I supposed to believe that?"

"Believe what you want. I can find the homeless man if you'd like to ask him yourself."

Oliver was rubbing an elbow patch with one hand; the other was half buried in the guardsman mustache. While he was composing a reply his phone rang. He let it ring.

I said, "Aren't you going to answer that?"

He said, "The machine will take it."

"That happened once before when I was here," I said. "The phone rang and you didn't pick up. You said something like 'Office hours are over. Let the machine take it.' That was the first time I ever saw a salesman refuse to take a call. How did you know it wasn't a customer for a million-dollar home?"

He planted his elbow patches on the desk and leaned over it toward me for emphasis. He made no effort to hide his irritation. He said, "There aren't many million-dollar customers these days, Caprisi. And the serious ones leave their names."

"Or they move on to a broker who answers his phone. No, here's my guess. That answering machine is on a separate line from your listed office number. If I check the phones out front I won't see any blinking lights. Will I?"

"It's a separate line. So what? If you don't tell me pretty damn quick what you're getting at . . ." He hadn't thought ahead to an appropriate threat, and the sentence trailed off.

I said, "I'm sure a few honest-to-God home buyers stumble on this number." I had his full attention and I took my shot. "But if the caller asks for a 'special' appointment with Sheri— or, I don't know, Diane?—I bet you can arrange a booking."

"Who told you that?" The bluster was gone and now his sagging face betrayed him. The big mustache was starting to look like a bad day in the rain forest.

"It doesn't matter who told me. I should have guessed myself last time I was here and ran into Diane in her Victoria's Secret undies. Hell of a gift wrap. I thought she was dressing to meet her husband, but now I know. Those were her working clothes."

He was back to stroking elbow patches, both of them now. And surveying me shrewdly. "What is your interest in all this, Caprisi? Why do you care?" He had given up the idea of bluff; his object now was damage control. "Are you doing research for an article?"

"I work for the senator. An article that mentioned your sideline would do him about as much good as it would you. There'll be no article, believe me. But for reasons of my own I've got to know the truth."

I waited while he figured out I was right about the negative value of publicity to Beaufoy's interests.

When he spoke, it was with quiet intensity. "You have to understand that everybody in this office sells real estate. And most of the staff are totally straight."

We were making progress. "How many aren't?"

"Three, besides Sheri. One she recruited. One I found. Diane was here." The silk scarf had worked its way out of his shirt in a kind of protest. It was billowing against his chin. While he tucked it back in he launched his apologia.

"Do you know what it's like for a woman in this field? Driving horny men from property to property while she puts up with a barrage of sexual innuendo? Sheri found a way to turn that on its head. The transition was entirely her idea, logical and maybe inevitable. Her income from real estate had dropped, and her husband's business was nearly down the tubes. One of them had to bring in some money."

"Why not him?"

"Bryce is a weak sister. They were a team—maybe out of habit, who knows about marriages?—but Sheri knew she had to be the rainmaker in that family. Why not? There've got to be a few wives in every big city who sweeten the family pot with a little discreet nine-to-five humping. Do I have to tell you what goes on? Do you see the ads for escort services in the Yellow Pages?

"Sheri and I fine-tuned the concept. A real estate person can go anywhere, no questions asked. And Sheri commanded big bucks. Deservedly."

His take on the setup was making him almost smug. I needed him back on the defensive. "And what was your cut for pimping—sorry, booking—this daylight recreation?"

Good, he didn't like that. But he rallied well enough. "Come see me when you're not making the nut and your expenses are mounting," he flashed. "When you've got a wife who practically lives at the club, and subsidizes a hairdresser to the stars. A horse that eats whether your daughter rides him or not. A sitdown dinner for nearly two hundred ravenous freeloaders."

He caught my look. "Basically all I did was help Sheri, Diane, and the others through a rough time in the home resale market. Yes, there was something in it for me—just enough to make up the shortfall in running this company. Without it, Clifton Oliver Realty and its nine employees would have gone belly up."

"Good for you, Cliff," I said. He had me close to alligator tears. Thank God for a free market economy: If your business is failing, find another; keep your staff working, even if it's on their backs.

My tone hadn't escaped him. But he was more confident

now; he saw himself as almost home free. "As for Sheri's murder," he said, "because that's where I think you're at—believe me, I'm as much in the dark as anyone. I came clean about what we do here, our little sideline. It's no big deal. Maybe I need a license, maybe I owe a fine. I don't know. But going public would hurt my daughter, kill my wife."

He laid it in. "And of course the senator. Maybe the senator would be hardest hit." He flashed his salesman's smile. "So back off, okay?"

"You did come clean, and I appreciate that." It was time I dropped the other shoe. "But Cliff, not entirely clean. Not French-dry-cleaner clean."

"What's that supposed to mean?" A manicured hand sprang to his mustache. His security blanket.

"Your tweed jacket? I felt bad about what happened to it. The trash can had messed it up and the homeless guy didn't help. I wanted to bring it back looking fresh, but today's dry cleaning prices are highway robbery."

He was staring again, wary of what was coming. The big nose seemed alive.

"There's a lab on the East Side we used once at the paper. The technicians are good, and they owed me a favor. I asked them to take out the stains."

I let that sink in before I hit him with, "They were surprised by what they discovered on the right elbow."

Oliver found his voice. "What the hell is this? What are you talking about? There wasn't a damn thing on the right elbow."

"Why do you say that? Because you washed it thoroughly, maybe compulsively? News flash, Cliff." And now for the Big Lie. "Blood holds on to the tight weave of British tweed. It clings like a drowning man to a life raft."

He should have known all along this was coming, but he looked as if he had been poleaxed.

I said, "Sorry, pal, there it is."

His fingers were exploring unknown territory in the mustache.

I said, "Listen, Cliff, you're in luck. So far this is all between you and me. If the police had the jacket they'd be running a DNA match with Sheri's blood."

"Jesus," he croaked. "Jesus."

He was on his feet, but not steady on them. He considered sitting again, but remained standing. At last he breathed, "I knew I shouldn't have done it."

My heart leaped. Was this Bingo? "Killed her . . . ?" I encouraged.

"For Chrissake, no! I didn't kill her. *I shouldn't have gone there.*"

It wasn't Bingo, but it was a giant step forward. I said, "Steady, Cliff. All in all, you'll do better sitting down."

He nodded, and I waited while he groped his way to his chair and fell into it heavily.

I said, "Okay, you mean the garage, right? At the senator's building? That's where you went, isn't it?"

He nodded.

"When you get hold of yourself you can tell me why."

He was hyperventilating and he took a few steadying breaths before he spoke. "She called me. On her cellular phone. I knew something was wrong as soon as I heard her voice—it was weak, gasping. All I could make out was, she was in Beaufoy's garage, hurt real bad. She scared the shit out of me. I jumped in my car. I was there in ten minutes."

By now he was weeping softly—real tears that didn't go with the guardsman mustache or the elbow patches. "I loved that girl. She had . . . I don't know, something. She lit up the room. She was the daughter I never had." He blurted it out. "Instead of the one I did."

He brushed the tears away with both hands. "I found her on the floor at the back of the garage . . . dead. She . . .

she looked awful. Crumpled in a heap, smaller than life. The blood . . ." He couldn't go on.

I tried to ease him forward. "It must have made a mess of her nurse's uniform."

His eyes widened. "You know about that? The uniform?"

He had been blocking out the image; now it came vividly alive to flood his consciousness. The horror showed on his face.

I could guess where the story was going; I would have to lead him through it.

I said, "Clifton Oliver Realty could have ridden out the death of a sales agent. She'd have been one more crime statistic in a violent city. But when your dead employee is dressed like a nurse? There'd be questions, a ton of questions. Followed by scandal. The country club . . ."

"My wife," he whispered.

Moving right along I said, "So you stripped off the uniform and the white shoes . . ."

He was finally ready to take over the narration. "I . . . I used the white dress to mop up the blood the best I could. I can't tell you how awful . . ." He stopped to shudder. "I took her car keys from her purse and opened the trunk. I figured her street clothes would be there and they were, in her dispatch case. I took out her dress and shoes and put the bloody things in the case."

He began hurrying his words; he was anxious to get through the ordeal. "I was afraid someone might come into the garage, and I needed concealment to finish what I had to do.

"I . . . my God, I carried the poor girl to her car. But that ridiculous sports car was so small I wouldn't have been able to maneuver in it to dress her. There was a larger car nearby."

"A Buick."

"Was it? I put her in the back seat and managed to get her dress back on. It wasn't easy. Especially avoiding the blood." Another shudder. "The shoes I couldn't do. Maybe I didn't try hard enough. Did it matter? I used the tissues in her purse to wipe every place I thought I'd left fingerprints. And then I got out of there."

"You stayed remarkably cool." I was thinking especially of his call to Sheri's cellular phone after his visit with her body. "Tell me, what did you do with Sheri's dispatch case with the bloody nurse's uniform?"

"What could I do? I brought it back here. It's upstairs in the room where I hung the jacket. Under a pile of junk."

"You didn't take the little black doctor's bag that was part of the nurse's outfit. Why not?"

"A doctor's bag? If there was one I never saw it."

That was the last question I could think of. And, just possibly, I already had the information I needed.

Oliver looked thoroughly wrung out. It wouldn't have surprised me to see the patches curl off his elbows.

I said, "You're going to be late for the caterer."

En route from Yonkers to Riverdale I picked up the tag end of a Herbert Turnbull commercial. I punched up another station and caught the same spot from near the beginning. The opposition was on a saturation campaign, blanketing the airwaves, and this was a prime hour for radio—drive time. Turnbull could only buy it up if the money was rolling in. The fat cats always smell a winner.

The spot may have been recorded that very morning. I came in on Turnbull's weasely voice: ". . . sincerely hope no one intends to vote for me because my opponent appears to have been involved—although I doubt as a principal—in a sordid, cold-blooded murder. The issue is not his possible connection with this loathsome crime. That is a matter for the police and the courts. The issue is simply, which of us is better qualified to represent the people of New York in the—"

I punched it off. The bastard. And that bitch.

22 The super, LaPierre, was standing outside the lobby of Mort's building with the doorman of the adjoining building, another Haitian. They were commenting with amusement on a couple of Dalmatians draped in sandwich boards who were ambling back and forth across the entrance in the gathering dusk.

La Pierre was unimpressed. After he greeted me he said, "If this matter concerned my people I could have a thousand Haitians here in an hour." The doorman nodded vigorous agreement.

The super drew me aside. "Senator Beaufoy did not look well when he returned from the city," he said. "His companion had to assist him to the elevator. I think he is sadly troubled that the death of the young woman is not yet solved." The unspoken question hung in the air.

"Soon, Mr. LaPierre. Very soon now." I could feel the tension building in me. Pre-show jitters.

The elevator was a long time coming. This was the hour the building's residents came home from work, and I could hear the car making stops all the way to the highest floors. When it returned it slid past the lobby on its way to make a pickup at the garage level. A minute later the door opened to reveal Ms. Kleiman. The thick clutch of cheery yellow chrysanthemums she held, probably excess inventory, made her look even gloomier than usual.

I nodded a greeting as I stepped into the car. "Mums," I said. "Can football be far behind?"

She pressed the Door Close button. "To me, mums are the first sign of the death of the year." Ms. Kleiman was straight out of Chekhov, a character in mourning for her life.

We rode in silence until the car bumped to a stop at five. "Do you have a minute?" I said.

"What about?"

"You may be able to help me. I was hoping I might catch you." That was true; my timing was perfect.

The car door had opened and we stepped out. Ms. Kleiman fished for her keys, somehow maintaining control over the shapeless mass of long-stemmed mums. "Help you how?"

"I'm not sure. But I think of you as the eyes and ears of this building."

"That's not so. I pay as little attention as possible."

"Still . . ."

She was opening her door, and her sad, bony face registered a grudging decision in my favor. "A minute," she said. "While I get these in water."

In the apartment she gestured to me to sit down. She walked back to the open kitchen and I sank back against the cushions of her convertible couch.

While she shed a sweater and unwrapped the mums I said, "You were good enough to clear up the misinformation about that supposed argument between the senator and the Bannerman woman the day she was killed. You let me know there was none. But I was wondering if you *did* see or hear anything out of the ordinary in the building that morning."

She had taken a large vase from a cabinet under the sink, and now she turned on the water full force. She started to roll up the sleeves of her blouse, then changed her mind.

"Mr. Caprisi," she called back to me over the sound of the water as she rinsed the vase and began to fill it, "I've been over all that with the police. Twice. I really have nothing more to add."

I hated going through this without her full attention, but I would have to make do. I said, "I believe there's something you didn't tell the police."

"I can't imagine," she said.

The Big Lie had worked once today; I was almost certain it would again. I launched it. "It's something I learned from the senator."

"What in the world would that be?" She had turned off the water. She was cutting the stems two or three at a time with a pair of shears and plunging the mums into the vase. "I can't even guess what you're talking about." Her voice had gone shrill.

Damn, I wished she would turn and face me. But then, maybe it was better that she wasn't looking at me while I ran my bluff. I took my carefully reasoned guess: "The senator said you met a woman who was on her way to see him."

"That morning . . . ?" The words floated vaguely from her.

"A nurse. White uniform, white cap, little black doctor's bag? She told him she ran into a neighbor. You were the only neighbor at home. Surely you remember. Or was the senator making that up?"

She carried the vase to the dining table. I saw now why she had brought the mums home. They were past their peak, beginning to droop. Unsalable. She set them down and sat in a chair near me. Thank God I had gotten past the lie.

Slowly, testing the words, she said, "Was that stupid of me? Forgetting that nurse? It didn't seem much at the time. . . ."

"Yes . . . ?"

"Oh, dear. Is this something I should have told the police?"

"I don't know. At the moment it's still something between you and me."

Now almost gingerly, "I suppose the senator told you . . . ?" When I didn't respond, she went on, ". . . whatever it was the woman told him . . . ?"

Good; she hadn't stopped to consider that possibly the senator had told me nothing. Cagily I said, "I'd like to hear it from you."

Still slowly, and now softly, "It was nothing more than what you might imagine. I was about to go down for the mail. The elevator opened and this nurse stepped out. I was a bit startled, is all. And, naturally, concerned."

"Because . . ."

"I knew the senator was just out of the hospital." She was gaining confidence; her voice was stronger, less tentative. "I was concerned that he'd had some sort of relapse. I know that back problems can be terribly painful."

"You and the nurse exchanged a few words." Had they? Since I had no idea I kept the tone vague, somewhere between a statement and a question.

"Did we?" She searched my face to see what I knew. "Not many. I asked if she was on her way to see the senator and was he all right, and she said—I remember now—yes, he was, but she was going to try to make him a little more comfortable. And please not to mention it to his wife, as he didn't want to worry her. That was all there was. She seemed in a hurry and I got in the elevator. Hardly a memorable encounter. I suppose she was going to give him some sort of physical therapy."

I said, "Or possibly a shot of morphine?"

"Why that?"

"For the pain. Physical therapy wouldn't have worried his wife."

"I suppose. Does it matter?" She stood up. "I hate to be rude, Mr. Caprisi, but I have things to do. . . ."

I got to my feet. "Of course. I'm sorry." It was now or possibly never. "And that was the last you saw of the nurse?" I started walking very slowly toward the door.

Ms. Kleiman was opening it to ease my way out. "Yes. Here in the corridor."

"Because when I saw you in the garage the day of the murder"—I stopped walking. "Do you remember?"

"Very little of what went on down there. I was terribly upset. Distraught."

"Yes. You and I talked about that. How you kept babbling about the dead woman in the green dress. That green dress."

"Did I? Yes, I do remember. I've blocked out most of that awful morning." She slowly closed the door.

I said, "At the time I didn't understand why you were obsessed by that green dress. Neither did you. Now I know."

I waited for her to ask, but she didn't. She looked at me steadily, the line of her bony jaw sharper than ever.

I said, "You didn't expect to see that dress on the dead woman when you came down to the garage for your car. Because she was wearing the white nurse's uniform when you stuck the knife in her two hours earlier."

She blinked, once, but she stood her ground and her voice was steady, and dry as dust. "Where on earth did you get such an idea? Why would I do something so hideous? What reason could I possibly have?" And then, with an attempt at passion, "You have no right to talk to me that way. Please get out of this apartment." But she didn't move to open the door again.

I pushed on. "Ms. Kleiman, you were so shaken up that day by the body in the green dress, I failed to notice you were also totally strung out—badly in need of a fix."

"What do you mean? I was upset."

"You were wired. Do you remember how you drove, leaving the garage? Wildly. Out of control. Your tires squealed and you scraped the walls of the ramp. You were desperate to make a score. And somebody—Felix Pacheco?—must have steered you to a new connection, because the next day you were nicely calmed down. Civilized."

The mention of Felix had widened her eyes for an instant, but she said steadily, "Is that what you think? You think I'm a drug user?"

"I know you are. Maybe back in your flower child years a recreational one, but you're an addict now."

She started to protest again but I rode over her. "Yes, you're steady, functioning, reliable. So long as you're supplied. I don't know what you're on, Ms. Kleiman, and it doesn't much matter."

I tried not to sound judgmental but I had to break down her protective wall. "I'd guess you've been through all the pills, and most of the permutations of heroin and cocaine. You've probably inhaled, ingested, and injected. A couple of minutes ago at the sink you started to roll up your sleeves. And then you stopped. A guilty reflex from a time when you had needle tracks? For all I know you have them now."

Without realizing she was doing it, she folded her arms. And as I spoke I could see her begin to fade like her over-the-hill mums.

I felt for her—a ninety-five-pound bundle of chronic unhappiness. I said, "I'm talking serious, longtime drug use. What happened, Ms. Kleiman? Life must have done you a really dirty deed."

"If it did, so what?" The words came from a black well. "In the end doesn't it do it to everyone? We'd all be addicts. You're making that up about me."

"Am I? You want me to ask my friend Felix, the drug retailer for this neighborhood? He's been off Rikers Island for a few days. But you must know that."

This time she was prepared for Felix's name, and her face didn't give her away. She said, "What are you getting at? That woman's death had nothing to do with drugs. Does it matter whether I use them or not?" But her voice told me she knew where I was headed.

"Yes, it does." I waited, hopefully. "Do I have to spell it out? Or will you do it for me?"

She still said nothing, but now her wafer-thin lower lip began to tremble. She bit down in an effort to still it. I wanted to fold my arms around that thin body and comfort her.

Gently I said, "Why don't you sit down?"

Dutifully, almost trancelike, she moved to the couch and sat. Now her whole body was trembling. Her world, such as it was, was crashing around her. She said, "I . . . I didn't . . . I never . . ." And fell silent.

Were we stalled again? I said, "Can you talk about it?"

She shook her head slowly.

I said, "Suppose I say what I think happened. And any place I go wrong, you just shake your head. Would that be all right?"

She was still too paralyzed to speak. She barely nodded. Knees pressed together, she stared, unseeing.

The words came easily to me. If this had been a story for tomorrow's *Ledger*, the eight hundred words would have scrolled from my computer with barely a pause.

I said, "Felix was in jail for weeks. I can imagine your agony waiting for his release. By the time you ran into the nurse at the elevator that morning you had to be desperate for a fix. While she was in with the senator you screwed up your courage. You waited, and when she left his apartment you confronted her. Here in the hall?"

She hadn't taken her eyes off me. Now she nodded. Slowly, once. Then again, quickly. Good.

"You stopped her in the hall and asked her to sell you morphine, pills, anything. For what? Unbearable chronic pain?"

She whispered, "I said my doctor was away."

"She must have told you she didn't have any drugs. You knew she had to be lying. Why else had she gone to see that pain-racked man down the hall? The more perversely she insisted, the more you begged and pleaded. You accused her of being a liar and a heartless bitch and you demanded what was in the little black bag she carried. I suppose you shouted."

"I didn't dare shout," Ms. Kleiman said, no longer in a whisper. "There was the senator in the apartment at the end of the hall."

"Sorry. Of course. The nurse escaped into the elevator and the door closed on her. By then you were in a blind, strung-out rage. It would have been such a small thing for that woman to give you relief. She was stubbornly, needlessly, cruel. In a panic now, half crazy with pain, you rushed back into your apartment and grabbed—what, a kitchen knife?"

Her eyes slid to the sink, and I said, "The shears? Nod if I'm right, Ms. Kleiman."

She nodded. Very good.

"You followed her down to the garage, caught her at her car. She had her keys out. My guess is, she was about to open the trunk. Your anger was boiling over. You brandished the shears and demanded the drugs. She backed into a far corner of the garage. Maybe she held the little black bag in front of her for protection. Maybe . . ." I was running out of steam. "Help me, Ms. Kleiman."

Thank God she took over. "Not for protection. She said, 'Take the damn bag,' and I thought she was swinging it to hit me. My arm . . . stiffened. I don't know, to ward her off. I never intended . . . But she was moving forward. I felt the shears go in." She took a breath. "The next I knew, I was in the elevator clutching the black bag, and the bloody shears were gathered up in my skirt."

She was shaking again, trying hard to cry and failing. Again I wanted to fold a comforting arm around her, but her body language told me that wasn't what she wanted. When she had gained control of herself she said, "I was out of my head. I wanted to scare her, yes, but I never meant the shears to touch her. I never meant to hurt her."

At last her tears came. She cried out, "And the bag? When I opened the black bag, it was empty." Her voice grew fierce with the injustice of it. "Completely empty!"

I had found Sheri Bannerman's murderer and established Mort Beaufoy's innocence, but at what price? As soon as Ms. Kleiman told her story to the police, the scandal of "The Senator and the 'Nurse' " would unfold in all its embarrassing detail and that would be the end of Mort Beaufoy. I had won a Pyrrhic victory.

If she held back on her confession until after next Tuesday, and if Mort should manage to win the primary, there was a slim chance—a *very* slim chance—he could patch up his image enough by the time the general election rolled around, and he could squeak through. A lot of ifs, but I had to root for them. Never mind that Mort was my employer. The choice for the voter was between a brilliant legislator with a not quite pristine record of marital fidelity and a hack politician with no real interest in the national welfare who also happened to be a not quite indictable crook. The faint blemish in Mort Beaufoy's personal life was hardly likely to affect his performance in the Senate. All it could affect was his ability to get elected.

After her confession Ms. Kleiman had collapsed, a despairing mess, into a corner of her couch. She seemed emptied of all emotion as she stared unseeing at her hands lying dead in her lap. I gave her a few minutes. When I saw signs of a return to life I brought her a glass of water and a box of tissues. She took them with a nod of thanks, dabbed at her eyes, then sipped the water slowly. When she had more or less pulled herself together she said, "I suppose you'll go to the police."

I said, "No, my advice is that you do that. If you go to the police yourself, things will go easier for you. Much."

She looked at me for the first time. "Suppose the police never find out . . . ?"

They would find out. Hap Nordstrom might move glacially, but he was thorough. He would piece the story together through Felix Pacheco, Cliff Oliver, Hal Vector—close to the route I had followed. Only slower.

How much could I do for Mort Beaufoy? I said, "The police will find out eventually. But if the truth comes from you first through a good lawyer, you'll have a better chance at a lesser charge. Maybe involuntary manslaughter."

"Prison . . . ?"

"Some, maybe. I don't really know. Why don't you talk to a lawyer?" I owed Mort, I decided, and my fellow citizens, this much: "But you might want to take some time first to think it over."

By some miracle she might take until after the polls closed on Tuesday.

23

I didn't bother to stop when Andres called to me from the desk as I hurried through the Stanley lobby. I didn't want to deal with messages, packages, or small talk. I wanted to get upstairs, fortify myself with a healthy jolt of bourbon, punish myself with a greasy dinner delivered from some brutal neighborhood joint, and pull my muddy suite up over my head until tomorrow morning. It was going to be a long five days until the polls closed on Tuesday.

When I cracked my door I saw a light on inside. Pushed wider it revealed Poppy Hancock. She was tucked up on my couch, very much at home with her shoes kicked off and her skirt hitched high, a pile of newspapers open beside her and a briefcase on the floor at her feet. She was scribbling on a yellow legal pad.

She looked up briefly, said, "Hi, you're early," and presented me again with the top of her curly head as she returned to jotting her note before she lost the thought.

I had a flash recall of those ugly, accusing signs held aloft earlier today on Seventh Avenue, and Mort's stricken look when he saw them. I felt trashed by Poppy's presence. I said, cold as ice, "How the hell did you get in here?"

"The idea came from you," she said mildly. "I'm your sister, remember? Didn't Andres tell you I was here?"

I was in no mood for cute exchanges. I said, "They have strict orders downstairs against exactly this."

She pretended not to notice my anger. "You know I can be persuasive. I'm the woman who last year got three hundred and ten thousand people to vote for a mayor most of them despised."

"Your methods of persuasion," I said, "make my flesh crawl."

She could no longer ignore my attitude. She nodded slowly and said, "I can understand that. And I suppose I respect it. You'll just have to put those feelings aside for the next few hours."

"Like hell I will."

She had pushed the legal pad off her lap and stood up. In her stockinged feet she looked more than ever the high school cheerleader. She would look absolutely right in sneakers, socks, pom-poms, and a pleated skirt that barely covered her crotch. Her body was built for cheerleading and vigorous sex.

She clearly had no intention of putting on her shoes. I said, "Poppy, I want you out of here. Now. Go run your cruddy campaign."

"It's running smoothly at the moment, thank you. Practically on automatic pilot."

"Bully for you."

"Is that what has you pissed? That things are going so well for us? I did have a few loose ends, but I tied them up here while I waited for you to show."

"I hope you found everything you needed."

My withering sarcasm went right by her. "Yes, thanks. Oh. I made a few calls, a couple upstate. I left a twenty next to the phone. If that doesn't cover it—"

"You've got a goddam nerve," I exploded, "after what you pulled today. Showing up here to get laid."

She didn't flinch. "What did you expect, a time-out till after the election? Or did you think we were a one-night stand? You know I don't do casual sex."

"To tell the truth," I partially lied, "I wasn't thinking about us at all. I was focused on my candidate. Making sure I got him the nomination."

Her voice became softer, almost pleasant. "Your working day is over, John. It's okay to get personal now."

Except for the senator and my parents, nobody called me John anymore. No woman since I was seventeen but my mother. The sound sent a low-voltage jolt through me all the way to my toes. When it passed I said, "Sorry. I'm afraid I can't do that with you. Not now. Probably not ever."

"Because Herbert Turnbull is going to whip Mort Beaufoy's ass next Tuesday? Believe me, in fifteen minutes that'll be the farthest thing from either of our minds."

"Don't believe it."

She had ambled close, and her million-dollar smell filled my nostrils. Damned if I was going to give an inch. She placed both her hands on the back of my neck and toyed with my hair. Her warm belly pressed against mine. A flow of alternating current passed back and forth between our bodies. I stared at her stonily.

But only for a minute. The bitch.

The ringing phone roused me from a post-coital twilight doze of surpassing sweetness. I had to disentangle flesh from unyielding flesh to reach the bedside phone. Poppy stirred resentfully as I worked to slide out from under. By the time I picked up she had fallen still again.

It was Hap Nordstrom.

I croaked, "What time is it?"

"Twelve-thirty. I woke you, huh? Sorry. But you'll want to hear what I have."

That brought me fully awake. "Wait. I'm going to the other phone."

I put him on hold and went naked to the living room to pick up. "Okay."

"I've got the office door locked," he said, "but I'm about to head for home, so please don't hold me up with a lot of questions."

He hadn't taken the time to crack wise about disturbing whoever was with me, so I suspected he had something of substance to tell me. His next sentence confirmed that: "As far as you and I are concerned, what I tell you now constitutes payment in full."

"You've made an arrest in the Bannerman case?" God, I hoped not; not yet. This business was going entirely too fast.

"Case closed as of a couple of hours ago."

"So who did it?" I was feeling a little sick.

"I think you met her. I know you did. The senator's neighbor who reported finding the body. Helen Kleiman. Can you believe it?"

She hadn't waited to spill her guts. Now I felt really sick. What was her all-fired hurry?

Gamely I managed, "No. You've got to be kidding. Are you sure?"

"She made a full confession. Called me at seven o'clock as I was leaving the office and poured it all out over the phone. She did the deed, all right. She had a bloody skirt at home and she had the murder weapon, a pair of florist's shears that fit the distinctive shape of the victim's wound."

"You never told me the wound was a 'distinctive shape.'"

"Damn right I didn't."

I couldn't complain that he'd held out on me after the way I'd been less than candid with him these past few days. I saw Mort Beaufoy's campaign crumbling like a sand castle under a thundering wave, but I had to continue my pretense of innocence: "What was it about, Hap? Why did she do it?"

"You have to understand, when she called me she was under heavy sedation. I don't know what she'd taken, but she was slurring her words, she rambled, some of what she said made absolutely no sense. The nearest I could tell, the killing had to do with some kind of misunderstanding over drugs."

What could I say? I said, "The Kleiman woman was into drugs?"

"She was a longtime habitual user. She ran into Bannerman on Monday when she was badly strung out because her supplier was in jail. Felix Pacheco. You want to hear crazy? She insisted that 'that woman' could have 'taken care of her' but refused."

"She thought Sheri was selling drugs?" My voice was dry as dust.

"I never did get that from her in a form I understood. She was having some kind of hallucination. I don't know, maybe she thought wishing Bannerman was a supplier would make it happen."

Grimly I said, "You'll sort it out when Kleiman comes out of her episode."

"Didn't I tell you? Kleiman's dead."

I dared not speak. Good God, could that be true?

Hap said, "You still there?"

"Yes." I was fighting nausea, my head was pounding.

He said, "I didn't know it, but when she phoned me she had already cut her wrists. All the while she was making the confession her life was oozing away. By the time I understood that and we raced out to her place, we had to break down her door. She was lying in a warm bath. She'd been gone ten minutes at most."

In mourning for her life, Ms. Kleiman—Helen Kleiman, to give her the respect of her full name—would mourn no more.

And Mort Beaufoy's reputation was safe.

I said, "Congratulations, Hap. And thank you."

After we rang off I sat numbly in the living room, naked and shivering. It took a while before it dawned on me that I needed warmth. I padded back to the bedroom and crawled into bed, a heat-seeking missile, and locked on to Poppy Hancock's body.

She stirred. "What was that?" she murmured, and pressed closer. "Why did you go into the other room to take that call? Who was it?"

"Nobody important."

"At this hour?" She wriggled free. "At this hour it had to be a woman." She sprang to a sitting position. "Are we going to have a problem?"

"Poppy, there's not a woman in the world who could go one on one with you. It was business. And none of yours."

"But who—?"

"Not now. Maybe in the morning." Why spoil the rest of her night?

Mine, I suddenly realized, was going better than I could have imagined.

Later, a good while later, we lay side by side in another rest-mode, separated only by a film of sweat. I don't know why—it was all chemistry and instinct and zero reason, because I believed I deeply loathed her—but as of that moment I had never felt so attuned to a woman, so sure of where I was, so securely locked on track. It wasn't all sex; the woman's mind held as much interest for me as her body. Ugly as were the uses she had made of it, it was a fascinating mind and I wanted to explore it as I had her body.

After a few moments of thoughtful silence Poppy gave me some hint of a possible confirmation of chemistry and instinct. She brought her mouth to my ear and uttered the first loving sentiment I had ever heard from her. It lifted me on wings of joy and filled me with hope.

She whispered, "I'll deny this if you ever quote me. Herbert Turnbull is truly repulsive. He is a snake totally devoid of morals, and beneath contempt in every imaginable way. I loathe him, and I deeply, deeply regret that he's going to whip the pants off your man on Tuesday."

I kissed her. Rest time was over.

E P I L O G U E

Although I had promised Bryce Bannerman I would be at his wife's funeral that Saturday, I was unable to make it because I had to spend the entire weekend out of town with my candidate. Between Friday night and Sunday we hit Rochester, Syracuse, Binghamton, and a half-dozen other cities upstate. Mort spoke in large halls and small and shook a million hands, give or take a few dozen.

As soon as the senator learned the Bannerman murder had been solved and his name no longer figured in the crime, his bad back took a dramatic turn for the better and he managed to stay fairly steady on his feet during the three days of whirlwind personal appearances.

After he won the primary the following Tuesday—by a comfortable, if not overwhelming, margin—the campaign did take its toll and he suffered a small, physical setback. He passed the next two weeks in bed at his home near Washington, where he declined professional nursing assistance in favor of full-time attendance by Clara Beaufoy.

I sent flowers and a note to the Bannerman funeral, and a week later I got a grateful and gossipy thank-you letter from Bryce. The outpouring of sympathy from many quarters had warmed his heart. Among those who spoke at the service, Sheri's boss, Clifton Oliver, could not have been more lavish in his praise of Sheri's generous nature and her fierce devotion to her work. The artistic director of the downtown theater company Sheri belonged to spoke charitably of her as an actress "tragically cut down before her talent came into flower." Bryce had returned full time to the antiques business, but he was getting along badly with his partner. He was thinking of selling out to Hilly Bailes and seeking new fields to conquer. There was the possibility of a joint venture in a mini-mall with Mac Puller.

I continued to work for Mort Beaufoy through the general election—he won that handily—but I went back to his apartment house in Riverdale only once more. The day after Helen Kleiman's confession and suicide I drove there to pick up the little black doctor's bag I had suggested the super turn over to the police. I told LaPierre I would take care of the bag myself, and I did. Rather than turn it over to Hap Nordstrom, I put it out with the trash Saturday morning at my hotel in Syracuse.

There was no point in giving Hap another loose end to speculate about. Late one night a month or two after closing the case he was going to wake up abruptly—or maybe catch himself in the middle of trying to create life—and wonder once again how come those murderous shears hadn't penetrated the victim's green dress before puncturing her midriff. Fortunately, after a minute or two he was likely to tell himself, The hell with it, why trouble trouble? And go back to whatever he had been doing. Particularly since his work on the Bannerman case had won him a transfer to Manhattan South, less than thirty minutes from home.

The slumlord had grown bored with being a press lord and sold the *Ledger* to a suburban newspaper chain that was at least run by professionals. The new owners made overtures to bring me back to the paper. I declined, having by then signed a contract to write a book on trash journalism. I found I liked working for myself. "The truth shall make you free," and the freedom allowed me to stick closer to the truth.

Jerry Scovil never did apologize in the *Ledger* for his story on the stage-managed audio tape the opposition had suckered him with. The tape was never again mentioned in the *Ledger,* and Scovil's byline didn't appear in the paper for a month. When it did surface, he had lost his column and been reassigned by the new management to reporting on education matters.

Poppy Hancock came out of the campaign with her reputation pretty much intact. While she had failed to make a silk purse out of a sow's ear, she had, one pundit observed, at least managed to fashion Herb Turnbull into a pretty fair plastic pocketbook. Turnbull had given Beaufoy a closer race than anyone had expected at the time he filed, and the pros recognized Hancock's cunning in managing him. In the following months she was eagerly courted by a variety of governors, mayors, congressmen, and wanna-bes who saw election trouble for themselves somewhere down the road.

A few months after the election, while Mort Beaufoy was burnishing his distinguished record in the Senate in what he called his "swan-song term," Herbert Turnbull was indicted by the federal attorney in his jurisdiction in a complicated kickback scheme involving government contracts to a multinational conglomerate. In a plea bargain just as complicated, Turnbull admitted no guilt and served no time, but was forced to resign his position as Boone County surrogate, a political plum he had planned to use as springboard for a return to national politics.

Turnbull angrily maintained that "the so-called incriminating videotapes" that showed him receiving a bulging envelope from a man in desert garb had been faked, and that he had been set up by political enemies who feared his growing popularity with the voters. Nevertheless, he withdrew from elective politics to become the registered spokesman in the United States for the government of Libya.

It was at about this time that I learned Turnbull was not only a crook, he was inept. The campaign episode involving so-called Dalmatian separatists trying to embarrass Beaufoy was entirely his invention, his brilliant contribution to campaign strategy. Over Poppy Hancock's strenuous objections, Turnbull had invested substantial campaign funds in a gimmick that brought zero returns.

When I went to work for Mort Beaufoy I started making notes for what I thought might be still one more book on the mechanics of an election campaign. I never realized just how interesting my involvement in this one might be—and how potentially awkward for the candidate. A month ago I heard from the senator in answer to a letter from me congratulating him on his skill in downgrading from dangerous to merely annoying a confrontation among three Central African nations. After thanking me in a letter he dictated, he appended a note by hand at the bottom of the typed page:

"In the confusion of the election process I never had a chance to thank you properly for the service you rendered my campaign, much of it behind the scenes and unsung. Dear boy, I do so now from the bottom of my heart, as does my wife, who is my partner in all my endeavors. When I retire from politics at the end of this term it is my hope that the voters of New York and of the nation, whom I am doing my damnedest to serve honorably and fruitfully, will say, 'I'm glad the old boy gave it one more shot.' If they do, I hope you, in the privacy of your home, will take a bow."

There is of course no way I can publish this chronology of the senator's final election campaign during his lifetime. Or, come to think of it, during my own. My account will go into a safe-deposit box until all the people I have written about are long gone (including Felix Pacheco, who still languishes in the state prison near Ellenville, in the wholesome air of the

Catskills). My children or grandchildren may one day interest a publisher in it. Or not.

Will I have children? It is beginning to look at least like a theoretical possibility. After a contentious, infuriating, passionate, on-and-off, cross-country courtship, Poppy Hancock and I cautiously announced our engagement four months after the general election. (The caution was all on my side; Poppy was ready to get married during the congressional Christmas break.) A few people were rattled by our announcement, but not many, and not deeply, I was surprised to learn. Paul McClintoch said mildly, "That could work. Try not to fight. Don't talk politics." Yeah.

What can I say? Poppy and I have an abiding respect for each other's minds; we rise to the challenge of a good argument. We are locked in a never-ending verbal tug-of-war. Never-ending, but exhilarating. The only place we don't fight is in bed, so we try to spend a lot of time there. Also on the plus side, I see evidence that my fiancée's flabby conscience is developing muscle. Her recent clients don't make me cringe, and now she has taken on one I actually respect.

Is this development out of conviction, or is it part of her campaign to overcome my reluctance to formalize our relationship? I haven't forgotten it was Poppy Hancock who said more than once: Everything we do has a political side—in life, in love, in the laundromat. I am maintaining a wait-and-see position.